LA ES

C predator. No tracks

HUNTED

The locations included in this book are real and reflect the true geography of Liverpool. The events of the book are fictional, and at times refer to sensitive content.

First edition published and printed in the United Kingdom 2023.

A CIP catalogue record of this book is available from the British Library.

ISBN: 978-1-7395022-0-1 (Paperback, printed by Mixam)
ISBN 978-1-7395022-1-8 (Paperback, Amazon)
Imprint: Conundrum Publishing House
Editor: Christine Beech
Typesetting: Matthew J Bird

For further information about this book, please contact the author at:
www.LauraGraves.co.uk

This book is dedicated to my grandparents.
They will never get to read my books,
but they always knew I could do it.

Prologue

Her face hits the ground, teeth first.

They scrape along the concrete as she tries to lift her head. She coughs, choking on the river of blood that runs from her nose, staining her lips. Her nails splinter as she crawls, burying them into the dirt. Her heartbeat resounds in her ears. Her face pounds like the skin of a drum being beaten until it rips.

She feels a blow to the back of her head. It strikes her like a bat to a baseball, a solid hit. The force spins her, leaving her blood-soaked face staring at the sky. Her breathing is shallow and her petite frame is limp. Her muscles give in to the numbness. She blinks, slower each time. Her eyes are heavy and her surroundings are out of focus.

Traffic and sirens are faint in the distance.

Unable to move, she closes her eyes and considers not opening them again. Tears roll down her cheeks. Her inner voice is screaming for help, willing someone, somewhere, to pick her up and carry her to safety.

She feels something move near her feet, followed by pressure on her body. Fighting to open her eyes one last time, Emily Spencer finds herself face-to-face with evil.

1

The streets of Liverpool are paved with puddles, but the rain begins to ease.

He walks ten metres behind her, trying not to move too quickly in case she becomes alert to his presence. It is midnight and, with everybody stumbling in or out of town, it is not hard to go unnoticed.

He watches the heels on her red shoes, as they complement the lean tone of her calves. As his eyes start to undress her, she makes an abrupt turn into Pembroke Street. He stops at the corner, watching her fumble for her keys whilst hordes of university students make their way home. Her deep brown curls rest on the nape of her porcelain neck.

He zips up his jacket as she enters her home. He hurries across the road and disappears into the woods that back onto her house. He watches, waiting for her to walk to her bedroom.

Pulling on a balaclava, he is almost invisible. He throws his body over the brick wall that parts the garden and woods. The wall is laced with shards of glass and broken bottles to ward off potential thieves, but he takes full advantage of a neglected spot and swings his body over with ease.

Crouching with the stealth of an assassin, he waits for a glimpse of her body. Impatient, he creeps towards the patio doors of the kitchen, stepping over the clutter. His breathing is the only soundtrack to the night. He watches her shirt lift as she reaches up.

Amy Tatton is unaware she is the object of obsession. Sweat runs down his neck as he thinks about sinking his teeth into her flesh, tasting her skin, and smelling her hair.

He presses his hands and body against the patio doors, looking with wide eyes and panting. Each hot breath steams the glass. As he tries to open the door, the metal clasp on his watch taps against the glass. He pauses and holds his breath. Standing still, every muscle in his body is tense.

Amy notices her cat staring out into the garden. She turns and looks through the glass doors. Despite her heart racing, she takes a step closer. Willing herself to be brave, she peers into the garden and sees nothing but darkness and her reflection.

He stands frozen, holding his breath.

After seconds of staring, her eyes adjust to the lack of light as they do with the stars at night. A pair of eyes stare back at her. Not flinching. Just staring.

Without taking her eyes off him, she gasps for air and stumbles back, heading towards the front door, turning only to grab her keys. She can hear him frantically trying to open the patio door.

She reaches for her phone and tumbles over her feet, hitting her head on the floor. She dials 999 but the phone falls from her hands and slides underneath a table. She can still hear him banging on the doors.

Sobbing with fear, Amy reaches for the phone, stretching her arm under the table, looking back to make sure she is still alone.

Has he gone? Is he in the house? Hiding in the garden? On his way to the front?

She sees the key swaying in the inside lock of the patio door. She runs to a small closet space under the stairs, closes the door and sits behind it, tucking her knees under her chin.

She listens for any noise that does not belong. The phone is her only lifeline.

2

Jolene Linnet swallows her last drop of whisky, discarding the empty miniature bottle somewhere between the toilet and the stage of the Epstein Theatre.

The audience applauses as she gives a friendly wave and a nod to the enthusiastic front row, all waiting to hear about the criminal mind and gruesome details of various cases.

"Killers, rapists, and thieves are everywhere. If I'm totally honest with you, there could be one in this room." Jo's voice booms down the microphone, causing some feedback. Already, the audience is eating out of the palm of her hands.

"We all get paranoid. We all experience rage. We all lose our inhibitions when drugs or alcohol are involved. We're all capable of committing crimes like the ones that horrify us. Acts of paedophilia or grave violence towards others."

The psychology professors look at each other, suddenly questioning their decision to book this student event.

"Both crimes can be a symptom of something darker. A brain tumour or hormonal disruption, perhaps. Even the most depraved people can be understood. Most people don't like to hear it of course, but it's true."

Students from different Liverpool universities have come to hear Jolene Linnet talk about her career; cases that she has worked on, and the gruesome day-to-day life of a knackered criminal profiler. They want inspiration, and Jo wants money to cover her rent, cigarettes and alcohol; the small pleasures in life.

Persevering through whisky-induced indigestion, Jo entertains the students for hours, reminiscing about difficult cases, gruesome crime scenes and the dark web. As everyone leaves the theatre, she sits in the front row, resting her aching feet on the edge of the stage. She closes her eyes but is disturbed by a small group of students who have managed to get back inside. They decide not to interrupt her. Wise decision.

Saturdays in Liverpool City Centre mean shopping or football, regardless of the weather. It also means a high footfall through the city, as tourists explore the '2008 Capital of Culture'. They take pictures of each other astride the Lambananas, outside the Maritime Museum, and with statues of the Beatles scattered across the city.

Since the late 1800s, Liverpool was the home port to many of the greatest ships, with links to the RMS Titanic. The music scene in the city was influenced by all those who travelled in and out of the port, creating a legacy of talent and musical magic.

Jo walks towards Dale Street, relieved to have her Sketchers back on. By day, Dale Street is synonymous with corporate business and government offices. Municipal buildings tower over the chaotic one-way roads. By night, the street is transformed into a hub of diversity where the only goals are to have fun and flirt.

The Vernon Arms and Rigby's provide the classic British boozer experience, just steps away from the GBar on Eberle Street, and a host of other eclectic places to spend an evening.

"Double whisky please," says Jo, as she sits at the bar of The Red Arms.

"Got any ID, Luv?"

"Fuck off, Dan."

The bartender laughs and gives her an empty glass and a bottle of Bond's whisky. "Do I look that bad?" she asks, pouring herself a generous glass. "On second thoughts, don't answer that."

The Red Arms is one of the dimmest and most miserable bars on Dale Street. A perfect place to stare down at the bottom of a glass.

"Don't mind if I do," says a voice next to her. "Danny Boy, pass me a glass please, and whatever the lady wants."

"I don't know what makes you think I look approachable, but do me a favour. Piss off and leave me alone," she says, without looking up from her glass.

"Approachable isn't the word I'd use," he says.

There is no response.

"I'm Detective Gillespie."

Jo looks up from her drink.

"Is that all I have to say to get your attention?"

"What do you want?" asks Jo, losing interest.

"I've been assigned to work with you on the stalking cases. You know, like a partner," Gillespie replies, as he smirks behind his glass, knowing he is already winding her up.

"First off, I don't need a partner, and second, what are you on about?"

"Don't you read the papers?" he asks. "Some idiot's following people and has the city spooked. Headquarters rang you this morning and left a message, asking you to come by. You didn't, so here I am." Gillespie feels the sting of whisky hit his empty stomach.

Jo switches her phone on. She keeps it off during lectures and when she is avoiding company. There is a voicemail from her landlord about rent increases, and a message from Chief Constable Bob Clarke.

"We've had a new case this week," says Gillespie.

"So? Why do you need me?"

"Come to HQ and we can go over it properly," he mumbles. "They don't like to admit it but they need all hands on deck, and that includes yours. The cases are too frequent. People are scared, and God knows what will happen next time."

Jo finishes her drink before saying, "I thought you were a student back at the theatre until you started following me. Then I just thought you were a fan."

"Well, my youthful looks can be deceiving," Gillespie responds, grinning from ear to ear. "What can I say? I look good for my age." He brushes his hair out of his eyes and leads Jo out of The Red Arms. As they walk towards Canning Place and the old Headquarters, he answers his phone and stops in his tracks.

"Perfect timing, Linnet. We've got another case already."

3

"Gillespie, Linnet; take a seat," says Bob Clarke, Chief Constable of Merseyside Police.

"You probably have questions, Dr Linnet, although I'm sure Detective Gillespie will have filled in some of the blanks."

Bob has been on the force since his rookie days in Leeds, back in the 1960s. Although eligible for early retirement, he is reluctant to leave without succeeding in becoming Police Commissioner, an ambition he has held for many years.

"Yes, but I'm not sure what you want from me," says Jo, who is aware of the cases from the news and a quick look through the crime reports confirms her suspicions.

"As you can see, someone, or a group of people, is causing alarm for Liverpool communities. I know as well as you do that this type of thing often happens in busy city centres, but things are getting out of hand. I'm under pressure from the media and from the powers that be to put these cases to bed one way or another."

He hands them a new file, explaining, "This case happened last night."

Jo and Gillespie open the file and read the call transcripts, victim statements and officer reports.

"Similar to the others. Someone watching the victim, no physical assault although here it looks like there was an attempt to enter the premises," reads Gillespie.

"The victim, Amy Tatton, called 999 but the operator could only hear screams and crying. She sent an officer round anyway," states Clarke.

"So, you have a string of cases like this one. No suspect. No assault. This case isn't dissimilar to the ones before it. What am I missing?" asks Jo. "Why do you need me?"

"Phillip Tatton, Amy's dad, owns a few casinos in the city. He has pull with influential people. Let's just say, this case needs a prompt resolution, so to speak. Get yourselves together and go through the cases. You have three hours before addressing our officers to give them some direction," says Clarke, as he stands to leave. His uniform is spotless, and his commendation badges sparkle with pride. "They're a good bunch. Some are just out of the academy, and some are just plodding along until they get their pension. Anyway, I'll leave you to it."

Gillespie pours two cups of coffee from a lukewarm urn. Reluctantly, Jo takes off her coat and settles into the desk to scour over the files and statements.

"Right then, let's start from the beginning."

4

Jo stands in the canteen at the old Merseyside Police HQ. The smell of greasy bacon and doughnuts lingers, despite most of the force having moved to new premises. Some operations, and officers, still operate inside the old building, reluctant to make the transition or leave the legacy behind. For Gillespie, the large brown building that sits on Canning Place will always be HQ. The smell makes Jo remember that she has not eaten since the night before.

Table by table, officers and detectives quieten down, ready to hear what the 'famous Dr Linnet' has to say. Most know her from their training sessions and a few old-school detectives look at her sceptically.

'Here we go. Get your second wind, Jolene,' she tells herself.

"Good evening, everyone. I'm Jolene Linnet, Criminal Profiler." She hears the whispers and mocking words from the back of the room. "I've been asked to lend my expertise on the recent cases."

Gillespie hands everyone a summary of their earlier conclusions. Despite her casual body language and slightly dishevelled appearance, Jo's presence is commanding. However, from the back of the room comes a comment from an angry, inexperienced officer.

"The Night Walker's gonna run out of luck soon and, when he does, we'll be there to show everyone that Liverpool doesn't let scum like that get away with anything." Several of the officers cheer along with this sentiment.

"The 'Night Walker' is a foolish tabloid name," says Jo. "Used to whip people up into a frenzy and I'll take the liberty of assuming that, due to your professionalism, you'll refrain from participating in the media's sensationalism."

She presents a map of Liverpool using a projector. "These blue dots are where we've had reports from young females who've been followed or watched from outside their homes. These green dots are attempted break-ins. No obvious pattern is emerging, although this may alter if more incidents occur. So far, we have nine unsolved cases, three of which occurred over the last three nights, including the attempted break-in at Amy Tatton's residence. This may not seem helpful, but it tells us that this guy, if it is a male, is growing in confidence. Escalating the frequency of intrusions means he may be ready to evolve."

The officers in the room are stunned into silence. All except one. "You can't possibly know that. That's just a guess," shouts Officer Mark Summers, from the back of the room.

"Shut the fuck up, Summers," shouts Gillespie. "Let her get on with it, and you might learn a thing or two about police work." The room breaks into laughter and Jo nods towards Gillespie, appreciating the support.

"Walking wouldn't have made for a quick getaway. We can't rule it out, but I don't think it's likely. You'll need to check camera footage at train and bus stations and taxi offices, and check who's been frequently renting the city bikes. Go back and talk to the victims and see if anything new comes to light. Speak to people in the community. Neighbourhood watch groups, that sort of thing. Someone must have seen something." Jo watches as the officers make notes.

"So far, these look like opportunistic crimes, which means that the offender couldn't have known where he or she was going to end up. They know the area and the shortcuts. They aren't going outside the inner-city centre. Not yet anyway."

"Are we done?" asks Mark Summers.

"Do I look done? Do you think I'm still standing here for the good of my health? Sit yourself down, Officer. Anyone would think you know what you're doing, and I think we all know that's a wild statement," says Jo, without breaking into a smile or losing eye contact with Mark.

She continues with her profile. "Based on victim statements, the chief has put the stalker in his thirties but let me be clear. This isn't a stalker. This is a voyeur. Voyeurism can be a sign of fetishism, or practice for something more violent."

The room falls silent. Jo knows she has their attention.

"The more the offender continues, the more they will grow in confidence. The attempted break-ins already indicate escalation. It's only an estimation, but we're probably looking for someone obsessive by nature. Look back through your records for unsolved cases that are similar and look for people in the area who have recently been released from prison. There won't necessarily be a history of failed relationships. Until we know more, we need to keep an open mind. This person might appear completely normal, or they could be isolating themselves from society."

The attention of the room begins to break as the officers vacate their seats with renewed focus.

"One more thing," shouts Jo. "We must remember he's not a typical voyeur. Usually, voyeurs are sexually aroused but no seminal fluid was found in any of the scenes. Either he was interrupted, or sexual gratification was not the primary aim."

Jo throws on her coat and takes out a cigarette. "Well, that was shit. I need a drink."

"We can get one on the way," says Gillespie.

"On the way where? I'm starving. My stomach thinks my throat's been slit."

"You can get something on the way to Pembroke Street. Amy Tatton and her dad are waiting for us," smiles Gillespie.

5

Jo knocks on the door, hoping that Amy Tatton is alone. It is hard enough to get answers from victims, without family members sticking their two-pence worth in all the time. Cases like this get under Jo's skin. Without physical evidence, there is no guarantee they will catch anyone.

She doesn't wish sexual assault to be a feature of the crimes, but seminal traces can speed up an investigation. It makes Jo sick to think about it, but she knows that their best break would be to wait for the perpetrator to get too confident and slip up.

Cases and sleepless nights have caught up with Jo, evidenced by the wear and tear on her face. The bags under her eyes are big enough to put your spare carrier bags into, and no amount of foundation cream can hide them. To the public, she looks mature, experienced and confident. In reality, she is worn-out, troubled and her own struggles keep her awake at night.

"Amy Tatton?" asks Gillespie as the front door opens. "I'm Detective Gillespie and this is Dr Linnet. I know you've been through all this before, but we'd like to come in and ask you some questions and look in the garden."

Amy nods and moves to allow them access to her home.

"Sorry to bother you again, Amy. I've seen your garden through a lens, but I always like to see the place for myself," says Jo. "We won't be long, so you go ahead and return to what you were doing, and we'll see ourselves out." She speaks sensitively and tries to be as reassuring as possible. She knows what it's like to have the police knock at your door time and time again.

"I don't think so," says Phillip Tatton, hurling himself down the stairs. He has an air of authority and arrogance, unique to men who think that everyone owes them respect. "Why don't *you* return to what *you're* doing, and I'll show you the way out when you're done."

"Mr Tatton. Hi, good to see you. Chief Constable Clarke sends his regards," says Gillespie, holding his hand out and attempting appeasement.

"He can shove his regards up his useless arse," retorts Phillip Tatton. "Until you lazy bastards find out who's got the nerve to invade my daughter's home, I don't want anyone's regard. I want answers. Do you hear me?"

He is dressed in a perfectly fitted three-piece suit, but it doesn't disguise his bruised knuckles or the scar running from his ear to his neck.

In the City of Liverpool, Phillip Tatton runs several high-profile casinos that are allegedly at the centre of drug trading and thugs for hire. There are rumours that the casinos offer female company to lonely businessmen travelling through the city from international lands. The casinos draw tourists and wealthy individuals, and generous donations have been made to significant leaders of the city. It is no wonder there are so many blind eyes when it comes to Phillip Tatton.

Aware they are being watched, Gillespie and Jo stand in the garden, silently looking for any clues that may have lingered from the night of the invasion. Jo knows that the passing of time reduces the usefulness of the scene, but it is always better to be safe than sorry.

"Glass on the walls," she notes.

"Oh, consider it a cheap security system. It means you can't jump over," replies Gillespie, who seems proud of the tradition.

"You don't say," she responds sarcastically. "Well, someone managed to jump over. Get swabs of each piece of glass and have them run tests for blood and fibres, assuming they haven't done that already."

"Er, I guess they have as the report said they found no blood at the scene." Doubt and confusion ring in his voice, as he says, "I'll just run them again anyway."

"Bet they love you, Gillespie. Duplicating their work unnecessarily."

"It's OK. I know a girl there," smiles Gillespie. Jo doesn't doubt that he knows a girl in most places. He is a good-looking man but could do with a shave and a scrub.

"So, have you got a family, Linnet?" he asks while gathering the evidence.

"Long story."

"Come on, might as well get to know each other. Could be stuck together for a while. Who knows? Maybe we'll get on like a house on fire."

Jo looks up at the roof, considering the possibility of someone scaling the house and accessing the garden that way. She tunes Gillespie out but realises that he isn't going to stop.

"I was married to a good man, divorced a year ago, got two kids and currently they are not talking to me. Happy?" she asks, shaking the mud from her boots.

"Cheat on you, did he?" prods Gillespie.

"Nope. I'm the cheat," she replies.

"Women. You can't live with them …" jokes Gillespie, feeling slightly awkward. "Remind me later to get more cigs." He tosses his stub on the floor and kicks it down a grid in the corner of the garden. Jo follows the trail of the cigarette stub, unamused by his contamination of the scene. She walks over to the grid and wraps her hands around the cover. Even with a strained pull, it doesn't budge and she feels something click in her back. She tries again before quitting and propping herself up on the wall, to catch her breath.

"Let's see what else is down there. Ring the council and have them come and lift this thing, then bring us the contents. Probably just shite and debris but who knows? We might get lucky."

"I'll get right on it," replies Gillespie, as he walks into the house.

Jo closes the patio door after him, and stands close to the glass, recreating Amy's version of events. She struggles to see past her reflection, so clasps her hands around her face to peer in more easily. She sees the glass steam up from her breath and feels her fingertips touching the glass. Flicking through her notes, she sees that no fingerprints were found at the scene, on the glass door or any item nearby, and there was no report of DNA traces taken from the door.

"All sorted," says Gillespie, hanging up his phone and re-entering the garden.

"How tall did she put this guy?" asks Jo, staring at the door.

"Approximately 6 feet."

"Do me a favour and get a swab of this glass from here to here." She draws a circle on the door with her finger, indicating an area where the perpetrator may have touched it.

"You want to tell me why I'm swabbing a glass door when we already know there are no fingerprints?"

"Fingerprints are good if someone's already in the system. Their DNA would also have to be in the system but it's worth a try. The intruder could have breathed or coughed over this door. You take the swab and I'll wait in the car," she says as she makes her way through the house, avoiding eye contact and dialogue with Phillip Tatton.

As she steps outside, clouds have started to move over the city, looking like distant mountains. The wind has picked up, blowing trees and leaves with an annoying hiss. Jo buttons up her coat and sits in the car, waiting for Gillespie, knowing full well that he will be taking the brunt of Phillip Tatton's impatience.

"Nice one, thanks for that," says Gillespie, as he gets into the driver's seat. "I get it. He's looking after his daughter, but still, he's an arrogant prick."

Unfazed by the silence in the car, Jo lets her eyes blur with the views that fly by the window. She dwells on the times when she was more sociable and easier-going. It has been a long time since she appreciated the happiness of children playing in a park or the beauty of nature on an autumnal day.

It has been a long time since she was able to forget what happened.

She has missed out on growing up with her sister, seeing *her* grow up, and all the overprotective big-sister rituals. Eddie Doran stripped her of these moments before the universe could set them in motion. Little Susie had waited for her big sister to pick her up from school. After waiting for half an hour, she had run down the path and out of the school garden to make her way home. At eight years old, she was too young to walk home alone but headstrong enough to think she was more than capable.

That evening, Susie clung to her oversized backpack, which was strapped to both shoulders, as she bounced down the road, singing her favourite songs and waving at people who passed by. Distracted by a dog on the other side of the road, she had tripped over her own feet and fell onto the gravel; her long blonde hair flopping like a mophead across her shoulders. Her bottom lip began to tremble as she picked the small beads of gravel out of her palms.

According to the CCTV from a nearby house, a man identified as Eddie Doran approached Susie and helped her to her feet. Some words were exchanged and, the next moment, they were both walking into the distance.

That was the last time anyone saw Little Susie.

6

Anne-Marie Swift is standing outside a bar on Mathew Street, one of the many tourist traps in the city. Liverpool is famous for its musical heritage and The Cavern is known the world over, with its links to The Beatles, Irish bars, and the iconic Rubber Soul.

Anne-Marie was celebrating her 21st birthday, in fancy dress, with friends. They decided to bar-hop down Mathew Street, dressed as cheerleaders. Short white skirts, tight-fitting white T-shirts gaping at the chest, and pigtails in their hair. Together, the girls turned many heads throughout the night but, after hours of drinks and flirtations, Anne-Marie and her friends were ready for bed.

"Mel, how long did your taxi say it'd be? I've got to text my dad, so he knows when to come and get me," says Anne-Marie. They have drunkenly made their way to a nearby fast-food hub and are waiting for a few bags of chips.

"The guy said as soon as possible, so probably in about 3 hours," laughs Mel. "You know what it's like getting a taxi around here. Just tell your dad to come now so you're not waiting here on your own. You're not getting any food, so you might as well."

Anne-Marie walks outside, pushing through the crowds of people as they pour out of the clubs, onto the streets. She lives in the opposite direction to her girlfriends, so sharing a taxi is not always affordable. She shakes her phone to get a better signal, but it doesn't work. She walks further down the littered street and tries again, but her phone dies. Just her luck. She knows that her dad will be waiting for her to get in touch, so she uses the nearest payphone.

"Hiya, Dad, it's me. Are you still OK to come and get me? I can get a taxi if I have to but I'm ready now."

"Yeah, where are you?" he asks, groggily.

"I'll meet you outside Moorfields station in about 20 minutes."

"OK, Love," he says and hangs up. She knows he doesn't mind coming to get her, but she still feels like a nuisance for bringing him out at this time of night. She pushes through the crowds and makes her way back to her friends.

Once the clubs play the last song of the night and put the house lights on, the atmosphere on the streets can turn dangerous without warning. Some people are ready to go home, and transition quickly from dancing to being pissed off that they can't get a taxi. No matter which camp you are in at the end of the night, the fight for taxis is as deadly as they come. Others are not ready to call it quits and look for somewhere to carry on into the early hours. Many find themselves starving and queue outside the Lobster Pot for cheesy chips.

Anne-Marie sits on a wall outside Moorfields train station, facing the main road to keep a lookout for her dad's car. It has been almost fifty minutes, but still no sign of her dad. She decides that, if she can flag a taxi home, she will probably find him asleep and, if not, at least she will be back safely.

Several taxis go by, full of lucky passengers. A car turns the corner and pulls over.

"Hiya, thanks for stopping. I'm soaked," she laughs. "Small Lane Cottage please, Croxteth."

The car does a quick U-turn and makes its way through the city centre. Anne-Marie is freezing. Her teeth are chattering, and she can't wait to get her oodie on and climb into bed. She rubs her arms and legs to get warm and reaches for the seatbelt. The taxi isn't the cleanest she has ever been in, and the driver is not as chatty as they normally are, but it's late.

She pulls at the seatbelt, but it doesn't budge. It got stuck in the door when she pulled it shut. When they stop at traffic lights, she tries to open the door a little so she can pull the seatbelt free, but it doesn't budge. '*Great, child locks,*' she thinks. She starts to get frustrated at the fact that her driver can see her struggling but shows no interest in helping.

"Sorry to be a pain but I think my seat belt's stuck in the door. Would we be able to stop for a second?" she asks, trying to be calm and polite. This doesn't elicit the response she is after. The driver doesn't acknowledge her request and the volume of the music is turned up. *'How rude,'* she thinks. At the next traffic light, she faces the door and runs her fingers along the top of the frame, searching for the lock. She flinches when her fingertip runs over a sharp ridge. Instinctively, she looks at her finger and sees a slither of blood emerging from the cut.

Her heart begins to pulsate, her legs tremble with fear, and the oddity of the situation dawns on her. The lock has been tampered with. She sits back in her seat and tries to rationalise the situation.

Trying not to raise alarm, she looks in the rear-view mirror and watches the driver, trying to convince herself that he is just one of those grumpy, odd drivers you get now and again, in a really shitty car.

She notices that his gaze is fixed ahead. His eyes are different colours; one blue and one green. She keeps looking, desperate to see a glimpse of kindness or humanity. He doesn't take his eyes off the road. He chews his gum like he is pondering what to have for supper, and she notices an old police scanner on the passenger seat.

"Do you think this will be more than twenty quid? Because I'll need to stop off at a cashpoint," she says, trying to elicit some response and a reason to stop the car. Without flinching, he begins to hum along to the eerie melody of Neil Young's 'The Needle and the Damage Done'.

Fighting back tears, she struggles to breathe and adrenaline runs through her body; her muscles tense, and her heart beats for its life. Her body has entered fight or flight with a bang, but there is no way of escape. She tries to switch on her phone, but nothing happens. She fumbles through her bag for anything she can use to defend herself, but she has nothing apart from bronzer and cigarettes. Feeling helpless, but still praying that she is overreacting, she stares out of the window wanting to attract the attention of others.

She doesn't recognise the road.

She squints, trying to read road signs as the car speeds past the unfamiliar buildings and land. She doesn't recognise any of them. The realisation of her peril hits her, like pieces of a deranged jigsaw clicking into place. Tears fall as she realises that she doesn't know where she is or how she is going to make it home.

"Excuse me," she says to the driver. "I think I'm going to be sick. Do you mind if we stop for a minute? I don't want to be sick in your car." She thinks that if she plays along and acts unaware of the situation, she can make a run for it. "Hello. I need to get out for some air. Excuse me, Driver, I think you better stop, I'm going to be sick. I'll pay you more if you let me out for a minute, please."

Nothing.

He carries on chewing his gum, humming to the radio and ignoring her requests.

"Let me out of the car! Stop the fucking car now! Please, please. I'll give you everything I've got, just let me get out!" she shouts as she starts to cry through sheer panic. "I won't say anything to anyone, please just let me out."

Still no response.

"Let me the fuck out of your car! Stop!" she cries, hyperventilating and no longer recognising her voice.

Suddenly, the car comes to a halt. She stops breathing and sits stunned as she watches him in his seat. She wants to look out of the windows, but they are all steamed up. He is no longer her driver, he is her captor. Kidnapped. Abducted. What is he going to do?

She shouts for help and tries in vain to open the back door of the car, banging on the window. They are in the middle of nowhere. The driver's door shuts with a force that shakes the whole car. She turns, terrified to see that his seat is empty.

She stops breathing again. She sits, for what seems like minutes, in deadly silence. Her heart pounds and each thud makes her feel close to fainting. Nausea is taking hold of her body. This is her chance to fight or flee but her own body is working against her, as it freezes.

The door opens.

Consumed by terror and anticipation, she watches as it all happens in slow motion. His fist rises above her and strikes her face.

Her body is flung onto the back seat and blood drips from her nose. Dazed and semi-conscious, she cannot focus and, as hard as she wills herself, she can't put up a fight. She drifts in and out of consciousness but can feel him tug at her body, pulling at her underwear. She feels a scratch on her thigh as he pulls off her skirt. She tries to kick her legs and fight him off but the blow to her head has left her disorientated.

He grabs her legs and pulls her out of the car. The back of her head thuds as it hits the hard stone ground and she can feel warm blood trickling down the back of her neck. He grabs her by the feet and drags her body across the rough ground for, what seems to her, like a mile.

The pain is too much to bear and her body is close to giving up. Weak and dazed, she tilts her head enough to hear him groan from the struggle of pulling her limp body and to see that they are heading for a row of industrial skips. He kneels beside her, swooping his arms under her legs and head.

She opens her eyes wide enough to see who is holding her life in his hands. She sees glimpses of his face as she drifts in and out of consciousness. He looks normal, like he could be someone else's dad. Dark hair, crooked teeth, and those eyes. He pants with excitement and, in one big haul, throws her near-dead body into a skip. She lands on her back with something digging into her shoulder blade. Unable to move, she closes her eyes and wishes upon the stars to die.

Before her final blink in her short life, she sees him vault into the skip and kneel on top of her numb body. He tilts his head and smiles at her, rips off her birthday badge, and strokes her throat with the blade of a knife. Her eyes bulge with fear as she tries desperately to breathe and grab something to smash over his head; tears of terror running from her once-innocent eyes. She tries to grab some scrap metal, but her nails break as she tries to lift it.

"Keep still and help me put it in," he whispers, as he puts her underwear in his pocket.

7

At the old Merseyside Police Headquarters, the atmosphere is bleak. Tired officers are still ringing around train stations and public transport hotspots for CCTV footage. Most offices are empty, and the sun is only just rising. Jo splashes water across her face and uses eye drops in an attempt to look fresh.

"Coffee?" asks Gillespie, pouring everyone a drink. "It's fresh and full, on account of us being workaholics today." He laughs at his sarcasm, knowing full well that he is happier being here rather than at home, alone. "Summers, you want one?"

"Officer Summers needn't be here for this catch-up. Anything he needs to know can be disseminated later. Isn't that right, Summers?" says Clarke, closing the door.

"Right, it might be early but there are still worms to catch, so what have you got?" he asks, placing his bag on the table, and searching for information from the room. For a chief constable in the middle of a city crisis, he looks fresh and well-turned-out. Only the papers and files bursting out of his bag indicate that he is as overworked as everyone else.

"New results just in from the scene at Amy Tatton's house," says Gillespie. "The council managed to remove the grid, although they weren't happy about it. It disrupted some of the pipework and the smell was shocking."

"That'll go down very well with Mr Tatton, I imagine." Jo notes that Clarke seems more bothered about Phillip Tatton than the lack of evidence from the grid.

"They did find cigarette stubs down there, but the labs are still looking for any DNA traces. They aren't expecting any useful results with them being soaked in sewage waste," continues Gillespie.

"What about the glass on the walls?" asks Jo.

"No joy. The initial investigation team had run it for fibres and blood and didn't get any hits. Neither did we. But we do have a message from the lab management team, something about 'speak to each other so you know what you already have and have not tested for'."

"So, let me get this straight. We don't have anything new. This is not the news I had hoped for. What about CCTV?" asks Clarke, shaking his head with disappointment.

"CCTV from a shop on the corner of Amy Tatton's house picked her up walking home, but it also picked up everyone else that walked that way. Nothing stands out," replies Jo, still pissed off about the comment from the lab. "Teams are still going through other CCTV from around the city to see if anything is suspicious. As well as ring doorbells."

"What about Amy Tatton? Did she have anything else to add?" Clarke digs for information and is increasingly frustrated at the lack of progress. "What about Phillip Tatton? He must have some enemies who'd like to cause him trouble."

"According to him, there are only jealous business rivals that would have an issue with him. The man portrays himself as a saint," replies Jo. "Amy doesn't have anyone in mind who would want to hurt her. She mentioned an ex-boyfriend from a few years ago who didn't take their breakup too well, but she said he lives in Ireland now. If you want my opinion, something is off about this whole case. Think about it. Someone has followed her, but there is nothing suspicious on CCTV. They jumped the glass-topped walls without leaving any traces and have been watching her without actually doing anything."

"Spit it out, Linnet. Get to the point," says Clarke.

"Just seems a bit, I don't know, odd. If Amy Tatton hadn't told us that this had happened, we wouldn't know. There's no evidence that it happened. Could she be making it up?"

"Bagsy not asking that question while Phillip Tatton is around," jokes Gillespie.

"Think about it, it's just her report. Maybe she got spooked by a rat or her reflection. Look, I'm not saying she's lying and I'm not saying she's wrong. It's my job to understand people and think of all the possibilities. So, if you ask me, there are two options. One, she's wrong about what happened. Two, she's right but this voyeur is a clever bastard and knows how to avoid being caught. If that's the case, then we have a serious problem."

"This is a real shit show," says Clarke, almost dismissive of her points. "I've got the press asking me for answers and demanding to know what we're doing to protect the city. All I can tell them so far is that we don't know this, and we don't know that. What the bloody hell *have* we got?" He opens his bag and takes out his glasses, files and a clean shirt. Finally, he removes and opens a packet of gum and tongues three in a single motion. "Well?" he asks, repacking his bag.

Jo stands and goes over to the city map that is spread across the table. "OK, let's assume Amy Tatton isn't mistaken. We know enough to advise people in the city. We know that these are the places where the voyeur has been reported so far," she states as she circles locations on the map. "We know this is where Amy Tatton lives; the last case reported, that we know of."

She stands back and looks at the markings on the map. "There isn't enough information to make this an official profile feature, but all these incidents have happened within a small circumference area of the city. This isn't a city-wide case. Not yet at least."

"And that helps how, Linnet?" snaps Clarke.

Jo fights the urge to snap back. "These geographical details could prove crucial to finding a suspect. The proximity of the incidents, so far, supports my instinct that the offender is local. Crimes like this, especially happening late at night, are not usually committed by someone who needs to organise travel to and from the scene."

She sits down, next to Gillespie. "I don't think these are random."

"Neither do I," says Gillespie. "If these cases were random, or opportunistic, there would be a bit more 'randomness' to them, right? The fact they're in the same area surely means the offender isn't doing things ad hoc."

"You're right," says Jo. "We have a marauder, not a commuter. Someone committing crimes near to where they live, or maybe near to where they work. Not someone travelling in and out of the city. The Circle Hypothesis is one method of investigative psychology.

Plot all relevant crimes on a map and measure the distance between the two that are furthest away from each other. Use this measure as a diameter and draw a circle. It will likely cover all the offences that are being investigated. There is a high chance that the offender lives within this 'Circle of Danger'. Great news for the police, not so much for the residents who fall within the circle."

"Right," says Clarke, standing and preparing to leave. "That's something, at least. Linnet, I'm counting on you to narrow things down and put this case to bed. We need a suspect. Gillespie, speak to Amy Tatton again. Find that ex-boyfriend of hers. If we're seen to have a suspect, then at least it looks like we are making progress."

Clarke leaves the room and Gillespie offers him a sarcastic salute. "If I get my head bitten off by Phillip Tatton again, you're buying me a drink tonight," he says, patting Jo's back and swinging the door shut behind him.

Jo stares at the map again. There are not enough cases to geographically profile the offender, but it is a starting point. All cases are in areas of deprivation within the inner-city centre. All locations are accessible by foot or public transport, although not all public transport runs late at night. Apart from Amy Tatton, no other victim reported the offender trying to gain access to the house. What is different about her? So far, no evidence has been found at any of the crime scenes. No blood, fibres or forced entry. Cigarette butts were found at some scenes but not others, and no DNA has yet been found.

Jo sits back in her chair and drinks the last of the cold coffee. Closing her eyes and trying to resist the urge to sleep, her mind wanders to Susie, as it always does. What she could have done differently, what life would have been like if she had picked her up on time, and what she would have been like if she had the chance to grow up. Presumed dead, Susie is a hole in Jolene Linnet's life that cannot be mended. As she pictures her sister's little face and smiles, her phone rings.

"Linnet," says Gillespie. "I hope you haven't had your breakfast yet. There's been another case."

"Where? I'll meet you. I need to stop off somewhere first though."

"I'll be on Rodney Street in fifteen minutes. Meet me there." Gillespie jumps into his car and starts the engine. Jo can hear it ticking over, refusing to start. "Make it twenty minutes."

"Where on Rodney Street?" Jo asks, with her pen ready.

"The morgue," replies Gillespie. "Our budding voyeur has just promoted himself."

8

Emily Spencer sits alone in the waiting room, staring at her feet. Her eyes reveal how lost she is. Her beauty is effortless, yet she covers her slim frame with cardigans and sweaters, pulled over her wrists to hide the battle wounds. She opens another message from her sister, Gina. *'Let me know how you get on at your appointment and make sure you're home straight after. The news has got me freaked out!'*

Gina and her husband, Graham Pierce, who is far from role-model material, are the only family Emily has. After the last incident, Gina is hell-bent on paying for therapy for Emily as long as she needs it. Emily looks at her wrists and gazes at the fresh scabs that have formed. The skin is still bruised and there are marks where the bandages have been taped.

"Hi, Emily, how have you been?" asks Sophie Sheridan.

"Fine. You?" replies Emily. She hates the small talk at the start and end of their sessions. Truth be told, she doesn't like the actual sessions much either. It is hard to open up and find the right words, especially when she doesn't know what she is trying to say, and there is limited time to say it.

"I'm very good, thank you, Emily. Is there anything you want to mention or bring up before we get started with today's session?"

Emily offers a shoulder shrug and gazes at the floor.

"Why don't you start by telling me how you feel today?" suggests Sophie, trying to elicit a response.

"I feel fine. Well, not fine, but you know what I mean. Things are fine."

Sophie nods sympathetically. "When you say 'things', what do you mean, specifically?" she asks, with her pen and notebook on her lap. "Do you want to talk about that?" Emily pulls her cardigan sleeves over her hands to hide her scars, and retreats into the couch. She wants to answer but it feels like she has lost the ability to speak and control her expressions.

"Some people do extreme things when they need help, but don't know how to ask for it."

Sophie always sounds concerned. Emily can't help but notice how confident and assertive she is, yet sensitive and nurturing. She favours the casual but smart look and wears just the perfect amount of makeup – ruby red lipstick and a touch of mascara. Every session, she sits in her revolving leather chair, with her hands resting on her knees. Emily stares at the floor during their sessions. She notes that Sophie always wears sensible shoes.

Sophie has to wear sensible shoes to walk from her car to the office each day. It's not a long walk, and some wouldn't call it a walk at all. Down the street, cut through the old derelict church grounds, and over to Liverpool Cathedral car park.

There is something grounding about starting and ending the day next to the cathedral. Religious or not, everyone is moved by the sheer magnitude of the architecture. Locals and tourists stand in awe outside it. Families share a picnic in St James Gardens. Children play tag up and down the footpath that circles the cathedral. Generations create memories there. Boys used to draw a line on the walls of the graveyard, seeing who could run up it the highest. Friends sit and absorb the tranquillity of the gardens.

"I don't know what to say today, Dr Sheridan," whispers Emily.

"That's alright, Emily. Take it slowly and, remember, there's no right or wrong thing to say. How about we start with you calling me Sophie? Dr Sheridan makes me sound old and stuffy," she says, smiling and pausing again for a few minutes. The sadness and empathy in Sophie's eyes are touching. Emily thinks that she would make a lovely mum.

"When I see you next time, I want you to bring something that you've written or drawn. I know you love art. It doesn't matter what it is. You could write down what you think other people think about you, or what you think about yourself."

"OK," says Emily, "I can do that. I just find it hard to get going, that's all. It's not you, it's me."

Sophie and Emily start laughing at the cliché and the atmosphere of the room relaxes and feels a little warmer.

"Don't worry, Emily. I know how hard it can be to talk about the past, especially when you have been through so much." Sophie gives a kind gentle smile and, with a tilt of her head, she lets Emily know that nothing could shock or surprise her. She knows about Emily's past. She knows that she has faced more rejection and trauma than most at her age and that it is being internalised now more than ever. With a half-smile, Emily takes her hands out of her pockets and makes herself comfortable on the couch.

"I still can't stop thinking about him," says Emily, nodding towards her wrists. "I try to use my affirmations and all the other things you have taught me, but I can't stop it." She looks at the floor, feeling embarrassed and guilty.

"You've done amazing to be here and to keep going when things are hard. Do you remember when you first came? You wouldn't look at me, let alone speak to me. I am so proud of you, Emily. You can't beat yourself up every time there is a day which is a little harder than others."

Sophie reinforces how safe this space is, and that they will focus on moving forward rather than going over the events that led Emily here. A true professional in every sense but, now and again, she invests herself in a case more than would be advised. This is one of them. What Marcus Gaines did to Emily is no less harrowing now than it was back then.

Six-foot, strong, dominant and charming Marcus Gaines.

Emily met him when she was fourteen and he was almost sixteen years older. He had introduced himself at the bus stop one day, appearing concerned that she was alone and in need of a friend. She kept the conversation minimal but he continued to show up now and again. The last time he approached her at the bus stop, he had invited her for coffee. Angry at Gina, Emily had agreed to go with him. They talked for hours about music and, for a while, she felt like she could be herself. She liked not having to be conventional or conformist. He was older and charming, and he wanted to spend time with her. He gave her attention that she wasn't getting from anywhere else. That's probably why, in hindsight, she agreed to meet him again, with his group of friends.

When she arrived at his house, she was excited to be on an adventure, especially since she knew Gina would not approve. After giving her a tour of the house, which was clean and modern, he led her to a dimly lit room at the rear of the building. Although she had hesitated, Emily was enticed by his smile. She had built herself up to kiss him back if he tried to kiss her. She wanted him to but felt foolish for allowing herself to think that such a mature and caring man would be remotely interested in her in that way.

She followed him into the room and the door closed behind her. If only she had told someone where she was going that night, they may have come looking for her. They would have known that she was in the grasp of a dangerous man, luring vulnerable girls into his home with charm and compliments.

When the door shut, she jumped and Marcus placed his hands on her shoulders. He had told her that no one understood her like he did; that there wasn't anyone who cared for her like he would. She began to believe him as he wrapped his arms around her but the video recorder in the corner of the room made her stomach turn and her muscles freeze.

He kissed her neck and started to undo her shirt buttons as she saw the small red light appear on the device.

9

Emily turns the radio down as the wind rustles through the trees and the rain thrashes against the windows. There are more reports about the dangers in Liverpool and areas are being placed on high alert. It's no wonder some people struggle to go out.

She reads what she has written and contemplates tearing it up and writing something else but knows it will not be genuine. She tucks her book under her pillow and turns off the light.

She is not a great sleeper. Too many thoughts and dreams occupy her head, and sometimes she lets herself imagine an alternative life where she has a happy family and goes off to college to make something of herself. She is 24 years old, still in a single bed, and relying on benefits and her sister's support. As she closes her eyes with disappointment, her bedroom door begins to creak open. Keeping her eyes closed, she listens as footsteps shuffle to the end of her bed.

"Emily, are you awake?" whispers a drunk, slurring voice.

She keeps still and silent.

"Emily? It's Graham, wake up." He places his hand on her duvet, on her thigh. She can hear his breathing getting heavier and the smell of alcohol drifts over to her pillow.

"Go away. I'm sleeping, and you're drunk," she says, willing him to go away or for Gina to wake up and disturb him.

"Come on now, that's no way to talk to the man of the house. Come here, I just want to talk to you, that's all." His hand is still on her thigh as he perches himself on her bed. "Let me look at you," he whispers.

Emily keeps still, shaking. Her eyes are scrunched up so tightly that her eyelids feel deprived of blood. Her palms are sweating but she knows that he will eventually give up and leave. Ever since she was young, this is what he's like when he is drunk. Gina told her to stop being silly and that she should be grateful that he was chipping in to pay for the sessions with Dr Sheridan.

"Graham. Is that you, Love?" shouts Gina from the bedroom next door. Emily feels him rise from her bed and he quietly closes the door behind him. He's gone. She lies on her back, staring at the ceiling, listening to the sickening noises coming from her sister's bedroom.

Picking up her journal, she creeps into the bathroom. She runs a bathtub of hot steamy water which burns her skin as she lowers herself into it. She begins writing whatever comes into her head. Thoughts about the irony of this world. Thoughts about life without Graham Pierce. Thoughts about how much she hates herself. Writing gives the thoughts a place to land.

She holds out her palms and runs her fingers across the scabs that decorate her wrists. She closes her eyes and tries to imagine how she had felt before she took the knife to her wrists. Her heart pounded like it was trying to break free from her chest. Her lungs had worked against her, and she felt like she was choking on fear. There was a force inside her that needed to get out and, at that moment, the only way to stop it all was to hurt herself.

Emily has been to more sessions with Sophie Sheridan than she can count. She is practically her best friend, although she knows that's not a healthy way to look at it.

She has friends of her own, but they don't consider Marcus Gaines anymore. As far as they are concerned, Emily has dealt with that and moved on a long time ago. It is a distant memory for them, but a daily demon for her.

10

Jo and Gillespie are waiting outside the medical examiner's lab on Rodney Street. Jo swigs cold coffee and Gillespie gorges on a hotdog. They are exhausted but determined to keep at it and grab power naps in-between waiting for lab results or darting to different locations.

Gillespie throws his sauce-covered napkin into the bin and checks his phone. "Just got a message from HQ," he says. "Amy Tatton's been in touch and wants to speak to someone as soon as possible. You OK to wait here while I give her a ring?"

Jo nods, glad of the minute to herself. The sound of metal tools clashing against the sink in the lab is strangely comforting. It is the sound of someone working to find pieces of a puzzle, to help the helpless and tell the story of their last moments.

Gillespie returns through the doors with a spring in his step. "Spoke to her. Seems her ex-boyfriend's back in town. Well, that or he never actually went to Ireland. He knocked on her door last night. Her dad scared him off."

"You get a name?" asks Jo.

"Michael Tanner. And get this, he's got a restraining order against him. Apparently, Phillip Tatton arranged it and paid for a few shortcuts, which is why Amy never mentioned it. She just thinks Tanner saw sense and left her alone." He shakes his head and says, "The things you can do if you have enough money, or scare people enough."

A woman shouts for them to come into the lab whilst she is drying her hands and putting on new latex gloves. Her glasses are on her head, keeping her fringe from falling into her eyes. She has a mug of coffee next to the sink and indicates that she is ready to start. She smiles at Jo.

"Anne-Marie Swift. 21-year-old female, Caucasian, cause of death unlawful. Facial muscles look like they're reaching the early stages of decomposition, so I put the time of death somewhere between midnight and 3 am," reports Dr Tara Howden, Medical Examiner for Merseyside. Jo and Gillespie watch and listen as she gives them the rundown of her findings.

The body of a young woman lies before them, with her torso stapled following the autopsy. The room is filled with dormant and musty air, with no windows to let out the stench of the devil's work. The floor tiles echo every step of the living whilst the cooling fan in the corner sounds like the screams of the dead. Jo stares at the girl lying lifeless, as flashbacks fleet before her eyes of when she had to identify a total of five bodies, none of them her little sister, Susie. Still, that responsibility and those sights never leave you.

"Her parents told us she was celebrating her twenty-first birthday with friends in town," says Gillespie, covering his mouth to fend off the smell of chemicals and death. When he was new to the force, he had vomited in Tara's sink almost every time he went to the examination room but, over the years, he has learned to fight the urge.

"Yes, Miss Swift's stomach contents reveal that she had consumed a considerable amount of alcohol. From the smell, I'd say she had been drinking champagne cocktails," Tara says, without noticing Gillespie turning green. She is matter-of-fact about business and has witnessed it so often that the smells and sights are familiar territories.

"You're good," says Gillespie, both disturbed and impressed as he flicks through his notepad. "I remember that being in one of the friend's statements."

"It's an acquired taste, but the champagne and brandy leave a distinct aroma and I also found traces of sugar cubes. Whoever made the cocktails stuck to a classic recipe. I must find out where this was. My future wife might be partial to a champagne cocktail or two." She makes a sarcastic face, thinking about how terrible her last few dates have gone. She smiles again at Jo, who doesn't notice.

"This is also interesting," she says, as she lifts the sheet covering Anne-Marie Swift's corpse, which is as much for her dignity as it is for officers with weak stomachs or those who wolf down a hotdog before coming in. She reveals a strange oval mark on Anne-Marie's left inner thigh.

"What is that?" asks Jo, bending down for a closer inspection, not fazed by the sight before her. Tara is impressed.

"My guess is it's a puncture wound. Technically, they could be from something that leaves an indentation like a belt buckle but, if you feel the grooves, they feel like teeth marks. They're a little uneven so I'm not completely certain at this stage, but she may have been bitten by her attacker. I've sent an impression to the lab," replies Tara, repositioning the sheet over the corpse.

"We've got ourselves a whack job, haven't we, Doc?" exclaims Gillespie, as he makes notes about the possible teeth grooves.

A giggle is overheard from behind the desk, and everyone turns to look.

"Sorry. Whack job. Whack to the head. He whacked her. Get it?" mumbles a young woman. She waits for someone to respond to her humorous and ironic choice of wording. Still waiting, she returns to the computer screen and pretends that it hasn't happened.

"Jenna Crook," says Tara, as she introduces her new apprentice, while looking over her glasses at her to signal a request for more professionalism.

"You should check with the labs about the other evidence. Maybe there are some answers in whatever was in the skip; aside from the girl, I mean," adds Tara, addressing Jo and Gillespie.

"Do you know the cause of death yet?" asks Jo. "Or where she died? I mean, I know where she was found, but ..."

"I thought you'd never ask, Jolene," quips Tara. Jo looks startled at the use of her name.

"She died in the skip, on her back. Her attacker was probably kneeling over her or applying some type of force to keep her down. I found bruises on her abdomen which are consistent with being restrained. You can see the mascara lines running behind her ears and towards the back of her neck. Despite everything that she endured, the cause of death was blood loss. He slit her throat with what looks like an average kitchen blade. See the slightly jagged edges? No trace left behind."

"And then he left her to die," concludes Gillespie, with a look of vengeance.

"She was dragged from a car. Tyre marks were found at the scene, and I found upholstery fibres on the heels of her shoes. Before you ask, they've been sent for analysis."

Tara pauses to give Gillespie a chance to write down the information. "Judging by the cuts on the back of her legs, she was dragged a fair way. He slit her throat after he had sexually assaulted her. There's no seminal trace but this girl had rough intercourse in her last hours, so I think it's fair to say that it wasn't voluntary."

Jo's eyes fixate on the girl. The body that lies before her isn't just evidence. She is someone's daughter, someone's friend. She is someone's victim. Yet, right now, she is a mere silhouette on the slab. There is no sign of the so-called afterlife to collect the precious soul of this child. No white light emerges from the heavens. She used to believe that, after death, good souls were taken to an eternal fountain of happiness. This job provides more than enough evidence that death is just an end and, for too many people, the ending comes too soon.

"I hope I get five minutes alone with him when we catch him," says Gillespie under his breath.

"You and me both. Right, thanks Dr Howden for those details, they were very helpful," says Jo.

"Call me Tara, and you're very welcome, Jolene," she says, smiling again. "Come back if you think of anything else."

Jo leaves the room, with the doors swinging shut.

"She likes a dramatic exit, doesn't she?" says Tara.

"Not like me. I'm as stealthy as they come," replies Gillespie, sticking out his chest. "You won't even notice when you're falling in love with me."

"Probably not. I imagine I'll be in the grasp of a stroke or a serious concussion if that ever happens."

"Ouch," laughs Gillespie, heading for the door. "You really are as mean as they say," he teases, making sure he gives the doors an extra swing on his way out. He runs down the street to catch up with Linnet.

"The car's this way," he says, out of breath and pacing the ground. His stride seems much smaller than Jo's, but small isn't always a bad thing, he has been told.

The traffic in the city is always chaotic. People drive up one-way roads the wrong way, park where they can dump their cars without paying, and overtake other cars on dangerous roads if it means they can reduce their journey by three seconds. Pedestrians are even worse, crossing roads where there is a high risk of being flattened by a bus. Why wait for the green light to cross if you can have a quick life-and-death thrill on your way to lunch?

"What now then, Jo? You see this type of thing before?" asks Gillespie.

"Now we talk to the evidence. But not to the press, OK. I don't want to find out that you're a bloody leak. Some details of this case shouldn't be revealed to the public for obvious reasons, but we also don't want this guy to be spooked and flee the city."

"As if you think I'd be a leak," says Gillespie. "I know I'm not the most organised or intelligent detective there ever was, but I love my job and I love this city. No one wants this creep off the streets more than me."

"I think Anne-Marie Swift's parents might disagree with you there, Gillespie," she replies. "Talking of which, don't forget to go and see them. Her dad must be wracked with guilt, and they might have thought of something else by now."

"Will do. Imagine losing someone in this way, because you weren't where you were supposed to be," says Gillespie.

Jo doesn't have to imagine. She knows too well what that weight of guilt and regret feels like.

11

Gillespie stands in the doorway of his office. Jo makes herself comfortable in her new partner's chair. On the desk is a typical family photograph and there are files of old cases scattered across the desk. She runs her hands over her face and takes a deep, exhausted breath.

"What do you think Tara meant when she said, 'Come back if you need anything else'?" she asks. "Was that a bit odd?"

"You think everyone's odd," he replies, and Jo couldn't disagree.

She stares at the notes she took from Tara's report and cross-references them with a list of evidence that was sent to the labs for testing. Jo is meticulous in her tracking of information, as being organised is one way to spot patterns and anomalies.

She has been asking herself the same questions all day. Why is he killing? Why kill when he could just rape his victim? What role is the victim playing for him? Some killers do it for the thrill of violence or the sexual climax. Killing is the best way to silence a witness. When the killer knows their victim, it can happen in a passionate outburst or frenzied rage. Others are visionary killers, who kill for a higher purpose or rationalise their kills as necessary.

Not all killers move bodies. Some leave them where they are, unafraid of them being found. Others take great measures to hide the bodies. Rose and Fred West hid bodies in their garden and home. Myra Hindley and Ian Brady buried bodies in Saddleworth Moors.

She looks at the young children in the family photograph on Gillespie's desk. "Yours?" she asks, nodding towards it.

"The kids are. She left me, shall we say. Can you believe it?" asks Gillespie, holding out his arms to model what a good catch he is. "The kids live with her parents. I wasn't in a good place, and they really like it there. Routine. Someone is always at home. I see them on video calls, but they have their own lives, and they don't want to look at my ugly mug all the time." Jo gives a sympathetic smile and makes a mental note to ask about the kids another time when lives are not at stake.

"What do you think about the whole thing, Gillespie? Does anything strike you as unique?"

"You mean apart from the whole rape and murder thing?" quips Gillespie, biting the edges of his paper coffee cup. "It's the first time I've ever seen anyone in a skip, living or dead. Kind of strange, if you ask me. And you know what else is strange? How there was no seminal fluid. Anywhere."

Despite signs of sexual violence, there was no environmental evidence of such an act taking place. No condom, no semen. Only the damage caused to Anne-Marie Swift.

"Sexual assault committed by a male doesn't have to be penetrative. It can be with any foreign object," explains Jo. "Get a hold of the crime scene investigators and see if there was anything nearby that could have been used. Can you ask someone to speak with the women involved in the first voyeur or break-in cases? If he made a mistake, it will be in those first incidents. Guys like this start and can't believe their luck."

"OK, but do me a favour and stay here. I've got Clarke on my back every hour and if he thinks I've lost you, he'll have my balls in a vice."

Jo analyses the crime scene photographs. The skip is rusty-yellow, half-filled with old slabs of wood and sand. The body was found with her arms above her head and her clothes torn. The tyre marks on the ground and the drag prints to the skip are barely visible in the images. There is an enlarged picture of the possible bite and neck wound.

She wants to see the scene for herself to get a feel for what happened. She believes that the best evidence is in the atmosphere of a crime scene. It is there where someone was terrified for their life, where someone may have felt power or remorse, where a soul may have lingered, and where there may be a stench of guilt.

This is evidence that you can't snap or tag. It can't be presented in the courts but, through experience, Jo knows it is this stuff that can make or break a case.

12

He sits on the edge of the park bench, on this crisp autumnal afternoon in Chavasse Park.

He could be mistaken for someone who loves the outdoors, taking in the busy scenes of the park. No one would know that this man, newspaper in hand, is thinking about the woman from a few nights earlier.

No one knows he is being hunted by the police.

He relives the way her skin had felt when he touched it and the smell of her hair when he had let it slip through his fingers, as she took her last breath. He smiles, recreating the mental context of the struggle. It had unexpectedly aroused him.

He feels aroused now.

The tears and muffled screams had made him erect. He was the dominant male. Even as he sits here now, he is the one in control. No one looking at him would suspect him of being anything other than an ordinary man. Respectable.

Chavasse Park is a green oasis in the city centre. A place to sit with friends and catch up over coffee or declutter your mind. It is surrounded by the daily hustle and bustle of Liverpool. The Hilton Hotel, Liverpool ONE shopping centre and the King's Dock, home of the Echo Arena, form its circumference.

"Excuse me, do you mind if we sit here?" asks a young woman, with an infant on her lap.

He moves up to gesture that he doesn't mind, and smiles at her. He can smell her perfume and the sweetness of her scent makes him look at her longer than he intended to. She smiles at him and starts to feed her son, unaware of the evil sitting beside them. She is wearing a tight-fitting shirt and jeans that cling to her skin. The two top buttons of her shirt are open and, as she leans forward to feed her child, he can see the pale skin of her smooth chest and the lace of her red bra teasing to be seen.

She looks at him and he takes his time to look away. He doesn't need to look at her anymore. He has seen enough. Enough to imagine what he would do to her and what he would make her do. He feels the thrill in his veins and the anticipation runs through his body like electricity.

"Cute kid," he says. "How old?"

"Thanks. He's 24 months old."

"So, he's two," he laughs.

"Yeah, I could have just said that, couldn't I?" she laughs. "You got any kids?"

"No, always wanted some but my wife couldn't have any."

Red Bra looks at him, apologetically.

"It's OK. We have kids in the family. Do you live around here?" he asks, knowing that he has disarmed her and can elicit all the information he needs.

"I do. Liverpool born and bred," she laughs. "Got to get him back for his bath, nice to meet you though."

He watches her walk away. Jeans cling to her hips and he imagines pinning her down. He is startled by the shrieks of laughter from students across the park. They sound like lambs, screaming to be freed from their capture and inevitable slaughter. As he looks back for Red Bra, she is gone. Frustrated, he throws his newspaper into the bin and looks at his phone, relieved to see that she is in the background of the photographs he took earlier.

13

The tyres of Gillespie's car jerk over the pebbles and grit on the ground. The docks along Chaloner Street are a far cry from the scenic Albert Dock, which is ten minutes down the road.

Chaloner Street is home to many industrial sites or, at least, it is for now. In another year or two, there will be bidding wars for the luxury apartments and penthouses planned for the area. A dead body found on a site can drive prices down or up, depending on the ability of public relations to turn a horror show into a unique selling point.

"We're here, so let's get a move on. We haven't got much light left," says Gillespie, pulling himself out of the car and giving Jo a nudge.

Police tape is sealing off the area, but the wind has blown some of it loose. It looks like an eerie photography scene. Gillespie crosses the tape line and takes out his notepad, as Jo follows.

"OK," he says. "This is where the tyre tracks were found. The rain's washed them away, but we've got photographs that were taken when Anne-Marie was found."

"Give me a hand to get into this skip." This elicits no more than a slow-motion shoulder shrug from Gillespie. "What? Too heavy for you?" she asks.

"No," he snorts. "I can lift 300 lbs in my sleep." He uses his hands to give her a step up and over the skip. "See? But you might want to cut back on the meatball marinara subs." Luckily, she doesn't hear him.

As expected, the skip is full of scrap waste and other materials that probably made the scene a lot harder to investigate. No wonder results were coming back from the lab in drips and drabs. "Got any gloves?" Jo asks. Gillespie passes her a pair of purple latex-free gloves.

"Allergies?" she asks.

"No, it's just all I've got. Swiped a box from HQ. What can I say? I'm a magpie," he laughs, holding his hands up. "You managing in there, or do I need to jump in?"

"I got it," Jo replies.

Relieved, Gillespie sits on a nearby rubble boulder and lights a cigarette. He may be an experienced detective, but some things still give him the creeps and being inside a skip in the middle of the Chaloner site, where a girl was murdered, is one of those things.

Jo holds up the photograph of Anne-Marie's body in the skip and tries to imagine what happened. There are stained outlines where she had been drained, and rogue leaves have started to cover up even this bit of her existence.

"The killer threw a body into this skip with ease before jumping in, and was carrying a weapon."

"So he was in and out of the skip like a blue-arsed fly. Maybe we're looking for a killer gymnast." Gillespie smiles to himself as he stands up and brushes his hair out of his eyes.

"Gillespie, run me through the lab reports again, please. Apart from the absence of semen and condoms, what else does it say?"

Gillespie flicks from one page to the next in his notebook.

"The only hair found at the scene was from the victim. The only blood was from the victim. Nothing under her nails, no skin or hair. Some false nails have come off, but there was nothing underneath them. Indentation marks on her thigh. Throat slit but no weapon was found. Animal fibres were found, assumed to be rats or whatever rodents you might find in an industrial site. No seminal fluid or vaginal fluid on anything nearby. Just the fibres on the bottom of her shoe. Gravel was found in cuts on her legs from when she was dragged here, but that doesn't help us since we already know the location."

Jo puts one foot on the side of the skip and jumps out, shaking off the dirt and the death. The crime scene looks too clean. To not find anything after a brutal murder, rape and struggle would suggest a level of forensic awareness that scares her. They get back into the warmth of the car.

"Maybe whoever killed Anne-Marie is not the same person as the voyeur?" suggests Gillespie. "Think about it. There's a big difference between someone watching other people for pleasure, and murdering them. Plus, you don't go from voyeur to killer in less than a week, right?"

Gillespie's car is as tidy as his desk. Old coffee cartons and sandwich boxes are on the floor and the ashtray is jam-packed with old stubs, some with lipstick on, Jo notes. It smells like a students' common room where the students smoke and drink whisky all day.

The smell gets stronger when he puts the heater on. "If I don't put the heater on, the clutch pedal sticks," he explains, driving down the road. "Where next then?"

"Back to the office. We need to regroup and go over everything again. We're missing something."

"You know what's bothering me?" asks Gillespie.

"I'm torn between the smell of your car or the smell of a dead cat coming from your heater."

Gillespie ignores her and continues, "I just don't think these crimes are related. You said yourself that offenders escalate over time, even a short space of time, but wouldn't voyeur to murderer be a leap rather than an escalation?"

"Maybe. Escalations do usually happen slower than this, but there could've been a triggering event that made him increase the violence. The risk has increased too. This wasn't an opportunity crime; it was planned. You can't find someone to take, go to Chaloner Street and find a perfect dumping site on a whim or stroke of luck."

Jo tries to open her window to let in some air and let out some stench but struggles to get it down. "Oh, yeah, it sticks. Sorry," he apologises, as he increases the air from the vents and changes the temperature to cold.

Jo runs through the facts again. Anne-Marie was picked up in the town centre, as CCTV captured her walking down towards Moorfields Station but lost her after she turned a corner and passed a takeaway food shop. There were no defensive marks on her and no skin or hair under her nails. There was a cut on her finger but that could have happened inside the skip on some waste material. She had got into a car on her own accord, and she had ended up at the docks, where she was brutally assaulted and had her throat slit.

"We need to see Clarke," announces Jo.

"If we must. The man's doing my head in. He might be the big boss, but he's got a stick up his ass. I don't know how he ever found a wife."

Jo takes a deep breath out of the window, as she says, "I think she knew him. I think Anne-Marie knew who he was."

14

Emily finishes her voluntary work at Tree View Court Nursing Home. She goes twice a week to visit the residents and play games with them. It's as much for her benefit as it is for them. It's peaceful and predictable, not like her therapy sessions.

"Hi, Emily. Lovely to see you again," says Sophie.

She runs through the agenda for the session and summarises the progress that Emily has made so far. She is so positive that Emily wonders if she has muddled up the patient files. She talks about her being strong, resilient and fierce. Not words that Emily would ever use to describe herself.

"How would you describe yourself, Emily?" asks Sophie, as if she has read her mind. "You tell me, and I'll write it down. It doesn't matter what the words are. Let's just get them out and onto the board for now."

Emily thinks for what feels like an intense, silent sixty seconds. She always worries that she won't articulate her thoughts accurately enough. "Useless," she says.

Sophie hesitates for a split second but writes it on the board. "Any others?"

"Annoying, miserable," Emily continues, with various other synonyms for these words.

"Great, Emily. You've done well so far. How does it make you feel when you look at the list? What would you say to someone else who described themselves this way?"

Emily can feel her face going red and her palms starting to sweat, as she replies, "I'd say it's probably not true."

Sophie nods in agreement and asks, "Would people who know you describe you like this?"

Emily shakes her head and looks at the floor.

"How would they describe you, Emily?"

"Friendly, caring, troubled," she replies, waiting to see what Sophie will say next.

"I think that's more accurate than the initial list you gave me, don't you? When we struggle with our mood, especially when we've been through trauma, the way we see ourselves isn't always an accurate picture."

By the end of the session, Emily has set herself some goals to achieve over the next few weeks. One of the goals is to look at different art schools and their entrance criteria. Emily has often thought about this but never followed it up, but there is something about Sophie's company that makes her feel safe. Like she could thrive, rather than just survive life, after Marcus Gaines.

Sophie doesn't know what worries her more. Whether Emily is getting too attached to her, or she is getting too attached to Emily.

Their sessions had started only a few months after the ordeal with Marcus Gaines. Sophie had read about the case in the papers. A local girl was prostituted and forced into making pornographic videos. It was all over the newspapers and broke Sophie's heart, but it was nothing to how she felt when she heard Emily talk about her experience.

It has been a long journey getting Emily to this point, and she doesn't want anything to jeopardise her recovery. She is Emily's ally, which is why she feels like she has betrayed her. As much as she wants to, she is not allowed to give Emily the information she received this morning.

There are reciprocal relationships between police and medical professionals, and Sophie is privy to some information whether she wants it or not. She doesn't know if she can bear the look on Emily's face when she finds out that the Restorative Justice Team has reached out, and that Marcus Gaines has asked to see Emily.

15

"Did you two get me up here to just look at me, or do you have something useful to tell me?" asks Clarke, with his usual impatience. "I was about to go for coffee and some very important people *might* have been there; people who say they *might* be able to make my promotion happen."

"Sounds promising," Gillespie says, sarcastically.

"Get on with it then," snaps Clarke.

Jo is leaning against the window, looking out into the city, as she says, "I think Anne-Marie Swift knew her killer."

"It's your profile, Linnet. If it's wrong, then it's on your head. Why the sudden change?" asks Clarke, in an aggravated manner.

"There wasn't anything under her nails to suggest she was abducted in a scuffle. If she was dragged off the streets, there'd be witnesses or defence marks. Surely to God, someone would have seen something. It was in the middle of the city centre, for Christ's sake."

She pulls up a chair next to Clarke, lowering her voice, but with just as much focus. "She didn't ring a taxi. We know she didn't. The phone records of her mobile and nearby public phones show us that. A taxi can't pick someone up unless they have booked the job. I'm telling you, she got into that car willingly."

"Could have been a black cab," says Clarke.

"Any that were operating that night have been accounted for," Gillespie responds, flicking through his notepad.

"Right, so spit it out, Linnet. What's your working profile now? If there's a change, we need to update everyone," says Clarke, searching his bag for a pen. He is sharply dressed, like he spent an hour under a lint removal machine. His uniform is crisp, and his shoes are not scuffed at all. A tell-tale sign of management. He takes out his glasses, pen and paper and places them on the desk, ready for the update. "Right, Linnet, go."

Jo goes over the profile that she has already given the officers but reiterates her thoughts about Anne-Marie getting into the car willingly. She suggests that she must have known the driver, or had some reason to think it was safe to get into the car. Perhaps it was someone she had met that night or someone that her dad knew. Maybe it was a taxi driver who had given her lifts several times before. Perhaps it was a friend offering her a sanctuary under false pretences.

"We've got a new name in the mix," says Gillespie. "Michael Tanner. Amy Tatton's ex. He's been bothering her, even though there's a restraining order in place. I've got people looking for him. He rang Amy Tatton a few times but had no joy with the number. Probably a burner."

"Sounds suspicious to me. Get him in. The sooner we can give the press some good news, the better." Clarke's phone starts to vibrate and he leaves the room.

Jo pours herself and Gillespie a coffee, cursing as she spills hot water over the cuff of her shirt. She wipes it dry with a tea towel, the cleanliness of which is questionable. Gillespie is swiping left and right on his phone.

"Thanks, that's the first coffee you've made me since we met," he says, without looking up.

Jo looks over at the whiteboard at the photographs of Amy and Anne-Marie, the crime scene pictures and the lack of suspects. There is a box of unsolved voyeur cases on the floor. They could all be related. The lack of evidence itself is a signature, left behind by the killer. Crime scenes don't need a pentagon drawn on the wall in blood or a shoe to be taken as a trophy. Killers don't need to make the dead body look tidy, and voyeurs don't need to satisfy themselves at the scene. Each crime, each victim, and each offender is different, despite stereotypes and infamous cases in the media.

Gillespie's phone starts to vibrate.

"Remember the grid you asked me to check out at Amy Tatton's? The team pulled out all the contents. Nothing in there. Some ciggy stubs but no evidence on them. The waste had washed anything usable away. I had labs check the brand. Royal Oak cigarettes. Same brand as Daddy Tatton." He knows that sounds worse than he had intended it to. "This is interesting though. The swab from the patio door came up with something."

Jo looks at the report on his phone, and the images attached to the email. "Gingivitis," she says. "Gum disease that causes the bacteria around teeth to build up and harden. Bad breath, receding gums, and loss of teeth in extreme cases."

She stops reading. Truth be told, the result is both science and luck. She remembers reading some research about dolphins' DNA. Scientists managed to capture a dolphin's breath and extract its DNA. The force of water and breath coming from the dolphin's blowhole meant that capturing breath inadvertently captured DNA from the lungs. The test on the patio door hasn't provided them with DNA, but it has given them some physical information that could be useful.

"If we could get past the whole 'medical records are private' thing, then we could access dental records and narrow things down," says Gillespie.

"Right, I'm off," says Clarke, coming back into the room. "I'll get that profile update to the team. If anything else arises, give me a ring and leave a message with Trish. She'll see to it that I get it. It's about the only thing she does well. Gillespie, I expect to hear from you later." Clarke is still speaking as he leaves the room and the door swings shut.

"If he wasn't so busy barking orders, he wouldn't forget his stuff," says Gillespie, putting Clarke's glasses on and crossing his arms. "Right then, Linnet. Where to next, old girl? I've got a promotion to get, so double time, lady."

Jo laughs at his imitation of Clarke. To be fair, it is spot on. The right amount of authority, sickening ambition and misogyny. Gillespie's phone vibrates again. He takes Clarke's glasses off to read it.

"Tech team have found Michael Tanner."

16

Graham Pierce and his friends are sitting in the living room, watching football. The sound is bursting out of the television speakers. Roars and cursing occur intermittently. Crushed empty lager cans surround overspilling ashtrays. The smoke fogs up the room and the stench of stale ale clings to the furniture.

Emily closes the door behind her as quietly as she can, trying not to draw attention of the Neanderthals in the front room. She tiptoes her way to the stairs. A burst of loud heckling comes from the living room, causing her to freeze and hold her breath. She can see Graham sinking into his oversized, stained leather recliner. He is like a mechanical toy that performs the same action repeatedly, leaning towards the television to shout at the referee and then slumping back in his chair in a silent tantrum.

Particles of ash drop from his cigarette and float in the air like dead fairies. Perched on the sofa next to Graham is Mick, who drives a small van delivering goods to warehouses. On the other side is Alan, the quietest of his friends. Quiet or intense, Emily doesn't care; they are all odd as far as she is concerned. She takes her chance to run up the stairs, hoping that the sound of her feet hitting the floor will be swallowed up by the coughing, flatulence and jeering from downstairs.

Lying on her bed, she flicks through college websites on her phone, looking for art courses. They all want to see a portfolio from potential applicants, which isn't an issue. The problem is that they want to see the portfolio in person and the thought of travelling and speaking to strangers makes her feel anxious.

The front door of the house slams shut. The lock goes on, and the key is turned. Mick and Alan have gone. It is just her and Graham. The television is still on, and the lights are still illuminating the house. She tells herself that she is safe in her own home but pauses her music to double-check. The pulse vibrates through her ears, and she hears the stairs creak. The handle turns and her bedroom door begins to open slowly.

"What are you still doing awake?"

Emily lets out a long sigh and catches her breath, before replying, "Hi, Gina. Just listening to music. Couldn't sleep."

"Not surprised," says Gina, "with all that racket down there. The place bloody stinks too. Never mind, I've got rid of them. We're going to watch a film in bed after he's cleaned up the mess. How are you feeling today?"

"Good."

"Good? Wow, that's a turnaround. You need to calm yourself down," says Gina, as Emily laughs and hits her with a pillow. "What are you doing?" she asks, as she looks towards Emily's phone.

"Looking at colleges, if you must know. Adult classes. I've decided to join and study art."

Gina pretends to fall off the bed in shock. They both laugh as it's a rare phenomenon.

"That's amazing, Emily. I know it makes you cringe when I say it, but I am so proud of you."

Emily smiles and pushes her sister away when she tries to hug her. "Thanks," she laughs. "I said I'm good, not emotionally available." The pair continue to giggle. "If there was anyone I would hug though, it would be you," she says, as Gina blows her a kiss and closes the bedroom door.

Emily opens her phone. *'Do you fancy a coffee tomorrow?'* Message sent. She has been meaning to reach out to Samantha, a friend from secondary school. Since Marcus Gaines, her friends have been few and far between, but those she has are keepers.

Her phone vibrates on the bed. '*Yes, but I can't tomorrow. Will give you a text soon to make a plan. xxx'*.

She throws the phone back on the bed and is startled by shouting coming from the room next door. Listening against the wall, she can make out that Gina isn't happy with something Graham has done or something he has said. Maybe both. He has been staying out until the early hours most nights and he has lost one of his regular taxi customers; a businessman who has decided that if Graham can't be somewhere on time, then he isn't good enough. He has also been given a formal warning from the taxi firm after returning a car in a terrible state one night and calling the manager an 'uptight bastard' when he was asked to clean it.

Gina went crazy when he came home a few nights ago at 4 am and left dirty footprints on the new carpet. She hadn't bought the fact that he was working late. She accused him of having an affair, but Emily thought it was more likely that he was sitting on his own in the car, watching porn.

Who would have him? He is big, scruffy, and lanky; hardly fighting off the affections of various women. His breath alone is repulsive, and no number of mints or gum can hide his vices and poor hygiene. Maybe he is having an affair with a man? Or maybe he just likes anyone but Gina.

The noise from next door lowers, and Emily chalks it up to another night of Graham being the worst thing to happen to her sister. She wonders if there is a trail of women that would say the same thing about him.

17

Gillespie bangs on the door of Michael Tanner's home. Jo stands back, letting the detective do the police work. An elderly woman answers, clearly unsettled by the noise.

"Can I help you?" she asks, peering over the top of her glasses.

"Yes, Love, sorry to disturb you. I'm Detective Gillespie and this is Dr Jolene Linnet. Could we speak to your son, please?"

"Son? Sorry detectives, but you're about ten years too late to see my son."

"Excuse me?" Gillespie looks at Jo, puzzled.

"My son died a long time ago, Love. It's just me and my grandson here now. It can get quite lonely, but we get by just fine. Cup of tea? You must be catching your death out there." She stands aside to wave Jo and Gillespie in from the cold. "I'll open a pack of M&S biscuits too."

"Thank you, that's very kind of you," replies Gillespie, taking a seat in the living room which is full of mismatched furniture. The television is blaring, and a cigarette is burning in the ashtray. They look around the room. There are enough pictures to excite an ancestry enthusiast. The only ones in newer frames are of the lady and a man. Surely, Michael Tanner.

"Thank you," says Jo, as she takes her cup of tea. "Should we call you Mrs Tanner?"

"You can call me Nora," she says, as she sits on the couch and waves to them to help themselves to the biscuits. "Lived here all my life. I was Mrs Pendle before I was swept off my feet by my beloved Bobby and became Mrs Tanner. But, I tell you what, I'll always be a Pendle at heart," she says, with a mischievous wink.

"Mrs Tanner, can I ask you about Michael?" asks Gillespie, pointing towards a photograph to get confirmation that it is him. "Do you know where he is?"

"Is he in some type of trouble? I've brought that boy up on my own since his dad died. His mum is of no use whatsoever unless she needs something. Is he alright?"

"We'd just like to ask him a few questions and see if he can help with a case we're working on. Where is he now, Mrs Tanner?" asks Gillespie.

"Work. Got himself a little part-time job in a charity shop. Oh, I am so proud of him for working there, let me tell you. Brings me home lots of gifts and spoils me rotten, he does."

"Glad to hear it, Mrs Tanner. Do you mind telling us where the shop is? We can pop by and chat with Michael there, save us from disturbing you again."

As Gillespie is getting the address, Jo realises that she doesn't know his first name. He looks like a Brad, with his hair falling into his eyes. Or a Jeff, with his casual style. She makes a mental note to ask him later.

"Has he been to Ireland lately, Mrs Tanner?" asks Jo, out of the blue.

"Ireland? No, Dear. The furthest he's been in his life is Blackpool. Poor sod. I don't get out much, you see. He's just a local lad. Out until all hours working in that shop. I can tell you now, there aren't many young men who would look after their nan the way he does."

"Thanks again, Mrs Tanner. We can see ourselves out. The biscuits were divine by the way," says Jo, taking one for the road.

The charity shop is just a few streets away. The shop door is perched open by a small box, presumably to let fresh air into the small, stuffy space. There are more items in the shop than the space can manage. Everything from clothes, children's toys, shoes that looked like they have walked a thousand miles, and a library's worth of dusty books.

"Can I help you?" asks a young man. "We aren't open today. We're just doing a stock check and putting out some new stuff."

"Michael Tanner?" Gillespie flashes his badge.

"Yes? Is something wrong? Is it my nan? I'll get my coat."

"No need for that. Is there somewhere quiet we can talk?" asks Jo, wanting to get down to questions.

Michael Tanner is a waif. He looks pale and his blonde hair makes his blue eyes look artificial. "What do you need from me then?" he asks, as he sends his colleague home and locks the shop door.

'A sign of guilt?' wonders Jo.

"We're hoping you can help us with an investigation." Gillespie takes the lead and Jo watches Tanner closely for any change in his body language. "Do you recognise any of these girls?"

Headshots of five victims are presented. Amy Tatton, Anne-Marie Swift and others from unsolved voyeur cases.

"Look closely and take your time."

"No, never seen them before."

Jo and Gillespie glance at each other.

"Oh, hang on. Yeah, I recognise one or two of them. From the shop."

"Well, is it one or two, Michael?" asks Jo, impatiently.

"Two. Definitely two," he says, pointing to two of the pictures, neither of them Amy Tatton or Anne-Marie Swift. "I'm sure they've been in the shop a few times."

"Do you know them? Talk to them much?" asks Gillespie. "Fancy them?"

"No, not really. I mean, they come into the shop and leave donations. Nice stuff, most of the time. That's how I remember people, by what they drop off. I don't fancy them. Never seen them outside of the shop." He is babbling and Jo has heard enough and asks, "Can you explain your relationship with Amy Tatton?"

As soon as he hears the name, he runs for the back exit. Jo is faster on her feet than Gillespie and manages to wedge a foot in the door before Michael can close it properly. He is stronger than she expects. Gillespie starts pushing the door alongside Jo, sending it swinging open, and Michael Tanner to the floor.

"That was mostly me," says Gillespie, brushing his sweaty hair out of his eyes.

Jo picks Michael up off the floor and throws him into a nearby chair. "That wasn't very smart was it, Michael? Let's try that again, shall we? And leave the athletics out this time."

"I panicked, OK? What's he been saying about me now? Whatever it is, I didn't do it."

"Why would the name 'Amy Tatton' make you panic? Something you want to share with us? Or would you feel more like sharing down at the station? Up to you, of course."

"I'm not meant to go anywhere near Amy, but I just couldn't help myself." Michael trembles and his T-shirt is starting to stick to him with sweat. "I stayed away for as long as I could."

"When was the last time you saw Amy Tatton?" asks Gillespie.

"I knocked the other day. I know I shouldn't have, but she came into the shop. She didn't see me, but I saw her from the back office. I missed her so much when we split up but she wouldn't talk to me. It was like I meant nothing to her. Her dad got involved and sent me packing. Said if I ever came back, I'd be hunted and put down like an animal."

"Apart from then, have you ever been to her house? Her garden?" asks Jo.

"No, I swear. I wanted to, but I was too scared. Have you seen her dad? Do you know who her dad is? He'd have killed me. That restraining order is fucking bullshit. Amy wouldn't have wanted me out of her world for good. She loved me. When she came into the shop it was like fate throwing us back together."

Jo has to agree. The restraining order does sound like bullshit, but it is legally binding nonetheless and, if she is honest, she wouldn't want Michael Tanner around her daughters either.

"Let's go, Michael. We can continue this chat somewhere that doesn't smell like old jumpers," says Gillespie.

"We'll have to drop him off and go," says Jo. "Clarke wants us to meet him. They've found another body."

18

The drive from HQ to the latest crime scene is a quiet one. Gillespie chain-smokes all the way. His cigarette nearly falls from his mouth every time they drive over a pothole in the road, which is often.

The tidiness and organisation of the crime scenes are bothering Jo. How can such violence and intrusion happen without leaving anything behind? She knows she is missing something but, right now, she needs a clear head for whatever they are about to walk into.

Gillespie parks the car over the road from an alleyway. The place is swarming with officers, most of whom are busy tackling nosey pedestrians, wanting to see what is going on. These days, people are less concerned about who has been hurt and more concerned about the pictures they can snap for likes on social media. Jo recognises that they are just around the corner from Amy Tatton's house.

The dark area appears abandoned. Broken glass, used needles and condoms litter the floor. Bushes of nettles and weeds are overgrown, making the area secluded.

"Nice of you to join us," says Clarke, walking over to them. "An anonymous person called a few hours ago. Looks like the body's been here a lot longer than that. Tell me you have something."

"Just dropped Michael Tanner at the station," replies Gillespie. "Reckons he's squeaky clean, but don't they all? He gives me a Norman Bates' vibe."

"At least we have a suspect to work with. Let's find a way to connect him to another victim. See if there are any links to this one." Clarke walks over to the body, where Tara is speaking into a dictaphone. "Dr Howden, find anything useful?" he asks.

"Maybe. The time of death isn't clear, but I'd say she's been here for over twenty-four hours. No more than thirty-six. We'd see more bloating if that was the case. The body's in an advanced stage of rigor mortis. No sign of external decomposition, but I might find some in the organs. I'll have to wait until I have her back in the lab for that."

Tara has a reputation for tough-talking and not taking any nonsense from chauvinistic officers who think they will be the ones to turn her off girls. Jo likes her. She likes that Tara is probably the smartest person at any crime scene.

The body is lying on top of weeds and surrounded by rubble and waste. Someone has discarded her like she was meaningless.

"Any ID on the victim?" Jo asks.

"Gemma Woodcock," answers Gillespie. "Officer Summers found a student ID card a few feet from the body. The photo matches the victim. 22 years old. That's all we know."

"Cause of death?" asks Clarke.

"I'll have more to tell you when I get back to the lab, but I'd guess it was a blow to the back of the head. Looks like her head hit this rubble with some force. I can't tell you whether that was intentional or not until I investigate," replies Tara, as she stands and brushes the dirt from her trousers. She signals for her colleagues to prepare transportation of the body. "She's been beaten, I can tell you that. There's significant bruising on her abdomen. And here, look at this." She moves the right leg of the victim to reveal a bite mark on the inside of the thigh.

Officer Summers steps closer to Clarke. He has been waiting for his chance to work side-by-side with the chief. "We've found multiple used condoms, lots of seminal fluids. All collected, bagged and sent off." He pauses for a comment but gets none. "There was some vomit not far from the body which looked fresh. That's been sent off too."

Clarke nods to dismiss him. "Thank you, Summers. I'd say that's a start. I'll put a rush on the labs and see what they spit out. With any luck, we'll find something that links Michael Tanner to this scene, and we'll have him nailed to the wall."

He summons one of the newer officers and gives him a telling-off for having loose laces. Even from where Gillespie and Jo stand, they can sense the fear and remorse in the young man.

"If he was any more wound up, he'd snap," comments Gillespie. "Look at the state of this place."

Jo uses her feet to unearth overgrown weeds and mountains of litter. The alleyway is an invitation for antisocial behaviour. She notices that Tara is looking puzzled as she re-inspects the body.

"Council have been reviewing this alley for some time. There are calls for it to be gated, you know, to protect the area and put people off coming here for dodgy reasons. The problem is, that there's no ownership of it. Look at it. No lights, no love, no tendering of the area. It's scrap land."

"Except it's scrap land around the corner from Amy Tatton's house which, of course, could be a coincidence, but I doubt it," says Jo, still with one eye on Tara.

"Everything alright, Jo?" asks Tara. "I'm heading back to the lab. "I'll be gone by 5 pm but should have something for you before then."

"What was wrong before, when you went back over to the body?" asks Jo. "It looked like you had lost something."

"Oh, nothing. Well, nothing I can say right now. I need to do an examination before I can confirm anything, but this one feels different."

"Really? Well, give me a ring when you have something. Or I can come to you," says Jo, curious to know what Tara is thinking. "Off anywhere nice?"

"I'm going on another date, for my sins. I don't have much chance of finding Miss Right in my lab, let's be honest. Got to take my chances where I can." Tara winks and walks off, carrying her coat in one hand and her medical gear in the other. Jo wonders how she can find the time or enthusiasm for dating after a day like today, with bodies piling up in the city.

'Perhaps I need love and life to equal the death and darkness of my job. Take a leaf out of Tara's book,' Jo tells herself, knowing full well that she can't be bothered.

"I'm going to see our friend, Michael Tanner," says Gillespie, appearing from nowhere. "I've got a feeling he can shed some light on a few things. I'll stop by with Mr Swift on my way through. He was a broken man when I told him about his Anne-Marie. He's heard things about his daughter that no parent should ever hear. The least I can do is check in and give him an update." As he walks away, Jo pauses, second-guessing whether she needs to remind him, but she takes her phone out and sends him a text message.

'Don't forget that Mr Swift hasn't been ruled out as a suspect. Keep your game face on.'

19

Walking through HQ is like walking through high school. Even after all this time, criminal profiling is still met with hesitance and scepticism. Jo blames Hollywood and TV shows that portray profilers pulling information and estimates out of thin air.

The history of profiling is shaky. Templates made by the FBI in the 1970s were based on notorious criminals such as Charlie Manson and Ed Kemper. Whether sceptical officers know it or not, these templates inform most of their work.

Recognising whether a criminal is an organised or disorganised offender stems from the templates, as does identifying the significance of body disposals and victimology. Each time police join the dots between evidence, the relationship between offender and victim, and whether cases are isolated or connected, they use the same principles of profiling. At least profilers are aware of what they are doing, and why, and the shortcomings of the techniques.

Jo was taught that the templates are a guide, based on data and patterns. After all, Charlie Manson and Ed Kemper are hardly representative of all criminals. Sexually motivated serial killers, yes. Thieves, fraudsters and thugs, not so much. Being a profiler is more scientific and mathematical than most people recognise, but hunches and instincts are still central to good police work.

Jo prepares to interview Michael Tanner. She enters the interview room with two cups of coffee. Pale and sweaty, he looks like he has been vomiting since he was arrested. He takes the coffee with trembling hands.

"How are you holding up, Mr Tanner?" Jo asks, spotting the video recorder become active. "Can I call you Michael?" He nods, his eyes darting between her and the files on the desk. "For the benefit of the tape, Mr Tanner is nodding. OK, Michael, let's go back over your history with Amy Tatton. In your own words, what's your relationship with her?"

Michael sets his coffee down and rubs his hands through his hair. "She was my girlfriend. We were in love." Tears form in his eyes as he says, "I thought we'd be together forever."

"Did Amy feel the same way?"

"I thought so. She said she didn't, but I think she was in denial."

"How so?"

"It's overwhelming, isn't it? Love. She didn't want to admit it and didn't want her dad to know either. That's why he had me sent away, the bastard. You know who he is and what he does, don't you? He's a thug."

"You had a restraining order filed against you which permitted you from going anywhere near Amy or her house. Tell me about that," says Jo, steering him back on track.

"Told you before, the restraining order is bullshit. Like Amy would need protection from me. I loved her and I wanted to keep her safe. Her dad hated me. Probably doesn't like it when anyone gets close to his 'little girl'. He arranged that restraining order without her knowing. He's dodgy. Everyone knows it. He has everyone in his pocket."

Jo considers the possibility of Mr Tatton being jealous, but Michael's accusation doesn't sit with her instincts. "Why do you think it reached the point of a restraining order? There must have been some cause for concern."

"I wanted to see Amy after she broke up with me. I needed answers to understand and figure out what I could do to make things right. Only she didn't want to see me, which was hard, you know. I rang her, I knocked at the house, and I text her. When she didn't reply, I emailed her. She wouldn't talk to me on the street, or even when I took flowers to her work."

Jo understands how things have escalated to a restraining order. She would have instigated one much earlier than Mr Tatton if it was one of her daughters. Michael is obsessive and doesn't see anything wrong in his behaviour.

"Can you tell me where you were the night that Amy's garden was broken into? We both know you never went to Ireland. Give us an alibi, and we'll check it out and, if all goes well, you'll be back to the shop in no time."

"I was at home, with my nan. Ask her. Pretty depressing really. We had microwaveable spaghetti bolognese and watched 'Catchphrase'."

"Presumably, you weren't watching 'Catchphrase' around midnight."

"Nan went to bed. I stayed up and played 'Call of Duty'. She kept coming in the room and telling me to turn it down."

"Do you recognise this place, Michael? For the benefit of the tape, I'm showing Mr Tanner photographs that were taken from this morning's crime scene in the abandoned alley."

Jo places two photographs on the desk and leaves enough silence for Michael to decide whether he wants to go down the route of truth or lies. He looks at the images but gives nothing away. She swaps the images for the ones that contain needles, condoms, and broken glass from the scene.

"Am I likely to find your DNA on any of these?" she asks. "And there's no point lying to me, Michael. The lab's working on it as we speak, so being straight up with me is the best thing you can do at this point."

"Couldn't say. Maybe, if I've walked through there. Who knows? No needles, that's for sure. Dirty, them things."

"To be clear, do you recognise the location in these images?"

"Yes, I've just said. It's not far from … Amy's house." The penny drops for him. "Which you already knew, didn't you? You come in here, acting all friendly, but you want to trick me into something. Have I asked for a lawyer yet? I'm not saying anything else until I speak to someone," he says, as he folds his arms and moves his chair back from the table. He hasn't asked for a lawyer until now and Jo feels bad that she hasn't reminded him. "For the benefit of the tape, I'm refusing to answer any more questions until I have my lawyer," says Michael.

"Fine, do it the hard way. I'll come back when you have a lawyer. I'll have the DNA results from the alley by then too, so maybe we can get this wrapped up, or you locked up, before the day is over."

Jo picks up her folders and walks out, frustrated with the lack of progress but satisfied that Michael Tanner is a good suspect.

Across town, Gillespie is sitting with Mr Swift and asks, "Silly question, I know, but how are you getting on?"

Mr Swift looks exhausted like he hasn't changed his clothes in days. Although there are photographs of the family and seemingly happy memories placed around the room, the house is a stark contrast today. Mrs Swift has left, blaming her husband for what happened to their daughter, Anne-Marie.

"Well, I'm here. So, I guess that's a win. How about you? Any progress?"

Gillespie is relieved that talk has quickly turned to the case. What else can you say to someone who has lost everything? What can you ask someone whose child has been viciously assaulted and killed?

"I know it doesn't feel like we're making progress, Mr Swift, but we are. We've got several leads that we're following up. We're speaking to a few people of interest, but I can't say any more than that at the moment."

"Will you find him, Detective Gillespie?" Mr Swift barely raises his head when he speaks. He stares into the distance. Gillespie isn't sure if this is because of the visions of his daughter's final moments, or if he has dissociated to protect his mind. Jo would know. "Will you find whoever took my Anne-Marie from me?"

Gillespie's heart is breaking, as he replies, "I can't promise you that we will, but I can promise that I'll die trying."

They sit in silence. Digesting all that has happened and contemplating what might happen next.

20

Sophie Sheridan sits in her office on Huskisson Street. It is based in the Georgian Quarter of Liverpool, an area recognisable by the almost-uniform historical offices. The precise right angles of adjoining houses and strategically-placed leafy trees make the area look picture-perfect.

Her office is full of character. A heavy blue door is framed by a brick arch and black iron fences flank the entrances. On an autumnal day, an assortment of red and brown maple leaves dress the footpaths. During the winter, the street looks like something straight out of a classic Christmas movie.

She looks through her appointments for the day. Dave is due in later this morning, suffering from obsessive-compulsive disorder, triggered after the death of his mother. After him, she will see Richard who struggles with trypophobia, an intense fear of repetitive holes in patterns, which makes it hard for him to find work. In the afternoon she is due to see Samuel who was diagnosed with schizophrenia as a child and is experiencing a relapse of persecutory delusions. He believes that his neighbour is whispering threats through the walls at night and sending cars to knock him over when he is out walking.

Sophie cares for her patients and is fascinated by the working of the human mind. The lack of definitive answers in psychology drives most people to frustration, but she is open to all possibilities. People present with various issues for ever-increasing reasons unique to them. In the sessions, her emphasis is on listening and understanding, and on guiding the patient to counsel themselves and find ways to cope with their difficulties. There is very little that surprises Sophie. However, Emily Spencer is a different case altogether.

Sophie has come in early to review the notes from her sessions with Emily, and her progress so far, as it is a complex case. '*History of self-harm and suicide attempt. The patient claims the suicide attempt was not intentional. Treated for depression with SSRIs and treated for anxiety with a short-term prescription for beta-blockers.*'

Sophie pauses to think about the effects of such medication on a young girl. Antidepressants that increase serotonin levels in the brain and anti-anxiety medication that inhibits the nervous system. She hopes that Emily's doctor is monitoring the prescriptions and dosage carefully, rather than leaving her to manage them herself.

'*Patient was groomed by an older male when she was younger and duped into being recorded performing sexual acts on herself and others.*' It is no wonder that this beautiful young girl is struggling to find her confidence in the world again.

'*Patient lives with sister and brother-in-law. Both parents are deceased.*' Sophie is aware of the lack of paternal instincts in

Graham, the brother-in-law. She has heard Emily speak about him on a few occasions, in a way that makes Sophie's hairs stand on end.

The phone rings. Her calls don't usually come directly to her, but she has given Molly, her secretary, the day off for her birthday and gifted her with a spa break for two. "Hello? This is Dr Sheridan. How can I help? Yes, that's correct, although I can't talk about patients and their treatment in person or on the phone."

She is frustrated. It isn't the first time that calls have been made to get information about one of her patients. Reporters ring, pretending to be family members, and family members ring to get information about loved ones. Usually, it's the overbearing, narcissistic parents.

"I have a client arriving any minute so, if you really must come, it will need to be an hour from now." She sets the phone down as Emily knocks on her door.

"Hi Emily, come in. Sorry about that. Molly is away for her birthday," she says, as she ushers her to the couch and pours them both a glass of water. "I can't wait to hear how you've got on this week."

Emily sips her water and makes herself comfortable. She has brought her art portfolio, excited to show Sophie some of her work and talk about the art courses. Sophie takes the sketches and looks at each one, amazed at Emily's natural talent.

"These are amazing, Emily. I love this one. Is it a tulip? And this one, a fox?"

"Yes, you can have one if you want. I've put together this portfolio for my art school application."

"Tell me about that, how's it going?" Sophie asks, delighted that Emily is leading the session and showing enthusiasm for the future.

If she is planning ahead it means that Sophie can be reassured that there are no imminent plans of suicide. A sad way to look at someone's joy, but a good indicator of where someone is up to when they have a history of self-harm.

She listens to Emily talk about the different courses she has researched and how she wants to push herself and go out of the city. Not too far, maybe Edge Hill University in Ormskirk, or Manchester Met; somewhere she can commute to.

"I'm thrilled that you've done all this. You have a great talent and express yourself well. I wish I had some of your talent, I really do!" she laughs.

Passing the artwork back, she asks Emily how things are at home. "Not too bad. Gina's working all the time, so I don't see her until late at night. I can't complain though, as she's supporting me so much. I text my friend for a catch-up, but she was busy, so we'll do something another time."

"And your brother-in-law, Graham?" asks Sophie, prodding Emily for more information.

"Same as usual."

"Anything going on I should know about?"

"He's just the same as always. Creepy, drunk and stinks all the time. He's been going out a lot at night, but I like that. It does my head in when he's at home with his friends. I just lock myself upstairs and get on with my own thing until Gina comes home."

"Has anything happened? Anything you want to tell me? You know you're entitled to feel safe at home, don't you? Regardless of who you live with."

"I know. He's just weird. I promise I'll tell you if something happens," she reassures Sophie, while trying to reassure herself in the process.

Together they set the week's goals. Last week, Emily completed a mood diary; this week she agrees to make appointments with colleges to discuss her options.

"Keep up the fantastic work, Emily, I'm proud of you. Thanks for my picture; I love it. Next time you're here, you'll see it on my wall."

As Sophie walks Emily out of the office, a man is waiting in the reception area. He holds the door for Emily as she leaves. If it isn't for his chivalry and semi-good looks, Sophie would be worried for her safety. The big building can feel so empty when Molly is off.

"You're prompt. Come in. My office is this way. I'm Dr Sophie Sheridan, but then I guess you know that already," she says, holding out her hand.

He shakes her hand and replies, "Thanks for seeing me at such short notice, Dr Sheridan. Hopefully, I won't take up too much of your time. My name is Detective Gillespie."

21

As he sits on the couch in Sophie's office, Gillespie can't help but notice how prestigious it is. Bookcases from floor to ceiling that also display her certificates and licences. Chesterfield furniture fills the room, and she sits behind her huge mahogany desk. Perfect décor for the Georgian Quarter.

"You might be more comfortable on this chair, unless you subconsciously sat on the couch to confess your deepest and darkest secrets, Detective Gillespie," she jokes.

"I'm here on behalf of Merseyside Police," says Gillespie, straightening his shirt and jacket. "Does the name Michael Tanner mean anything to you?"

"You already know that it does, Detective. I don't think I can say any more than that though. Patient confidentiality, you understand."

"Of course. Perhaps you could give me just enough without crossing the line? A few simple questions are all I have, and it would help with our inquiries." He takes out his pen and pad. "You're familiar with what's been going on in Liverpool? The attacks?"

"I'm working right in the epicentre of it all, but what's this got to do with me, or Michael?"

"Michael Tanner's in our custody at the moment and, on his record, it says that he attended some sessions with you a little over a year ago." He looks to Sophie for a response, as he continues, "Can you confirm or deny that?"

"I can confirm that. I'm not sure where this is going, but I don't make a habit of using patient information for anything other than their treatment and welfare." She takes off her glasses and he is struck by the colour of her eyes. If he hadn't just witnessed her wearing glasses, he would swear she is wearing cosplay contact lenses.

"Let me give you some information and you can chip in if you want. How does that sound?" he suggests, as he holds his hands out to appease the situation. "Michael Tanner is a suspect in the attacks that are happening in Liverpool. He has a restraining order against him, and it seems he's broken it several times. There's reason to believe that his DNA will be found at an active crime scene, and his alibi is shaky, at best."

Sophie doesn't interrupt or indicate any surprise.

"Does that fit in with your knowledge and impression of Michael Tanner?"

"I would love to help you out. It's been a long time since I met with Michael, and he was only here for a short course of sessions. Off the record, I've no idea what he might be capable of. On the record, he was troubled but willing to work with me. That says a lot about a person and their intentions, in my book."

"Ok. It was worth looking into but, hey, not every lead takes us somewhere, right?"

He stands and walks over to one of the many bookcases in the room. He doesn't recognise any of them. "Impressive collection."

"If you don't mind, I have another patient due in," says Sophie, as she stands and opens the door, signalling the end of their meeting.

"Of course. Thanks for your time, Dr Sheridan. Please take my card in case there's anything you think of that might help me."

He hands her a card after scribbling his personal mobile phone number on it. He pauses to allow her to respond but she takes the card and smiles, waiting for him to leave.

He walks out through the reception, passing a man who is repetitively turning the lights on and off, as he waits for his appointment.

22

Jo is sitting on Rodney Street, waiting for Gillespie and watching people pass by. It is an occupational habit.

Businessmen and women walk past, on their phones, without glancing up at the landmark architecture nearby. Elderly people walk hand-in-hand. Students walk in large groups. The street is home to private medical clinics and high-end offices. It is a short walk from Central Station.

A little girl runs past and drops her teddy. Before Jo can get up, a man catches up with her. Jo feels her heart begin to race. Is the little girl walking off with someone she knows, or someone who is tempting her away? She knows this is an unfair response to a man with a small child, or perhaps it is a stereotypical response, rooted in evolutionary survival instincts. The little girl disappears across the street with the man, laughing and hopscotching down the pavement.

Susie used to hopscotch and jump across crooked or broken pavement squares, playing 'broken biscuits' as she was careful not to step on any lines. Jo wonders what she might look like now, whether she would be happily engaged or married with children. No one will ever know. Eddie Doran stole her sister, and walked off with her one day, promising her God knows what to go with him. Jo dreads to think about what happened to her after that. She has investigated enough cases to know that children who have disappeared rarely walk off into a happy-ever-after. Was she killed instantly? Was she killed at all? Was she sold and trafficked? The possibilities make her feel sick.

Inside the medical lab, Tara is finishing her investigation of Gemma Woodcock. She has removed, weighed and inspected the internal organs, made her notes and returned everything to where it belongs. Respecting the dignity of the patient and regarding the feelings of the bereaved families goes beyond finding out what happened to their loved ones.

Tara is thorough in her investigations, in her record-keeping, and in ensuring that the families of her patients are none the wiser about what happens during a post-mortem. Once the body is clothed and prepared for a funeral, there will be no evidence that she has cut them open and taken them apart.

"Jenna, care to summarise?" asks Tara.

"Gemma Woodcock, homicide. Cause of death, blunt force trauma to the back of the head," replies Jenna, proud of herself.

"Good, but you're not on a word limit, so try again. What's the science? How did we reach that conclusion? What have you just watched me do?" asks Tara, as she scrubs her hands and cleans her kit.

"Gemma Woodcock. Cause of death, homicide. A single excision to the back of the head was made and the top of the skull was removed." Jenna pauses to swallow the excess saliva or stomach acid that is forming in the back of her throat. "The brain was examined and there is evidence of a traumatic brain injury. There's a contusion that indicates blunt force trauma to the back of the head, likely to be the cause of death." She pauses again and looks at Tara, who is now standing next to her.

"Much better, well done. So, you do listen to me after all," she laughs. "One thing though, TBIs aren't necessarily fatal and, when we're faced with a deceased person, it's not really an injury, is it? Other than that, not bad at all." She smiles and gives Jenna a heavy-handed pat on the back.

"How do you know it's murder though? Could she not have fallen and hit her head?" asks Jenna.

"Possibly. In cases where we aren't sure, we can state an 'undetermined' cause of death. From the size and depth of the contusion in the brain, it's more likely that Gemma Woodcock was pushed with some force, hitting the back of her head. Plus, the alcohol level in her blood indicates she wouldn't have been aware of anything that was going on."

"What if she did fall, but accidentally? Or whoever did it, didn't mean to kill her?" Jenna pushes with her questions, determined to reach a satisfactory conclusion. "I mean, I know it was an attack and a gross assault, but how do you know that murder was intentional?"

"We can record the death as accidental if the evidence suggests so. But the blood alcohol level, and the force of the head trauma, both suggest otherwise. The bite mark appears to be consistent with the other cases. The bigger picture is what matters and it's our job to look at all the facts and the science holistically and come up with a narrative of what likely happened. That's all we can do."

"Someone order a man in uniform?" asks Gillespie, as he walks into the lab. "Mine's with the dry cleaner, so will this do?" He spins around to showcase himself and Jenna laughs along.

"Detective Gillespie, if I ordered a man in uniform, I can assure you there would be a good reason. Like a blocked pipe or a fault in the wiring but, now that you're here, I suppose you'll do," says Tara, smiling at Jo.

"Why am I never enough for you, Tara?" Gillespie winks at Jenna, who winks back.

"You're just not my type. Florence Pugh, on the other hand, is right up my street," smiles Tara. Gillespie shrugs his shoulders in defeat.

"You know I'm only joking though, don't you? In a charming, sarcastic way." Gillespie wants to remind everyone in the room that he isn't a sleaze, just a joker.

"Of course."

"Right. And you're joking with me too, aren't you, about me being repulsive?" he laughs.

"Of course," replies Tara, with a serious look on her face which breaks into a slight smile. "Shall we get started?"

She tells Jo and Gillespie about her conclusions regarding Gemma Woodcock. The head injury and contusion in the brain suggest she was pushed with force, hitting her head on the rubble or rock in the alley.

"Nothing significant about stomach contents, and no needle marks on the body so she wasn't using any of the hypodermics found at the scene. High blood-alcohol level, but no indications of liver cirrhosis."

"Seminal fluid?" asks Jo.

"None."

"As expected then," says Gillespie.

"Not quite," replies Tara. "This case didn't sit right with me at the scene. Now that I've finished the examination, I know why."

She shows them a close-up photograph of the bite mark from Gemma Woodcock's leg and displays it next to one taken of Anne-Marie Swift.

"These aren't a match. The impressions are different in size and shape, and those on Anne-Marie Swift are deeper - a bite with intent. The marks on Gemma Woodcock are faded and don't even come close to breaking the skin."

"What does that mean then; a coincidence?" asks Gillespie.

"Maybe. Or a coverup. I also found evidence of old bite marks, the same size and shape as this one, on her arms. Fetishism, maybe. Self-harm, perhaps. Whatever it is, they aren't from the same person you're looking for."

"Results just came back from the alley," says Jo, reading a document on her phone. "Latex condoms at the scene, some empty and discarded, some used and discarded. Between them and the needles, there are too many DNA sets to get through today, but they did get a hit on one. Michael Tanner's DNA was found in one of the used condoms."

"Christ, that's him banged to rights then," says Gillespie.

"It puts him at the scene, but not in contact with the body. We still need more. Clarke said there was blood found on some of the broken glass, but no match. Various animal fibres were found near the body. Let's be honest; the place is a breeding ground for junkies, rats and drunks. There must be something else," says Jo.

"Just to be clear. The bite marks don't match, it may or may not look like an accident, and there was no evidence of sexual assault," summarises Gillespie, as he scribbles furiously in his notebook.

"And the body was found in a public walkway. Very different to the seclusion of an abandoned area where we found Anne-Marie Swift," adds Jo, sitting down on a cold metal stool next to where Tara is standing. Their eyes lock.

"What is it?" asks Gillespie.

"Gemma Woodcock might not have been killed by the same person as Anne-Marie Swift." Jo pauses, collecting her thoughts. "So, that means we could have two killers in the city, operating at the same time. Not impossible, but absolute shit luck. On the other hand, it means it's completely irrelevant and we've been chasing a dead duck."

"Or …," interrupts Gillespie, "… it is the same guy, but he was interrupted, or something went wrong. Michael Tanner's DNA turns up next to Gemma Woodcock's body, and he's got a restraining order stopping him from going anywhere near Amy Tatton. I'll bet my last cigarette that there's also a link to Anne-Marie Swift."

Tara watches as Gillespie and Jo talk about the possibilities. She is fascinated by how Jo's mind works and is glad that it is more straightforward to work with bodies and utensils. She likes answers and evidence, not hypotheses and possibilities. She interrupts their discussion to give them the results of the bite analysis from Anne-Marie Swift's case.

"Report came through earlier on the bite analysis. Nothing that gives us a name, but the report does clarify that the incisors of the biter are false." She points to her two front teeth and the ones on either side and explains, "They leave a different impression than natural teeth."

"That's something," says Jo. "Gillespie, let's ring all the dentists in the inner-city centre. See if anyone has a history of patients that match this description. They'd have it on record, right?" she asks Tara.

"Sure. Everyone would have a mould for false teeth, or to have braces made. That'd be on their history, but I doubt they'll hand over information about patients. Also, it's not uncommon for people to have false front teeth. Diet, acid, oral hygiene and bruxism, to name a few, affect more people now than ever." Tara fastens up her coat, signalling that she must leave. "Your best bet is to get an impression of any suspects and see if it matches the details from the forensic odontologist's report."

"We could get Tanner done and see if his gnashers match these," suggests Gillespie. "We would have his teeth, his DNA in the alley, and his history with Amy Tatton. Clarke would have this case closed as fast as you can say 'Prime Suspect'."

"Just remember that bite mark analysis is useful, providing it's accompanied by other compelling evidence," says Tara. "Alone, it can be misleading. Jenna, what do you remember about the issues with forensic odontology?"

Jenna joins the table and gives her summary of notes. She has been studying bite analysis as part of her apprenticeship, and the issues with its methodology. She explained, "There are numerous cases where people are found guilty based on bite mark analysis, only to then be exonerated because of a lack of other evidence, or DNA found that didn't match the 'guilty' party. It also depends on how bite marks are analysed. A case in 1991 led to the arrest of a man for rape and assault but the bite marks on victims were photographed without a ruler for reference and examined with infrared lights *after* the wound had started to heal. Eventually, the evidence from the bite mark analysis was overturned."

"We can speak to the dentists and get the ball rolling with a mould of Michael Tanner's teeth. That does give us something to go on, at least. Thanks, Tara," says Jo, heading for the door.

"Just one more thing to add," says Tara. "Some of the biter's teeth are fractured. Might be useful to think about dietary or behavioural habits, stomach acid issues or dental hygiene issues."

She doesn't want to be the bearer of bad news, but there are many problems in modern dentistry. Braces, veneers and corrective procedures for chipped teeth and the advancements in science can sometimes be a barrier to investigations. She fears that Jo will not get the clarity she wants from the bite marks.

"We found evidence of gum disease on the patio door in Amy Tatton's garden. No DNA evidence, but it's starting to form a picture. You're sure there's no DNA from the bite marks?" Jo asks, as a last effort to walk away with something.

"No, for there to be DNA from a bite mark, there needs to be a puncture wound. The bite would have to be much harder, and saliva transferred into the skin."

Jo nods, digesting the information, daunted by the thought that if the killer strikes again, she hopes that he will bite the victim harder.

23

The rain has subsided, but the ground is a maze of puzzles. It is hard to tell whether a puddle is just a puddle, or whether it is masking one of the many potholes in the city. Gillespie and Jo sit in the corner of Ruby's Bar on Brownlow Hill. She orders a steak ciabatta roll and he orders pie and chips, with a whisky for each of them. The food arrives suspiciously quickly but, after not eating all day, the concern soon passes and the food is devoured.

"What time's Clarke coming?" asks Gillespie.

"Any minute now. He wants to review where we're up to, to be ready for a press conference tomorrow. There's been pressure from local universities and colleges to release information to the public."

"All he's going to hear is that Tanner's the killer. You know that right?" asks Gillespie, swigging back his whisky like it was juice.

"We can only rely on the facts, and they don't look good for Michael Tanner."

As Jo is about to voice her concerns, Clarke walks in and orders drinks for the table. "What a bastard of a day," he says, placing his bag and jacket on the seat next to him. "I've got numerous people trying to make me look incompetent and a shitload of paperwork coming at me from all angles. Tell me something good, something that'll satisfy the media hounds."

The chief looks pristine, yet haggard. Jo swears that he is looking older each time she meets him.

"There's enough to make connections between Michael Tanner and more than one victim," says Gillespie.

"Yes, and I bet there are more victims we can tie him to if we look hard enough," says Clarke.

Gillespie gathers his thoughts out loud, for the table. "OK, so we know that Tanner has a restraining order in place but broke it several times by going to the property of Amy Tatton. We know he was in the alley where Gemma Woodcock was found, confirmed by his semen in a condom. That places him at, or near, two crime scenes."

"We also have bite marks from Anne-Marie Swift's body," adds Jo. "We're waiting on some more information, but we can take an impression from Tanner and see if it's a match. We'll have to get past his lawyer though. He lawyered up this morning."

"Fuck his lawyer," snaps Clarke. "We've got enough to place him at two crime scenes and I'd bet my arse that he's in this, up to his neck. An alibi from his granny isn't going to cut it either and I'm sure his lawyer is regretting taking the case on, as we speak. I'll tell the media we have a suspect. I won't name him, but I'll say he's being detained and helping us with our inquiries. Why aren't you looking happier, Linnet? Who pissed on your chips?"

"I've got reservations about Michael Tanner. Nothing substantiated just yet."

"His semen was in the alley, a few feet from a dead girl. What more do you want?"

"I'm just playing devil's advocate. There's no evidence to suggest he killed Gemma Woodcock. The Tattons have a biased history with Tanner. There's nothing, so far, relating him to Anne-Marie Swift. He's the best we have, but we need more."

Jo takes another drink and Clarke is hanging on her every word. "What we do know is that the guy we're looking for has poor oral hygiene. Possibly fractured teeth, false teeth and gum disease," she continues.

"Christ, Linnet. That could be half of the city. You could be describing Gillespie, or me for that matter. But at least it's something. Hold Tanner for another twenty-four hours and let's take it from there. His lawyer will try for a release, based on lack of DNA, but fight it. If he's our guy, then we don't want him being a flight risk."

As Clarke walks out of the bar, Jo checks her phone for messages but doesn't hold her breath. The last time she heard from her daughters, they were still angry with her. Although, not as angry as when they were sending insults and warning her to stay away from their dad. That was a year ago and they are starting to come around, but there is a long way to go yet.

"Anything interesting?" asks Gillespie.

"Nope. What about you and Jenna?" she asks. "You two seem friendly."

"I'm a friendly guy, but I'm unavailable. I'm married to the job," he replies, as he signals for more drinks to be brought to the table.

"She likes you; I can tell. It's my job to notice these things." They look at each other and laugh, knowing full well that he is the opposite of unavailable.

"Why don't you ring them?" asks Gillespie. "You check your phone more than I check mine. I assume it's your kids you're waiting for. Or your ex."

"There's more chance of hell freezing over than my ex getting in touch with me. In fact, if I got knocked down by a bus and never got back up, he'd be more than happy. The kids will be in touch when they're ready. They just need space."

"Jesus, what the hell did you do? Sell their kidneys and keep the money?" he jokes.

"I think there'd have been less fallout if I had." She drinks her whisky in one swift gulp, before saying, "I cheated."

"Tall, dark, handsome and in uniform, was he?"

"More like tall, blonde, beautiful and in a dress," she replies. "And your face is not too dissimilar to my ex's when I told him."

They laugh, which helps Jo fight back the tears that threaten to come when she thinks of her daughters. When her ex-husband found out what she had done, it tore a hole through their family. It didn't matter that it was only one woman. He was heartbroken and the emotional infidelity was harder to forgive than the physical. Jo had moved out to give him some space, but that turned into separation, and anger turned into hatred.

"What about your other family?" asks Gillespie.

"Mum and Dad died a long time ago. I've got aunts and uncles, but I can't tell you what they look like. You've probably arrested some of them, I wouldn't know."

"So, no sister that might like a man who is good on the inside but a little rough around the edges, and carries a detective badge and protects the city like Batman?" he asks, running his hands through his floppy, greasy hair.

"Truth is, I wouldn't know," replies Jo, as she tells him about Eddie Doran.

"Shit, man. I remember hearing something about that case, a long time ago." He wants the ground to swallow him up. "Where is he now?"

"Walton Prison," she replies. "I went to see him a few times before I joined the police. He's probably why I got into the field. I pleaded for him to tell me where she was, something to confirm that she was either alive or dead. He never said a thing. Not knowing is the worst bit, but I think that's what he enjoys the most. Eventually, Susie was declared dead, in the absence of a body."

"What do you think happened?" he asks. "Tell me to mind my own bloody business if you like, but you must have a theory."

"More than one. Do I believe Susie is dead? Sometimes I hope she is, rather than the gruesome alternatives. Sometimes I like to think that she was passed onto a happy family, in some type of fairy tale version of trafficking."

"That's fucked up, Mate," says Gillespie, rolling a cigarette. "I don't blame you though. The stuff we see and hear every day. Worse for you, you're in their minds."

Jo sighs, and says, "That's right where I want to be."

24

The morning rush of traffic starts early, with people driving out of the city and many driving in for work. Gillespie doesn't know which is worse; the cars doing battle on the roads, or the pedestrians who don't let anyone get in the way of their commute. Today, he votes for the pedestrians.

Some walk aimlessly, staring at their phones, surprised and full of scorn when they bump into someone else. Others walk with serious intent to get from A to B, without smiling or making eye contact with anyone. Commuting to work in Liverpool is a skill. Cups from 'Costa Coffee' or 'Café Zero' are a staple part of the morning commute, but Gillespie will always vote for 'Starbucks', given the option. Usually, he takes whatever is offered.

As he reaches HQ, he receives a message. It's from Clarke, reminding him to get what they can out of Michael Tanner and to make connections with the voyeur cases. He shakes his head and walks into the interview room where Jo, Michael Tanner and a fresh-faced lawyer are waiting for him.

"For the benefit of the tape, Detective Gillespie has entered the room," says Jo. "Peter Walsh is representing Michael Tanner. Anything you would like to say to start us off, Mr Walsh?"

Peter Walsh looks through the files that he was probably handed less than an hour ago. He is a police-appointed lawyer, and a young one to boot. He shakes his head.

"Right then," continues Jo, "let's kick this off with some questions. Gillespie?"

"Michael, we've reason to believe you were in Amy Tatton's garden on the night she reported an attempted break-in. Can you tell us where you were that night?" asks Gillespie.

"No comment," replies Tanner, looking over to his lawyer.

"For the record, you've already answered this question yesterday, Michael. I just want to ask you again, seeing as though I wasn't there." Gillespie remains friendly, appeasing cooperation from Michael, whose lawyer nods and indicates that he can answer.

"I was at home. Watched 'Catchphrase' with my nan. We had tea, she went to bed, and I played on my game. She came down several times around midnight to ask me to turn it down. Said it sounded like the house was turning into the bombed-out church in town. I was playing 'Call of Duty'."

The bombed-out church on Berry Street is an iconic Liverpool landmark. If you ask anyone for directions in the area, they will always be given with the church in mind. 'Opposite the bombed-out church' or 'You know where the bombed-out church is? Well, it's a few minutes up from that'.

St Luke's Church was hit by a bomb during the 1941 May Blitz, causing catastrophic damage and fires. Only the external features of the church were left standing. For the next sixty years, it stood derelict. An emblem of Liverpool's strength and a beacon of hope.

"See, the thing is, Michael, your alibi isn't as strong as you might think. We asked your nan, who's lovely by the way, and she said she was disturbed by your game, but couldn't be sure of the time," says Gillespie.

"What do you want me to do about that? You asked me, and I told you. Not my fault if the old bat can't remember."

"Do you have any reason to keep my client any longer?" asks the lawyer. "It seems like you're at a stalemate with this alibi. It's your responsibility to prove Michael wasn't at home that night playing games and, so far, you can't."

"We'd like to take a dental impression from Michael, to rule him out of another case. We can get that done now," says Jo.

"I don't think so. You don't have enough on my client to demand that level of cooperation," says the lawyer, packing up his files.

"Mr Walsh," says Jo. "Your client is in a worse predicament than you're yet to realise. He doesn't have a solid alibi, he's broken the conditions of a restraining order on more than one occasion, and his semen has been found in a used condom where a young girl's dead body was found. I think it's in Michael's best interests that he cooperates, don't you?"

Peter Walsh whispers to his client and they both nod. "We agree to the dental impression but, for the benefit of the tape, would like it on record that Mr Tanner is being compliant to help clear his name." He leans over to hear what else Michael is trying to say to him. "My client would also like to explain why his semen was found in the alley, although it's my advice that no comment is sufficient at present."

All eyes are on Michael Tanner, waiting for the revelation about why his semen was found at the site of Gemma Woodcock's body.

"I was waiting for Amy. The alley is around the corner from her house, and sometimes I see her near there."

"The semen?" prods Gillespie.

"I can't help it. Sometimes I go there waiting to see her and get excited. Nervous too. What if her dad sees me there? He's seen me there before. Battered me, he did. I wouldn't be surprised if you found one of my teeth in that alley somewhere."

"OK," says Jo. "So, you go to the alley, waiting to see Amy. You're excited and scared, you're aroused and masturbate. Why the condom?"

Michael looks confused. "It's a public place. I'm not an animal. I just don't know what to do with it once it's, you know, full."

"Do you recognise either of these girls?" Gillespie places several photographs on the table, including a picture of Anne-Marie Swift and the college identification image of Gemma Woodcock.

Michael looks at the images, and then at his lawyer. "I don't think so. They look familiar, I guess, but I don't know them. Who are they?" he asks, as his lawyer rolls his eyes.

"Yesterday, you didn't recognise this one," says Jo, pointing to Anne-Marie Swift.

"I don't know her. Look, I work in a charity shop in the city centre. People come in and out all the time. They drop things off, they stay to look around; it's thrifty nowadays. Cost of living, isn't it?" His behaviour is erratic, and his answers are too on-the-nail to be fabricated. His use of restricted vocabulary and speech is frustrating, and half of the stuff he is saying is irrelevant. Despite this, Jo thinks he is telling the truth.

"What about this one?" asks Gillespie, pointing to Gemma Woodcock. "You recognise her?"

"Same. Might do, might not."

"I think what my client is saying is, that he doesn't know these girls, but he can't be certain that he hasn't at least encountered them. If he has, he doesn't remember but he doesn't want to say that he's never seen them since he can't possibly remember every customer that has come into the shop," says Peter Walsh, looking at Michael, who confirms this with a confident nod. "You've got what you need from him or will have it by the end of this interview. DNA, blood samples, and he's agreed to this dental test. So, I don't see any reason to find Michael unhelpful or a flight risk and ask that you let him go home as soon as the test is done."

Jo and Gillespie look at each other knowing that, as long as Michael is cooperating and does not leave Liverpool until further notice, they have kept him as long as they can.

"Fine," says Gillespie, "but I want you to check in here every morning by 9 am so we know you haven't left the city. Deal? Fail to do so and a car will come and get you as fast as you can say 'donation'."

"Deal," says Michael, slapping his lawyer on the back in agreement.

"Wait here. The dental team will come and take an impression and, as soon as they're satisfied, you can go. It'll take a day or two for the mould to come back and be investigated," says Gillespie, as he and Jo stand to leave. "One more thing, Michael. You work at the charity shop part-time, yes?" Michael nods in response and Gillespie continues, "Tell your lawyer about any other work you do for money, cash in hand or not, I don't care. We'll get the information later."

Michael and Peter Walsh nod and begin to chat together.

"What do you think, Jo?" asks Gillespie, as he pours a cup of water from the dispenser.

"I think he's guilty alright, but I don't know if he's guilty of murder. How about you? Did you see the way he looked at the pictures? No remorse or fear. Like he'd never seen them before, let alone raped and murdered one of them."

"Still suspicious to me," says Gillespie. "I reckon we keep our eyes on him and see what he gets up to in his spare time. If he's got the time to hang around getting himself off in alleyways, he has the time to travel across the city, getting up to no good."

He doesn't like the way Michael looks or speaks, as if he is frustrated and excitable at the same time. It is hard work getting information out of someone who uses 'no comment' as a staple answer to most questions, but it is harder to decipher what is relevant when someone like Michael answers questions inconsistently. Either he is good at appearing confused and dim, or he is one of the oddest people that Gillespie has come across in a long time.

"The team are in there now, getting the dental impressions. If it's him, we'll soon have a match that ties him to Anne-Marie Swift," says Jo. "You go look at the files in the office and see if there's any connection between Tanner and the other cases."

Gillespie walks back to his office, stopping to speak to everyone he passes. He has a reputation for being friendly, flirty and funny. He isn't recognised by his peers as the ambitious type but is a solid detective who you can count on at any time.

By the time he gets to the office, Peter Walsh has emailed over the other jobs that Michael Tanner has been doing for extra money. A few weeks delivering pizzas, before he was fired for not returning the delivery bike. Cleaning local pubs but dismissed on account of not being a good cleaner. His most recent appointment was at 'Cable Cars', a local taxi firm. A few weeks into the job, the car he rented from the rank was clamped. On a second occasion, his car was removed from a walkway by police after it was left overnight, obstructing the middle of town. Gillespie makes a mental note to go to the taxi firm and ask some questions.

There are boxes of cases for him to go through. Cases of voyeurism that had happened before Jo got involved. Many women had reported being followed and watched, but none were able to provide useful information about who it was or what he or she looked like. CCTV is inconclusive. Most people have fake CCTV in their gardens and homes to deter intruders. The only thing they have in common was reporting someone being in their garden, seeing an outline of what looked like a stocky man, but no attempted burglary. No semen at any of the sites, just like Amy Tatton's. Jo had got lucky with the swab of the patio doors and the gum disease evidence, but there is no way they can go back and look for that in the previous cases.

Gillespie sticks a map on the whiteboard, an aerial view of the city centre. He is making it up as he goes along but has seen Jo do the same with the other cases. He places a pin on every location where a case has been reported.

The first pin for Hood Street, near St John's Gardens. The second pin is for School Lane, near The Bluecoat Centre. The third pin is for Henry Street, off the main road, and the fourth pin is for a ground apartment on Cooper Street. Finally, one for Pembroke Street, where Amy Tatton lives.

He stands back and looks at the map, waiting for something to jump out at him, the way it does for the characters in 'Criminal

Minds'. However, the pins are telling him what he already knows. The cases are mainly focused in the city centre, as are numerous train stations, taxi ranks and a national coach station. Amongst these is Lime Street, an international train station.

'*Could be commuting into the city from anywhere.*'

25

Gillespie leaves the map where it is so he can go through it later with Jo. After all, geographical profiling is above his pay grade and right on hers. He leaves the HQ and heads for the taxi rank that Michael has recently been sacked from. A taxi rank next to James Street train station seems like a good investment, especially when disruptions cause many trains to terminate there.

"Anyone here?" he shouts, as he enters 'Cable Cars'. The room is cold and smells of greasy sandwiches and cigarette ash. The smell makes him feel sick. He considers sitting but the chair looks like it will give way, or disintegrate if it is touched. It looks like no one has waited for a cab there for a long time.

"Hi, I think I spoke with you on the phone," he says, as a man approaches him, with a cigarette in one hand and a phone in the other.

"Not me, Mate. What are you after? Where do you want to go? You're better waiting outside, you know. The cars pull up out there and it's first come, first served."

"Thanks, I'm not here for a taxi. I have questions about an employee that used to work here. I'm Detective Gillespie." He holds out his hand, instantly regretting the germs he is potentially going to pick up.

"Boss isn't here, I'm supervising now. Will I do?" asks the man, who has surprisingly sat in the chair that Gillespie was sure would crumble. The man is stocky and unkempt, with ash from his cigarette falling to the floor.

"Michael Tanner. He worked here not long ago, and I believe he was dismissed."

"Tanner, what a wrong un' he was," says the man. "Didn't last long. Managed to get his car clamped in week one. A week later he came back without his car at all. It was taken by police, or someone like that, for obstructing a walkway. Silly sod left it there while he went into the shop. He was caught short; dodgy prawns or something. Anyway, he left it there for a few hours, got himself to the chemist and home, and didn't give two shits about the car. Pun intended. Next thing, it was gone. Boss got a letter telling him where he could pick it up, and that he needed to pay five hundred quid to have it released. He wasn't happy, let me tell you that. The car probably wasn't even worth that much to begin with." The man laughs, coughing and spluttering at the same time as taking a hit from his cigarette. He makes it look like such an unattractive habit.

"Did he get the car back?"

"Paid the money, but the car came back in a right state. It was towed to the pound and the boss drove it back. Apart from that, no one's touched it. Looked like Tanner hadn't cleaned it since he took it over. We're meant to give the cars a good clean, inside and out, whenever we've time in the week. We have a reputation to keep up, you know," he says, as more ash drops to the floor and onto his trousers which bulge at the hips and belly.

"Right. Where's the car now? Any chance I can take a look?"

The man looks at him, puzzled. "It's out back. Not been used since Tanner was fired. Needs decontaminating, and a set of new wheels. Came back with two punctures from gravel and a crack in the windshield. Fuck knows what he was doing."

He pauses for a second and looks Gillespie up and down. "You know, on second thoughts. I think you had better come back with a warrant. I've probably said too much already, me and my big mouth. I don't want to lose this job.I've got dependents. Besides, it's a cushy job here. I don't want to be next on the boss's hit list."

"Not a problem, you've been very helpful. We'll want to look at the car as soon as possible. I'll get someone over right away, as it's part of an ongoing investigation. I'll come back as soon as I can with a warrant and that should satisfy your boss. How about that?"

"Sweet," the man says. "What investigation?" He is suddenly aware that he hasn't asked why a detective is so interested in the taxi before he started spilling the beans on Tanner.

"Can't say, not until we get that warrant and get back here with a team. Might be able to shed more light on the situation then."

Gillespie stands to leave, unaware that he too has sat on one of the questionable chairs. He brushes his trousers and shakes off some of the cigarette ash that has fallen onto his shoe. "Thanks for your help, Mate," he says, approaching the door. "Who should I say I spoke to, if your boss asks?"

"Graham. Graham Pierce," the man shouts, as he walks back to the rear office.

26

"Faye Williams, don't you dare storm out of this house, young lady! You come back here and talk to me and your father with some respect!" shouts Mrs Williams.

"I wish I wasn't your daughter," cries Faye, throwing her phone against the wall in anger, and slamming the living room door so hard that the whole house shudders momentarily. She grabs her jacket from the bannister and attaches Jasper, her German Shepherd, to his lead. Within seconds, she is standing on her doorstep with her iPod blasting out her favourite tracks and the rain beating down on her head. She doesn't care if she spends the night walking and soaking wet, she is not going back to the house anytime soon. The sky is darkening, and it seems that the gloomy weather is keeping most people indoors.

She leaves her home and heads down a shortcut towards Festival Gardens, where Jasper can run off-lead. The area is over a hundred acres of land and is usually home to oriental gardens, waterfalls and pagodas. What once hosted the nationally treasured garden shows is now a building site, surrounded by overgrown weeds. Police signs are positioned at every closed entrance to deter people from entering. That doesn't stop everyone, of course. Where there is a will and a flimsy fence, someone will find a way.

Mountains of stone and concrete waste are dotted across the land. New trees have been planted in the distance as part of the green regeneration plan. Local business flyers are pasted to the fences like art.

"You love me, don't you, Baby?" she asks, looking at Jasper who is already dripping wet.

Faye feels sorry for herself, but she feels sorrier for shouting at her parents. She knows that her mum is only looking out for her, but the constant invasion of privacy and overbearing lectures about life have been driving her mad.

The stars in the night sky illuminate the landscape. In a few hours, the area will be full of gangs, smoking weed and drinking whatever alcohol they can take from home. For now, it is a clear, long run for Jasper who loves nothing more than being off-lead, chasing birds or rats, and digging holes.

Festival Gardens is Faye's happy place; anywhere she can listen to music and be free from drama. She considers texting her mum and apologising, but she doesn't. For one, she has left her phone at home and, secondly, she is sick of apologising to keep the peace.

It is getting darker and her wet clothes are starting to sting her skin. In the near distance, she spots a tall stack of wooden pallets and decides to sit there and catch her breath before going home. She sits for a few moments and tries to stretch her wet jeans so that they cling to her skin a little less. She squeezes water out of her ponytail.

The rain falls on her forehead as she looks up to the sky. Shivering, she takes the dog lead from her pocket and looks around for Jasper.

She sees a dark shadowy figure lurking in between two mountains of rubble. It is hard to make out with the heavy rainfall, but it looks like an odd place for a scarecrow. She wipes the water from her eyes and takes another look. Her heart starts to beat faster and her muscles tense, as she realises that someone might be watching her.

Looking over her shoulder to see where Jasper is, she sees him squatting on a small patch of grass, going about his business. She turns back around to find that the shadowy figure has gone.

With no phone to use as a torch, she regrets coming here this late. She decides to find Jasper and leave as fast as she can. It won't take long to get back to the other side and onto the main road. She will have to walk through puddles and mud to get there more quickly, but she is already soaked through, so it doesn't matter much.

"Jasper!" she shouts, looking around and is aware that she might not be alone. It's probably someone looking for a safe space to skin up.

"Jazz, come on. Walkies!" She listens for the sound of Jasper running towards her, the splashes in puddles or the panting as he leaps, but she doesn't hear a thing. She can see his caramel-coloured tail poking out of one of the bushes and starts walking over to him.

"Jasper," she says, as she approaches. She keeps looking around to make sure that no one is creeping up on her. She has seen too many Halloween movies. Pulling back branches, she sees Jasper lying in the dirt, with his eyes struggling to stay open. He whimpers like a helpless puppy and his breathing is irregular and erratic.

"Oh, my God, come on boy. Please, get up. Please."

She rolls Jasper over to help him to his feet but it is no use. His front legs have been snapped and blood is leaking from the right side of his little neck. She takes her jacket off and holds it against the wound, but it is soon dripping with blood. Jasper yelps with the pain, desperate for comfort and help. Faye tries to pick him up and carry him home, but he is too heavy. He is soaking wet, coated in mud, and whimpers each time he is moved.

She cries, still trying to keep her hand firmly against the wound. "Help! Someone help me, please! Help us!" She shouts with fear and desperation. Jasper stares at her with pleading eyes that begin to roll back and forth, as more blood is lost. As Faye kneels beside her best friend, trying in vain to keep him alive, Jasper becomes restful. His breathing slows down. His eyes remain closed, and his muscles become limp.

"Jasper, please wake up. Please, please, please!" Faye cries so hard that she almost faints. Her heart is breaking into infinite pieces. Covered in blood, she turns and vomits. She tries again with all her strength to pick him up but his dead body is too heavy for her slender frame. Out of options, she sits beside him. She squeezes him tightly and cries, but her screams fail to come out.

She is disturbed by a sound from somewhere nearby. She holds her breath and listens, trying to reassure herself that it could be a rat, a fox, or even the wind. As she tries to remain inconspicuous, she listens again.

And there it is, a whistle. Not the wind. Not the cries from the trees. A whistle, an eerie melody.

She lies Jasper down gently and peeks from behind the branches. Her pulse races and her imagination is running wild. Adrenaline is already surging through her body. She decides to run home for help and come back for Jasper.

She runs as fast as her heartbroken body can carry her. Puddles of mud splash up her legs. Rain falls into her eyes, and she trips over something hard. With her hands covered in wet gravel and soil, she picks herself up and runs even faster. Suddenly, she stops. Frozen. Fight or flight no longer keeps her moving.

"What do you want?" she yells.

In front of her stands a man, hooded and disguised by darkness. He sways slightly as if he is waiting for her to come closer. Still whistling, he tilts his head to the side as if curious as to what move she will make next.

He has been watching her.

He saw her leave her house. He watched her let the dog off the lead. He saw her wipe the rain from her beautiful face, and the way her clothes clung to her body. He watched her walk, dodging puddles and humming to her music. He saw her looking sad and scared. The dog had run over to him and he had no choice but to eliminate the risk. Snapping its legs seemed like a quick fix, no matter how sick it made him feel. A stab to the neck would put the dog out of its pain and let him get back to business. It isn't as effective as he has planned, but these things happen.

Faye is frozen with fear. There is no point in running. She is exhausted and Jasper's blood is all over her. There is no way out except ahead, through him. She takes a step forward, trembling with terror. Maybe she can run and push past him. Knock him over. She takes another step and another, until she sees a silver object glistening in his pocket. Her legs are numb with fear, but they make a sudden run for safety.

She shouts, as she hurls her body at his, fighting for her life. Like she is paper and he is stone, he strikes her. She falls to the ground and starts crawling away from him. He grabs her hair and throws her face to the ground. Her jaw hits a plank of wood; waste from old bonfires. A nail pierces her cheek, cutting through to her tongue. She loses strength and is blinded by the pain. She grips the ground in one last attempt to drag her stunned body across the ground.

"Please," she begs, choking on her own blood. "Please, stop."

He grabs her by the feet and flips her over. She can feel him tugging at her clothes, and a sharp sting on her leg. Drifting in and out of consciousness, she sees his face. His eyes. She smells his breath. It is stale.

She sees the silver object again. Not a knife. Not a weapon at all.

27

Gillespie and Jo arrive at 'Cable Cars' taxi rank. Graham Pierce is agitated that they are there and have brought a small team with them. The taxi of interest remains untouched since Gillespie was there yesterday. A uniformed officer has been monitoring it to make sure it isn't tampered with. A forensics team will investigate it thoroughly for anything that looks suspicious but, for now, a small team starts to inspect it.

They brush for fingerprints and are not surprised to find it riddled with them. They need to find a set that matches the suspect, Michael Tanner, or the victim, Anne-Marie Swift. The seats and floor of the taxi are inspected, as they search for anything that doesn't belong. Fibres from clothes, dropped items, earrings, waste, and anything else that might prove to be relevant. The team looks for evidence of blood, no matter how much or how little.

Michael Tanner is unreliable. Untidy. Unprofessional. Judging by the state of the taxi, he was a threat to the reputation of 'Cable Cars'. It is no wonder he was sent packing and the car was off-road.

"Mr Pierce? Does your manager normally stay away when police are investigating the place?" asks Gillespie.

"Dave's on holiday. A couple of taxi firms and, somehow, he's Alan Sugar. Sends his regards though. Says you can look at anything you like, as long as it's quick."

"Do you keep records of who uses each car? Drivers and customers?"

"Most drivers have their own car but some, like Tanner, pay a weekly rental fee for one of Dave's. Got to be insured obviously. We keep a rent book for the cars. Here, take a look."

Graham passes Gillespie a rent book that looks like it has been used as a coaster for the last few years. Details inside confirm that the car was rented by Michael Tanner and that he was the last person to use it.

"What about customers? If we wanted to know if someone booked one of your taxis, can you tell us? Can you tell us who picked them up?" asks Jo.

"Sure. If the operator takes a call, the details go into the system. Name, pickup address, paying cash or card, that sort of thing. The drivers can all see the jobs as they become available and it's first come, first served."

"Can we see entries for a particular time and date on the system?" asks Gillespie.

Graham demonstrates how the system works and pulls up all calls made to the rank the night that Anne-Marie Swift was murdered. Her name doesn't appear on any list, suggesting that she didn't call the rank and that no one had picked her up. A dead end.

"What about you, Mr Pierce?" asks Jo. "Did you get on with Michael?"

"As much as the next person," Graham replies. "He was odd but nice enough. Complete waste of space though, as a driver. Nervous around customers, especially the pretty ones."

"Is it possible for the operator to assign a job to someone, or to change the records?" asks Jo.

"I guess so. Sometimes a driver might be stuck in traffic, so we manually change who is taking the job. Or a customer might cancel or change their pickup address, so we manually edit that. So, yes, I guess so."

"Were you working the night Anne-Marie Swift was taken?" asks Jo, trying to catch him off-guard.

"Eh? I work most nights. In fact, I've worked every night since Dave's been away."

"So you have access to the system? You could manually change some of the information on there?"

"Listen, Love. I don't know what you're getting at, but I haven't changed anything. Nothing that didn't need it anyway. Are you nearly done here? I've got a job to do."

Jo makes a mental note about checking up on Pierce when she gets back to the office. She doesn't like him. Not just because he needs a good wash and a shave, or spits when he speaks. His smile makes the hairs on her arms stand on end.

"Gillespie! We might have something," one of the forensic team shouts from the back of the taxi rank, calling him and Jo over. The investigation team found a small amount of blood on the rear passenger door. There are some minute clothing fibres on the rear seat and an earring on the floor. The front tyre on the driver's side has a puncture from some sort of industrial bolt that is wedged deeply into it. The team prepares to move the vehicle back to HQ.

Pictures of nude women hang on the walls of the 'Cable Cars' operator's office, torn from newspapers. A calendar of semi-naked women leaning on expensive cars is pinned to the door, and ashtrays overflow with stubs and old chewing gum. Empty packets of crisps and sandwich boxes scatter the desk and floor.

"You done? You shouldn't be in here on your own. GDPR and all that," says Graham, leaning against the door frame.

"Any CCTV in this place?" asks Gillespie, walking back over to Jo.

"Nope," replies Graham, no longer wanting to cooperate.

"What about GPS tracking on the cars?"

"Nope," Graham laughs. "This isn't 'Fast and Furious'."

"Mr Pierce," says Jo, "you said Michael got in trouble once, after the taxi was 'towed to the pound'. Where was it taken?"

"Chaloner Motors. Private firm up on Chaloner Street. Probably make money hand over fist. The car was left on their 'private property' and they took it. Simple as. Extreme, if you ask me, but these private companies make their own rules."

"How long was it there for?" asks Gillespie.

"Not sure. A couple of days, I think. The boss thought Tanner was just being a lazy prick. Turns out the car was in the pound the best part of the week."

As the forensic team clears out, Jo and Gillespie follow them, leaving Graham Pierce to return to work. No discussion is needed as Gillespie enters Chaloner Motors into the sat nav.

28

"What's your first name, Gillespie?" asks Jo.

"What do you want it to be?" he replies, flirting and smiling.

"Gross. You know a fair bit about me, more than I've shared with others, and I don't even know your first name. Is it something embarrassing? Please let it be something embarrassing."

"Harry Gillespie, at your service." He smiles and shakes her hand.

"Nice to meet you, Harry. Suits you," she smirks, as they pull up at Chaloner Motors, which looks like a cross between a scrapyard and a car park. Gillespie taps on the window of a small reception area and is greeted by an elderly man, wearing a flat cap and folding up a newspaper.

"Hi, there. I'm Detective Gillespie, and this is Dr Jo Linnet. Wondering if you can help us."

The man shrugs his shoulders, barely interested. He signals for them to come in and shows them what they want to see. Records taken the night Michael Tanner's taxi was brought to the pound and records of release when Dave came to collect it. Graham Pierce was right. It was in the pound for a couple of days.

"Any CCTV?" asks Jo. "Might be something and nothing, sir, but if it's no trouble then a quick look wouldn't harm us, would it?"

The man shows them to a small room with no windows. Computer monitors show the camera footage of the pound, and an old VCR player sits in the corner.

"Welcome to 1969," says Gillespie. "At least the videos are organised. Try this one."

The man stops him from reaching for a tape and hands him a different one from the top shelf. "This is the one you want, Lad," he says. "Catalogue them myself, don't I? Only keep them for a few weeks then reuse the tapes. Can't get them anymore. Shout me if you need anything else. I'll be out front."

Fuzzy images appear on the screen, like a rolling montage, from the different cameras around the pound. Cars come and go more often than either of them have realised. Dogs run in, do their business, and run out again. Michael Tanner's car is brought in, exactly when they expected it. No surprises there. Jo fast-forwards the tape to see who picks it up. Dave appears on screen and drives the car out. Everything Graham Pierce reported is accurate, so far.

"Wait, go back," says Gillespie. "What was that?"

Jo rewinds the tape to the moment the car was brought in. She presses fast forward to watch it on double speed. "Stop, leave it. Let it play," says Gillespie.

They watch the tape. People come and go; workers, cleaners and customers, looking like they have paid a ransom to get their cars back.

"There. Look," says Gillespie. "It can't be."

Jo pauses the tape. "It is. But why? Why would he be at the same place as Michael Tanner's car?"

"I don't know. But I'm sure as hell going to ask him," says Gillespie, taking his phone out. Jo looks at the screen. Phillip Tatton is standing in his long trench coat, passing an envelope to someone else.

Bob Clarke.

29

"It's not what you think," says Clarke, addressing Jo and Gillespie in the office at HQ.

"Phillip Tatton is giving you money for something dodgy. It's exactly what I think," says Gillespie.

"OK. But it sure as shit isn't anything to do with your investigation."

"So, it's a coincidence that you're doing dodgy deals in the same place that our number one murder suspect's car is?" asks Jo. "You'll have to do better than that, Sir, and don't give me that 'need to know basis' crap. I'd say we need to know. Don't you think so, Gillespie?"

Clarke takes a deep breath and places his bag on the desk. He takes out a notebook. "The owner of the pound has a criminal record. Minor stuff. I helped him get his licence for the pound. In return, he lets Tatton use the grounds from time to time. You know, to rough people up a bit. Scare them. That sort of thing."

Jo and Gillespie aren't satisfied so far. They don't interrupt, keen for Clarke to carry on.

"Only it went beyond that. He took a car one night. Brought it back a few hours later. Turns out it was used in a robbery. I hit the roof. That wasn't the arrangement. Made me take a few hundred quid for it and said I was involved, whether I liked it or not. That I was to turn a blind eye, or he'd see to it that I never made commissioner."

"So, you just let him get away with it?" asks Gillespie.

"What else could I do? I was stuck. I keep records in this notebook. Dates I know about. Crimes that the cars have been used in. You know, for insurance."

"But they don't implicate Tatton," says Jo. "Christ, Clarke, what about Michael Tanner?"

"Irrelevant. Coincidence. You can see on the tape that I take the money from Tatton and go. What are you going to do?"

"I don't know," says Gillespie. "Report you. Let you resign and bow out."

"There's another option," says Jo. "Delay our decision. Do nothing. This might be a way to watch Phillip Tatton. We have the records and the cars used in the crimes. All we need is something to directly link Tatton to criminal activity. When are you seeing him next?"

"Don't know. He calls me. Are you suggesting I spy on him?"

"I'm saying that you carry on as you are. Keep taking records. See what we can get him to do on camera at the pound. If you find out something's happening, get a team there to catch him in the act. It won't save your career, but you can bow out doing the right thing."

"There goes my chance of being a commissioner. It's all I ever wanted. Let's nail this son of a bitch. I'll do it, but on one condition. Nothing changes. We still crack this case, nail Tatton, and then I'll go." Jo and Gillespie look at each other, uneasy about what has been decided and suspicious that there may be more to the story than Clarke has told them.

30

Tara arrives at Festival Gardens. A group of stoners found the body last night. Considering the area is taped off and the public is prohibited to go on the land, there are a lot of cars in the car park.

She spots Jo near the body. "Morning. What's happened here then?" she asks.

"Dead dog, dead girl," says Clarke, who appears from nowhere. "Faye Williams, 19 years old. Out for a walk after a row with her family."

"Anyone spoken with them?" asks Jo.

"Gillespie's over there now. Ruling them out," answers Clarke. This was standard procedure. Rule out the family as potential offenders, especially where a motive is apparent.

Tara puts her medical gloves on and offers a spare pair to Jo or Clarke. Jo accepts although she doesn't plan on touching anything. Clarke takes a purple pair from the CSI equipment box.

"Poor girl. She's young," Tara says to Jo, as they walk closer to the body. "What's going on over there?"

"The girl's dog. Legs snapped and a puncture wound to the neck," replies Jo. "Sick bastard."

"You OK?" asks Tara.

"Me? Yes, I'm fine. Well, as fine as you can be at this time of the morning, looking at a dead body and a tortured dog." She pauses and looks at Tara. "Sorry, I'm OK. Really, I am. Are you?"

"All the better for seeing you," replies Tara, as she picks up her pace towards the body.

Jo scans the scene, looking at the small crowd that has formed. Something horrific and nightmarish always draws a crowd. The thrill of seeing something which is usually on television or in films; something they have bad dreams about or hear on the news. These people will go home and phone everyone they know to tell them what they have seen, adding their details to make it more gory or traumatic, and posting it on social media, while the real victims of the crime are too terrorised to speak. News vans have parked up and are shouting for Clarke's attention.

"Ladies and gentlemen, I'll make a brief statement and take one or two questions, but that'll be all," bellows Clarke, as he addresses the reporters. "I'm sure you're aware that there has been a string of offences committed in the city and, although they're still under investigation, I want to assure the people of Liverpool that we're doing all that we can to keep them safe."

"What happened here?" asks a voice from the back of the crowd.

"A young lady has tragically died. It appears to be foul play, although we'll have to let the autopsy and investigators determine that. I'm sure you can imagine that there's a family who are devastated today, and I ask that you give the officers space to conduct their work, and the family time to grieve and support each other."

"Is it the Night Walker? Is he a serial killer?" shouts another voice.

"It's too soon to tell if what happened here has anything to do with previous cases and the words 'serial killer' haven't been used by us. We'll endeavour to bring those who committed these terrible crimes in our city to justice. That's all."

Clarke waves the reporters away and two officers escort them towards the main road, away from the crime scene.

Jo watches as the bodies of Faye Williams and Jasper are placed in bags and carried away. The area is secluded. The body was somewhat concealed, although it looked unintentional. Faye was found behind one of the mountains of land waste. Anne-Marie Swift was found inside an open skip. Both were young girls out on their own, late at night. Although there are similarities, Jo needs more evidence to suggest that they were killed by the same person.

"Tara!" she shouts, as she walks over to the medical examiner team. "Found anything?"

"Obvious sexual assault. I don't need to wait until the autopsy to tell you that. Unfortunately, no seminal fluid that I can see just yet. Bite mark on the leg. Clothes torn. Throat slit," replies Tara, as she packs up her bags. "This one is more consistent with your other case."

"Shit," says Jo.

"Sorry to be the bearer of bad news. I'll have more for you back at the lab. Give me a few hours?"

"Sure. Thanks. See you soon," replies Jo, patting Tara on her arm. "Drive safe."

Mark Summers jogs up to Jo, handing her a phone and indicating that the call is important.

"Don't you ever answer your phone?" asks Gillespie. Jo checks her phone. It's on silent. "I just left the family. They're in bits. Remind me next time to let you do this bit. You can use your psychology on them."

"What are you ringing for Gillespie?"

"I spoke to her mum and dad. There was a brief argument and Faye stormed out with the dog. Not uncommon according to Dad. Mum's in bits. I've left them with an officer. Got out of there as soon as I could. My gut says they don't know a thing."

"Did you check her bedroom?" asks Jo. The silence answers her question. "Go back. Go and check the bedroom. See if there was a boyfriend, girlfriend, or anything that surprises the parents. We need to check everyone. There must be something these victims have in common. We just aren't seeing it."

"I'm sure you hate me," Gillespie says as he hangs up and goes back into the house. He pulls on his gloves and walks into Faye's room. A typical teenager's bedroom, but tidier than he expected. The walls are bare, with no posters or photographs. The only things on the desk are books, folded clothes and a jewellery box which houses a few rings, but nothing that seems important.

He feels uncomfortable going through the girl's bedroom. He has done this a thousand times during his career but this feels different, like he is rooting in her room without knowing what to look for.

He fumbles through the wardrobes and underwear drawers, trying to be discreet and leave things as he finds them. Nothing. He looks under the bed in case there are storage boxes full of mementoes. Nothing.

He sits at the desk and flicks through the books he saw earlier. Faye had enjoyed reading, and it saddens him that she will never finish this one, 'To Kill a Mockingbird'. She will never get to the end and see justice through. The irony is not lost on Gillespie.

He puts the book back and picks up another; 'Frankenstein'. As he opens it, a slip of paper falls to the floor. He picks it up and opens it carefully, pinching the corners with his gloved hands. It's a receipt.

"Sorry to disturb you again, but I've one more question," he says to Mr and Mrs Williams.

"What is it?" asks Mrs Williams, as she blows her nose and wipes away some of the endless tears.

"You said earlier that Faye didn't have a boyfriend or girlfriend."

Mrs Williams nods.

"Does the name Michael Tanner mean anything to you?"

"Is that who did this to my little girl?" asks Mr Williams, which is one of the few times that Gillespie has heard him speak since he arrived.

"I don't know, sir. I'm just asking if he's familiar to you. I found this receipt in one of Faye's books. It's from a charity shop that may be significant. Do you know anything about a Michael Tanner?"

Mr and Mrs Williams look at each other and shake their heads. They embrace with desperation as if holding each other is all they can do to feel safe. Gillespie nods to the officer to take over and leaves the house.

"Jo, call me back. I found something."

31

Jo and Gillespie sit in the office, drinking coffee and reviewing where they are up to.

"A receipt from Michael Tanner's charity shop in a book owned by Faye Williams. A restraining order against Amy Tatton. Semen found at the same place as Gemma Woodcock's body. Potentially something in the taxi that links him to Anne-Marie Swift," summarises Gillespie. "I'd say our case is building up quite nicely."

"Seems so," says Jo, reluctant to accept the tidy conclusion.

"You don't seem happy about it."

"I doubt CPS will dance for joy either. Loads of people will have a receipt from the charity shop. It's a link, but it doesn't mean he killed her. What would his motive be, anyway? And don't forget Gemma Woodcock doesn't quite match the other bodies. Something's not adding up. What came back from the dentist?"

"Oh, not much help. Too many patients match the isolated conditions. Can't give us names but I did find out that not many have the full set. Gum disease, false teeth *and* fractured teeth."

Jo looks around the room and focuses on the map of the city. The one Gillespie has started putting pins in, to represent the location of where the victims were found. "See this area here?" She draws a circle, connecting all the pins. "This is the 'Circle of Danger'. Anyone working or living within this area is at risk."

"Can't we just find the intersecting area from all sites? X marks the spot kind of thing. Like they do in 'Arachnophobia'," asks Gillespie.

"Not quite." Jo adds a pin for Faye Williams's location. "We know we're looking for a marauder. Someone living or working within the area. What about victimology?" she asks, rhetorically. "Similar ages. All female. All alone at the time of the incident. Most are students, studying in the city. Amy Tatton might be embroiled in her dad's world. Faye Williams rowed with her parents. Anne-Marie Swift didn't get picked up by her dad. This guy has a type, but we aren't seeing it."

"Just to play devil's advocate, what if we're on the wrong track completely? All I'm saying is, what if we should be looking for a female criminal? Or a tag team?"

"The physical strength, combined with the damage to the bodies, doesn't indicate a female offender. Statistically, crimes committed by females are more subtle and less exhibitionist. The biting, the penetration, the lack of modesty when disposing of the bodies; it's more than likely we are looking for a male. And the consistency between the killings and the voyeur reports doesn't indicate more than one person."

"I'll get someone from uniforms to check the danger area. See if any ex-offenders are known to us or have just been released; that sort of thing," says Gillespie, sending a message on his phone. "What about Tanner?"

"He's not the only person who could've given someone a receipt. Let's get the entire payroll of the charity shop questioned and see if anyone else stands out."

Gillespie leaves to coordinate the uniformed officers working on the case, while Jo sits and stares at the map.

The 'Circle of Danger' isn't small enough to narrow down where future crimes might happen. There are major train lines and bus stations right across the city. Anyone could hop on a train at Central Station and be on the Wirral, or the other side of Merseyside, within twenty minutes. CCTV hasn't picked up anything suspicious so far.

As she sips her coffee, it occurs to her that Liverpool isn't just transport, clubs and universities. She takes out a pen and starts listing all the major landmarks. Places that aren't residential areas or neighbour the crime scenes. It's not a long list. Theatres, cathedrals, business centres, police headquarters, fire stations and other places that are dotted within the 'Circle of Danger'. She takes a picture of the list and sends it to Gillespie. *'Ask someone to compile a list of everyone who works in these places or has recently left or been fired.'* She sends a follow-up message, *'Please'*.

He replies almost instantaneously. *'Will do. Got more info from the lab. Animal fibres from the skip and alleyway are similar species. Too many to narrow down but the obvious suspects are rats and mice. Some fox and lamb hairs. Who knew Liverpool was a safari?'*

Jo takes out her cigarettes and wonders whether Tara smokes or has any bad habits. She doubts it. Tara's teeth are near-perfect and she always smells fresh and fragrant. She puts her cigarettes back in her pocket and flicks through photographs on her phone. Silly memes and awful jokes that Gillespie has sent her. Pictures of nice sunsets across the city skyline. Pictures of her two daughters.

Ashley, the sensitive one, sends her a text message every now and then to check in and let her mum know they are all OK. Darren and Becky barely get in touch. Darren is still angry; rightly so. Becky was always a daddy's girl, so she is still holding a grudge.

Her phone pings and brings her attention back to the room. It's a message from Tara. *'Hey! You free?'* Jo smiles and feels nervous as she rings her. No answer.

Another ping on the phone. *'Can't talk right now. With someone. Come see me asap though. X'*

32

Jo walks down the corridor to Tara's medical lab.

"Hey! You got changed," shouts Gillespie, chasing her down the corridor. She is surprised and disappointed to see him. She has changed, wanting to be presentable and not knowing what Tara might want her for.

"I got a message from Tara saying she wants to see us. Probably has an update. Let's go," Gillespie says, as he slaps her on the back and races ahead. She feels foolish but follows him into the lab, taking a deep breath as she walks through the swinging doors.

Gillespie already has the file of Faye Williams in his hand, flicking through it and looking at photographs of the body. Tara pauses to greet Jo, but senses something is off as Jo walks past her and looks at the pictures, over Gillespie's shoulder.

"What have you got for us?" she asks Tara, without looking up.

"I can confirm what I said at the scene. No seminal fluid was found there, or on the body. Bite marks on one thigh and her throat was slit, just like Anne-Marie."

"What about the fingernails?" asks Jo.

"Mud. Signs of a struggle. Possible trace evidence on clothing has been sent to the labs for testing. Swabs from the dog reveal an unidentified compound which might reveal something about the Night Walker."

Jo huffs at the sound of the tabloid name and Tara can tell something is wrong. There is tension in the air and even Gillespie picks up on it. Tara senses that she should carry on. "The substance has similar properties to sweets."

"Just when I thought this case couldn't get any weirder," says Gillespie.

"The same substance was found in the skip from the Swift case but didn't seem significant at the time. Now that it's at another crime scene, it's worth a look," explains Tara. "Ingredient one is gum. Ingredient two is diazepam, and ingredient three is Xylitol, which is found in mouthwash."

"I'd like some of that!" shouts Jenna, looking up from behind her desk. Jo and Gillespie have not spotted her there. "What's not to like. Gum for nice breath, a little diaz to lighten the mood, and a little lubricant. Sounds like something you pop before a date."

"Lubricant?" asks Jo, focusing her attention on anything other than Tara.

"Well, not quite. Xylitol is found in all sorts of dental hygiene products," explains Tara, yet to make eye contact with Jo.

Gillespie decides to follow his detective's nose and see what else Jenna thinks about the case and clues. She may be an apprentice, but she is also privy to the bodies and evidence. He perches himself on the edge of her desk. "So, do you know much about lubricant?" He realises his poor choice of words and tone as soon as the question falls from his mouth. He and Jenna both giggle quietly.

"Nothing really, I was being silly," she replies. "It just reminded me of a guy I used to date. He had a bad case of the devil's breath, if you get me. The smell was awful. I'm not shallow though so I did what any kind-hearted soul would do and took him to the pharmacist."

Jenna is animated, and her hands and voice tell a story that Gillespie is struggling to follow. He watches her more than he listens to her, with his mouth agape.

He scribbles some notes on his pad. If there is something in it, it is a lead for the detective of this partnership. Jo can follow the hunches, but Gillespie is a stickler for good old-fashioned detective work, picking up clues and solving puzzles like a point-and-click computer game.

"Anything else on Faye Williams?" Jo asks Tara, as she scrolls through her phone, looking busy.

"Nothing else about the dog, just broken bones and a fatal wound. Appeared to be cut with a similar object to the girls. I'm confident it was a knife. Typical sharp kitchen knife. Nothing special. But why kill the dog?" asks Tara, attempting to initiate mutual conversation, rather than just giving facts. "Why kill anyone, of course, but the dog is an anomaly."

"Who knows? It was in his way, I guess." Jo puts her phone away and looks at Tara for a split second, before moving her gaze to Gillespie, who is laughing with Jenna. "What do you make of the animal fibres at the scenes. Uncommon?"

"Not really. Rats and other rodents are all over the city centre, especially one that's almost surrounded by docks. Foxes too, although they'll cluster in the centre and anywhere there's waste outside."

"Lambs?" asks Jo.

"Sorry?" asks Tara. "Jo, is everything alright? You don't seem yourself."

"Myself? Course I am. Well, as much as I can be with dead bodies turning up across the city."

"Have I upset you?" Tara asks, moving closer.

"How would you have done that?" asks Jo, finally sustaining eye contact with Tara. "What about the traces of lamb fibres?"

A few seconds of eye contact and silence linger between them. It is Tara who breaks first. "Lamb fibres are obviously strange. I'd be inclined to put them down to anomalous testing. Research has shown some genetic similarities between humans and sheep, not many, but enough to throw a DNA programme sometimes. We can rerun the samples."

"Great. Let us know what you find."

Tara begins to say something as Gillespie comes over. Unaware that he has interrupted, he tells them snippets about the story from Jenna.

"How did your date go, Tara?" he asks.

"I don't think there'll be a second date," she replies, casting a glance at Jo. "Still fun though, and home by a reasonable hour, of course."

"Sure. I believe you, thousands wouldn't," he says, as he leaves the room. Then he shouts to Jo, "You coming?"

"Thanks for that. I'll wait to hear from you. Or Gillespie will. Just let us know when you have something, OK?" says Jo, as she leaves without waiting for a response.

33

Jo sits on her couch with a bottle of red wine for company. It is the first time she has spent more than an hour at home since she joined the case. She is frustrated, and the bottle of wine is not going to be the solution, but it will make a good Band-aid.

Murder programmes, robberies and deaths. Every TV channel reminds her about the realities of life. She settles on 'Love Island', despite feeling inferior to the contestants who have tanned, toned bodies and perfectly styled hair. She feels like a frump; pale and dishevelled in contrast.

She looks at the slightest hint of a tan line where her wedding ring used to be and wonders whether Darren is still wearing his. Doubtful. He probably took it off and threw it to the bottom of a pond in Sefton Park on the day she left. What a shitshow that was.

He had come home from work one night to find her asleep, with her phone in her hand. He had taken it to put it somewhere safe. That was when he saw the photos of her kissing someone else, looking happier than she had in a long time. When he woke her, he shoved the phone and photographs in her face and demanded the truth. The tears fell from his eyes and she couldn't tell whether it was with confusion or heartbreak. Probably both.

Jo had met Kirsty at a training event that took place three times a year and, over time, they got to know each other well and enjoyed their time together. They would text and call throughout the rest of the year and Jo eagerly looked forward to seeing her, more than the training events. One time, the night before they were to say goodbye again, Kirsty asked Jo to go away with her. Somewhere with a hot tub, massages and nice food. She jumped at the chance of time away from her job and family, even though she loved them dearly. Plans were made, trains were booked and the time came around quickly, much to Jo's delight.

It took her by surprise when Kirsty kissed her. Her first instinct was to put an end to things there and then, and go home. But she didn't. She kissed her back.

From that moment, things were different. Text messages were flirty, there were more trips away together, and she missed Kirsty every time they were apart. Through no fault of his own, Darren was no longer the one she was in love with. Married life became a chore. A miserable chore. Each moment was spent thinking about Kirsty, being on the phone with her, or being away with her.

When Darren saw the pictures, Jo wasn't scared for her marriage. She was relieved. She had some explaining to do, especially to Ashley and Becky but, at that moment, she could finally be open. When Darren gave her an ultimatum, to stay and stop seeing Kirsty or to leave and never come back, there was no hesitation. She packed her bags and left. Her marriage had been over for a long time. She would come back for the girls, but she chose Kirsty over Darren.

She didn't expect her daughters to be so angry. Deep down, she thought they would understand and be happy for her. Happy that she had met someone. But, when faced with their questions, she couldn't answer them. She didn't love women. She just loved Kirsty. She didn't hate men. She just fell out of love with Darren. Since then, they barely kept in touch with her, choosing to champion their dad. She didn't blame them. She was the villain, even if she had chosen love and happiness.

A few months later, in a cruel twist of karma, Kirsty met someone else and Jo found herself single again. Her heart broke, the same way she imagined Darren's had. She experienced guilt like never before. At least she had her job to throw herself into. The world of murder and psychopaths was not about to dry up.

The phone rings and Jo answers, muting the declarations of lust on 'Love Island'. It's Gillespie. He has been keeping an eye on Clarke and the situation with Phillip Tatton.

Clarke hasn't heard anything from Phillip Tatton, but he took it upon himself to interview Michael Tanner again. He is keen to name Michael as the main suspect for the murders and is speaking to the CPS to instigate arresting him, on suspicion of murder. Gillespie has also been looking into Clarke's background to see how far back the corruption with Phillip Tatton goes. Everything appears to triangulate with what Clarke has already told them but Gillespie has noticed something else and invites himself around to Jo's place, promising to bring food.

It's not long before they are exchanging information over vegetable spring rolls and char siu chow mein. Already tipsy, Jo recounts her affair with Kirsty, and a shocked Gillespie almost chokes on a bean sprout. He saves his own woeful love story for another time and focuses the conversation on Clarke.

"Did you know he has closed more cases than any other officer in Liverpool since he started here?" he asks, with a tinge of resentment. "Since he came back from Scotland, he's been on a roll. No wonder he has his sights on being commissioner."

"Scotland? Clarke's Scottish?" asks Jo, shoving a whole spring roll into her mouth.

"No, he's Liverpool born and bred. From what I can tell, he went on secondment to Glasgow but came back six months later, a few months earlier than planned. Not sure why. Got any kitchen roll?" he asks, as he has spilt soy sauce down his shirt.

"Find out why. I know I'm being nosey, but he's such a misogynistic dick. He can't talk to us without calling us 'guys' and staring at my chest. Not that there's much to see."

"I don't know, I'm sure you look quite fetching to him in your crinkled oversized shirt. And the way you throw your hair up in a messy bun with an elastic band is quite a skill."

"Dickhead. Go on. What else have you come to tell me? Pass me the kitchen roll, please. Actually, fuck it. This top can go in the wash."

"Clarke's got Tanner riled up. He's told him that he should expect to be arrested in the next twenty-four hours and that his nan will never see him again. Tight bastard."

"Michael isn't the brightest firework in the box, but any evidence is circumstantial. Even the stuff with Amy Tatton doesn't lead directly to him, although it seems like someone wants it to."

"What do you mean?"

“I’m just saying it could be a complete coincidence that he’s got this restraining order and can be placed at, or near, Amy Tatton’s residence. Take away the restraining order and Michael Tanner is just a random creepy bloke who works and lives in the city centre.”

“Why’s Clarke got it in for him then?”

“If a man like Phillip Tatton can bend Clarke, then who knows what else he is capable of,” replies Jo. “Anyway, my head’s banging. Are you crashing here tonight? The sofa’s comfy.”

“Sofa’s good, thanks. You go up, I’m going to dig a little more. If you get scared or lonely, you know where I am.” He winks and laughs, then winces with pain from a slap around the head.

‘Let’s see what you were up to in Glasgow,’ thinks Gillespie, as he settles into the couch and opens his computer.

34

"I can't believe you're even asking me this."

Emily sits on the couch in Sophie's office, her jumper sleeves pulled over her wrists and her arms wrapped around her body.

"I'm sorry, Emily," says Sophie. "I know this must come as a shock. I'll support you, whatever your decision. Restorative justice has been shown to help survivors as well as offenders and …"

"I don't give a shit about helping him. You know what he did to me."

"I know. He hurt you in ways most people can't even imagine." Sophie sits in her chair, desperately wanting to hug Emily and tell her to forget she ever mentioned Marcus Gaines' request to see her.

"He didn't *hurt* me, Sophie. He raped me. On camera. Sold the videos and did it repeatedly. He destroyed me." The words are barely audible over the tears and frustration. "Why would I ever want to be in the same room as him again, let alone *help* him? Even now, he's showing he has the power to get to me."

Sophie moves to the couch and sits beside Emily, holding her hand. "You don't have to do anything you don't want to. Do you hear me? Nothing at all." Emily cries and lets the weight of her body and trauma fall into Sophie's arms. "I've got you, you're safe here."

Sophie feels like the worst therapist in the world. Her heart is breaking for Emily, and at this moment, objectivity is just a word. She wants to say, *'Fuck Marcus Gaines and his rehabilitation.'* Instead, she holds Emily tightly, fights her own tears, and reassures her that she is safe, knowing that somewhere along the way she crossed the line from therapist to friend.

There is a knock on the door and they both jump. "I'll get rid of them," says Sophie.

"It's OK, I need to go anyway. Gina will be wondering where I am."

"Please don't leave like this. I won't sleep tonight unless I know you're alright. Just give me a minute." She walks to the door and opens it slightly, unsure who would be knocking at this time. "Oh, it's you. This really isn't a good time. Can you come back later?"

Gillespie smiles. "I'm sorry to bother you, but I could use your professional opinion on something. Are you OK? You look upset. Blink once if you're in danger."

Confused, she opens the door to show that she is safe and busy with a patient.

"Oh, sorry to interrupt. I can wait outside," he says, sheepishly.

"It's OK, I'm just leaving anyway," says Emily, as she picks up her coat and walks towards the door.

"Emily, stop, please. What are you going to do when you get home?" Sophie needs some reassurance that she isn't going to harm herself. "Will you come back tomorrow?"

"Yes, I'll come back tomorrow. And no, I'm not a danger to myself and I don't have any plans to harm myself."

Sophie puts her hand on Emily's arm. "You know me too well. First thing tomorrow?"

"Sure. Are you going to be OK here? With him?" asks Emily, staring at Gillespie.

"Yes, thank you. He's a detective and won't be here long, will you?"

He starts to answer but quickly realises it was a rhetorical question and settles for smiling at Emily. He makes way for her to leave the room and then follows Sophie in, closing the door behind him. He watches her as she goes to the mirror and straightens herself up.

"Rough session?" he asks.

Sophie is about to ask what he wants, but her eyes fill with the tears she has been fighting for the last hour. She holds her head in her hands and cries. Gillespie watches her, conflicted between how beautiful she looks and the right things to say.

"Want to talk about it?" he asks, passing her a tissue and sitting in the chair opposite. "It's Emily, right? The girl who just left."

"She's been through some of the most horrific things," says Sophie. "If I ever get my hands on Marcus Gaines …" She stops herself from continuing, knowing that she has said too much already.

Gillespie doesn't probe for information, but he is aware of who Marcus Gaines is. One of the most sickening criminals Liverpool has seen. He didn't investigate the case, but he knew people who did. People who were broken by what they had to watch when reviewing the evidence from crime scenes and online videos.

"I'm sure you've done everything you can. You heard her. She'll be back tomorrow. A night at home with family, crap television and food and, before you know it, she'll be back."

"I hope so. I wish I could know she was OK at home. She doesn't have the best home life. Her brother-in-law, Graham, is a piece of work. It makes my skin crawl hearing about him. Honestly, between Marcus Gaines and Graham, I don't know where she gets her strength from. She's remarkable."

Gillespie offers to check in on Emily and make sure she is OK. Sophie is appreciative but declines. She can't give Emily's information to anyone unless there is an emergency, and she must have faith in Emily and her progress.

"Not to be rude, but did you want something? What did you come here for?"

"It's Michael Tanner. I was hoping you will be able to shed some light on a few things. I know you said you can't divulge information but he's our prime suspect in several murders."

Sophie lets out an exhausted breath and searches her computer for Michael's records.

"What did you want to know? I can't tell you specifics, but I might be able to offer something." She has already crossed several lines tonight, so why not?

"He had a restraining order taken out against him, to stop him from going anywhere near his ex, Amy Tatton. I'm wondering whether a Phillip Tatton was ever brought up in your sessions?"

Sophie uses the 'find' function on her records and searches for any references for the name. "Yes, several times. Again, I can't tell you specifics or the exact context, but I can tell you that every reference to Phillip Tatton was amongst profanities." She looks up at Gillespie, peering over her glasses. "Does that help?"

“Not really. What about Bob Clarke? Was he ever mentioned?” he asks, knowing it is a long shot.

Sophie used the ‘find’ function again and, after a few minutes of shaking her head, she pauses. “Just once. Again, profanities. Does that mean anything to you?”

“Actually, yes it does.” Gillespie doesn’t know what it means exactly, but it can’t be a coincidence that the lead suspect in a murder case has mentioned Clarke by name, long before these crimes started.

35

"Of course, he knows me," says Clarke. "I issued his bloody restraining order, for fuck's sake."

Gillespie has forgotten about that, but it does triangulate. Clarke isn't a stranger to Michael Tanner; they have a history, courtesy of Phillip Tatton.

"Whilst I've got you on the phone, Gillespie, you might be interested to know I'm about to meet our friend, Mr Tatton. He's asked for an update on his daughter's case."

"Where? I'll meet you and we can do it together. No offence, but you're not my number one most trusted person right now. I don't trust you not to throw Michael Tanner under the bus prematurely."

"You're naïve if you think Tatton hasn't had eyes on Michael Tanner since day one. Secondly, people in glass houses shouldn't throw big bastard stones. I might've made a mistake but I'm not the only one, am I *Detective* Gillespie? It wasn't that long ago that I was covering your arse. Remind me, how is your wife?"

Gillespie hangs up and throws his phone across the desk, in a temper. He opens his bottom drawer and takes out a bottle of Maker's Mark whisky. He is separated from his wife, that is true, but she is the mother of his kids and, when she needed an alibi, he gave her one. Clarke found out and brushed it under the carpet, knowing it won't look good if one of his officers appears dodgy. The alibi was only for one night, and just in case she was asked questions about an assault. In hindsight, if Gillespie had known that his wife was involved in drug trafficking and having an affair with one of Liverpool's most notorious dealers, he probably wouldn't have agreed to lie for her.

On the other side of Liverpool City Centre, Tara is preparing for another date with a brunette thirty-something hairdresser. She chooses to wear a grey tailored suit with a white shirt, which has a stiff collar and is open at the top to reveal her toned collarbone. She puts her hair in a messy bun and walks through a mist of Tom Ford's 'White Patchouli', wondering what perfume Jo wears when she isn't at work. A classic probably, like 'Jean Paul Gaultier' or 'DKNY'.

She takes one last look in the mirror before heading out the door, fixing her lipstick and giving herself a wink for confidence. Her date is probably already there but she likes to be fashionably late. Jo would hate this trait and be surprised that someone so clinical can be unpunctual.

The taxi pulls up on Stanley Street. Usually, Tara would have pre-drinks in the Lisbon and a warmup dance in the Masquerade but, tonight, she heads straight for The Navy Bar to meet her date.

Stanley Street sits in a cosmopolitan area within the city. Drag queens hold centre stage outside gay bars and clubs. Alluring, enchanting and downright gorgeous, they set the standard for all to aspire to.

The sound of the bass line pulsates from wall to wall. The DJ spins her soul on the decks, giving Tara a nod and wave. The atmosphere is pure hedonism and people move to the same rhythm. Hands are in the air, bodies are fluid and the heat from the low ceiling ensures that some bodies are less attired than others. After handing her jacket to the cloakroom attendant, Tara stands in the centre of the club, leaning over the balcony to the dancefloor as if the room is hers. Like a lioness studying for prey, she smirks as she watches the crowd. The red-headed woman by the DJ box who sips through her straw teasingly whilst giving a head-tilt to a blonde. The crop-haired brunette who edges towards the bald bouncer as she seductively wraps her lips around her bottle.

Tara shuffles through the bodies that seem to be never-ending and dances her way out of tight spots. Once through to the other side, she scans the bar that is situated at the back of the club, looking for a place to reside. She notices a woman sitting at the bar who looks agitated, whose red high heel almost slips off as she sways her ankle from side to side frustratingly.

Tara walks up to the impatient lady, noticing something more beautiful about her with each stride she takes. Approaching the bar, she gives a nod to the barmaid, who immediately brings her over a bottle of lager, and takes a seat next to the woman.

"Your hair is beautiful. You must be a hairdresser," she says.

"Predictable," replies Megan, laughing. "What time do you call this anyway? I've been here almost half an hour, trying not to look like I've been stood up."

"Telling me off already? I like you. Besides, I'm here now, aren't I?" she asks, as she slips her hands around Megan's waist and kisses her cheek. "Tell me that's not real fur." She points at Megan's coat which is draped around the chair.

"Synthetic and straight from the catalogue, if you must know."

"OK, then. You can stay," Tara laughs and checks her phone.

Jo hasn't texted her back, so something must be wrong. There was a chill in the air the last time they saw each other, more than usual for a medical lab. She sends her a message. '*Hey, you OK? Not heard from you in a while. Just checking in. x'*.

"Boring you already, am I?" laughs Megan.

"Sorry, just work stuff. I'm all yours. What do you want to do?" she asks, putting her phone on the bar, in view. They talk and decide to stay at the Navy Bar for more drinks.

Megan talks about her family and her job. She manages a beauty salon on Smithdown Road, as a hairstylist, and has two dogs; Rover, a German Shepherd, and Benny, a Yorkshire Terrier. *'Original names,'* thinks Tara, who sits and listens, with one eye on her phone, waiting for it to light up.

"So, what is it you do, Tara? You said you worked in medicine?"

"I do, I'm a medical examiner."

"Like a GP?"

Tired and distracted, Tara smiles, nods and continues to listen to Megan who flicks through umpteen photographs of her dogs and cute videos of her baby nephew. A text message comes through on her phone. *'I'm fine. You?'* A message from Jo, which doesn't alleviate Tara's gut feelings. She replies. '*Yeah, fine,'* annoyed with herself for such a juvenile reply but doesn't know what else to say. Maybe Jo is fine after all. It's not like they are friends and confide in each other. It's not even like they really talk outside of dead bodies, labs and crime scenes.

"Back in a minute, just going to the toilet. Stay here?" asks Megan, who looks picture-perfect and has a massive smile. *Or is it lip filler?* Either way, she is the nicest date Tara has had in a while.

She flicks through her emails while Megan is in the toilet. Several have come through in the last hour. One confirms that Jenna will be staying on for at least another six months. Another confirms that the bite marks on Gemma Woodcock are not a match for the ones on Anne-Marie Swift and Faye Williams, as she expected. The verdict is that the bite marks on Gemma Woodcock are old and from various people, likely to be part of a sexual act. As she is about to put her phone away, another email comes through, confirming that the unusual substance from all crime scenes has a main ingredient of Xylitol, used in the treatment of some dental conditions.

Tara orders another drink and wonders whether Jo would have a lager or whether she was a cocktail drinker. She orders Megan an 'Old Fashioned'.

"Thanks, cheers to us!" says Megan, sipping her cocktail. "That's disgusting. Thanks for the thought but maybe a 'Woo Woo' or an 'Aperol Spritz' next time, Babe. You want it?" Before Tara can answer, Megan swaps their drinks and is gulping down a lager. "Anyway, my mum just messaged me these pictures of Rover and Benny. Here, look at this."

"I'm surprised you have a fur coat if you love animals so much," says Tara. "I know it's not real fur, but why bother? Shouldn't you be visibly against that sort of thing if you're an animal lover?"

Megan looks confused. "It's fake fur. Not remotely animal-related, or trying to be. I'd understand if I was walking around with a baby sheep or goat on my back but feel it, it doesn't even feel like fur." Megan is right. It feels wiry and bits of synthetic fur come off in Tara's hand.

"You OK?" asks Megan. "No offence, but you're much more fun on the phone."

"Sorry, I've got to go," says Tara, picking up her things. "Something's come up. Maybe we can do this another time?" She kisses Megan on the cheek, knowing full well there won't be another time.

Outside, Tara puts her hand out for a taxi whilst the rain falls hard. She dials a number on her phone, nervous and excited.

"Hey, I need to see you. Where are you?"

36

Tara sits in her living room, waiting. Her computer is open, the fire is on, and she has changed out of her wet clothes into loungewear and slipper socks. It has been an hour since she spoke to Jo on the phone and arranged to meet her at home.

"Hi, come in," she says, moving so that Jo can squeeze past her through the doorway. The intense smell of 'Joop!' lingering in the hallway takes Tara by surprise. "Can I get you a drink?"

Jo is still wearing her work clothes and feels overdressed or underdressed for this meeting; she can't tell which. "Sure. Whatever you're having." She takes off her coat and sits furthest from where she presumes Tara is going to sit. "Must have been a bad date if you rang me to get out of it. Something sounded urgent," she says, taking a glass of red wine. It would be rude not to accept.

"The date was OK. Megan was her name."

Jo sips her wine, waiting to hear why she has been summoned. The house is nice. Tidy and clean, just as you would expect from a medical examiner. Everything has a place. Even the wine glasses are clinically clean. Not like Jo's house. It is survival of the fittest for tableware and glasses, which is probably why nothing matches in her cupboards. Who cares though? Wine goes down the same way whether it's drunk from a glass or an IKEA mug. She drank it out of a cereal bowl once, with a straw, but she doesn't publicise that fact.

"We were having drinks in the Navy Bar. Do you know it?"

"No, should I?" replies Jo. Of course, she knows the Navy Bar.

"It's a bar in town, but anyway that's not important. Megan, she wore this fake fur coat, and I challenged her on the promotion of *any* fur, whether it's real or not."

"Sounds like a great date. Is this going somewhere? Only I didn't think we knew each other well enough to swap dating stories," replies Jo, immediately hearing the bitterness in her voice.

"Long story short, it was synthetic fur. It got me thinking." Tara places the laptop on Jo's knees, sitting next to her. "Look at this." Jo looks at the screen as Tara flicks through emails, reports and attachments, reaching over her as if the last few frosty days haven't happened. Perhaps they didn't happen, and it was all in Jo's mind.

"What am I looking at that we haven't already been through?"

Tara pulls up the Anne-Marie Swift case and highlights a sentence in the lab report. She pulls up the Faye Williams case and does the same. Finally, she opens the lab data from where Gemma Woodcock's body was found. "Do you see it?" she asks.

"Animal traces, we already know this. What am I missing, Tara?" Jo puts her wine glass down and looks at her, the sudden intimacy catching her off-guard.

"Until now, we assumed the animal traces were just the usual suspects. Rats in a skip and foxes in the wasteland. You questioned the reports of lamb fibres, remember? I got the labs to check them again because some research suggests humans and lambs have similar DNA patterns, enough to occasionally throw a computer program. Improbable but not impossible."

"And?" asks Jo, keeping up but still not connecting the dots.

"The fibres *are* lamb. Found in the skip where Anne-Marie Swift was killed, in the Festival Gardens where Faye Williams was found, and in the alley near Gemma Woodcock."

Jo is disheartened. She had expected a big revelation, something that would give them direction in the case and lead to catching the killer. She finishes her wine and stands to leave. Waste not, want not.

"It's a link between them all. All the murdered girls were sexually assaulted and, at each of those scenes, lamb fibres were found. I know why we haven't found any seminal fluid."

37

Tara and Jo sit in Ruby's Bar with Gillespie, who is eating a burger and fries. Sauce covers both corners of his mouth as he chomps like he hasn't eaten in days.

"Lambskin?" he asks. "What about it?"

Tara recounts everything she told Jo at home and on their way to the bar. Jo watches Tara, in her element, talking about all things medical and weird. She has to admit though, as strange as it is, it is a much-needed lead. Despite the sexual assault experienced by each murder victim, no seminal fluid was found at the scenes or on the bodies.

"Lambskin condoms. It occurred to me while I was on a date."

Gillespie looks at Jo, who subtly shakes her head to say, *'Don't ask.'*

"Lambskin condoms? This is starting to sound like some 'Silence of the Lambs' type-shit," says Gillespie.

"It's not as unusual as you'd think," says Tara, again in her element. "Animal physiology has been used in a variety of ways in medicine. Before it was made synthetically, insulin from cattle and pigs was used to treat medical conditions. Tarantula bites have been used to treat asthma in some countries, and compounds found in funnel spider venom are used to reduce brain damage in stroke patients."

Gillespie looks at his food and pushes his plate away in mild disgust. "OK. Why would someone wear lambskin condoms?" he asks. "Fetish?"

"That's what I said, but it's obvious now," explains Jo. "Allergies. If someone's allergic to the materials in typical condoms, like latex, they would need an alternative. Latex is fluid from rubber-based plants, and some proteins in latex cause allergies. Asthma, itching, hives and even anaphylaxis."

"You can get plastic-based condoms, but they're prone to tearing more than others. Lambskin condoms are a tougher alternative, made from lamb intestines," says Tara.

"This changes the profile," says Jo. "This allergy only affects one per cent of the population. Allergies don't always occur in isolation either, so we could be looking for someone with a medical history of various ailments. Food allergies, maybe."

Like a double act, Tara elaborates on Jo's point.

"Research has found links between allergies to latex and allergies to foods, like kiwi, banana and avocado, although I don't know how that helps your profile. Xylitol, the substance found at the scenes, is natural sugar from birch bark but can also be found in raspberries and strawberries."

With this additional medical information about the offender, Jo explains the impact it has on the profile. They are looking for someone who must take precautions in his social life and at work, and may have long periods of absences or hospitalisation. The prescriptions for treatment and latex-free products, like condoms, require a lot of money, especially if the killer is also having dental treatment.

Jo's mind is racing. "Gillespie, did you get anywhere with checking out local sex offenders in the area?"

"They are too many to mention, unfortunately. However, most have alibis for the dates in question. Those that don't are being tested for DNA and compared against the items, and general shite, we found in the alleyway where Gemma Woodcock was killed. Officers are still working their way through the staff lists you asked for, with nothing turned up so far."

"Ask them to focus on professional staff. Medical professions, educational lecturers, solicitors; that sort of thing. If someone is paying out for dental treatments and lifelong prescriptions, there may be a trail through health benefits or schemes at work," says Jo.

The three of them look at each other as if there is too much information for them to process tonight. Gillespie knows he needs to get an update from Clarke, but that can wait until tomorrow. Right now, he needs to share his concern about the cases. What if there are other cases that have been missed? With the new parameters of absent seminal fluid and the presence of lamb fibres, he is concerned that other cases could be linked to these.

"Worth a look. Can you have someone search previous crimes by those parameters?" asks Tara.

"I know a guy," says Gillespie, smiling. "I always said it was weird how someone can go from voyeur to killer so quickly. I still don't think we have the bigger picture."

Jo looks at Tara, who is staring at her phone. The way the light bounces off her face emphasises her jawline. Her look of concentration is familiar and impressive. Perhaps Jo needs to make more effort with her hair and appearance. The 'run-off-my-feet' profiler look is effortless, but tired. She gets a text message from Gillespie. *'Stop staring.'* She looks at him from across the table and gives him a quick middle finger.

"Got some new results from Michael Tanner's taxi," says Tara, sharing her phone screen.

The report shows that there is no match between the blood on the back of the earring and the victims, nor is there a match for any clothing fibres. The industrial bolt that was stuck in the tyre is traced back to a company that is contracted to do landscape clearance across the city.

Gillespie is already searching the internet for the owner of the company and their most recent contracts in Liverpool. "The company was opened five years ago," he says, as he continues to scroll.

"Who's the business registered to at Companies House?" asks Tara.

Gillespie smiles and looks up at her. "Phillip Tatton."

38

Jo and Clarke pull into the Edge Lane Enterprises car park. The rain is falling like pellets of iron and there is darkness in the sky. *Could this be a sign?* They sit for a moment as they watch who comes in and out of the office. Clarke chain-smokes, nervous about meeting Phillip Tatton again. Jo drinks coffee and stuffs a doughnut in her mouth to satisfy her empty stomach.

The silence between them is welcome. Jo doesn't have anything to say to Clarke right now but, when he suddenly speaks, she jumps and spills her coffee down her shirt.

"For fuck's sake," she says, wiping it with her sleeve.

"I said, 'How are you and Gillespie getting on with the case?' I'm still your chief."

"Right you are, *Chief,*" she replies, sarcastically. "As it happens, things are moving in the right direction."

"Such as?"

"You know how it is, *Sir*, small steps and leads to follow up. People to see. That sort of thing."

She doesn't want to piss him off but she also can't forget that he is only still on the case because he agreed to work against Phillip Tatton. "What about you? Anywhere with your mate?" she asks.

"He's not my mate," says Clarke, realising he is taking the bait. "He's frozen me out. Reckons I've been asking too many questions. I'll keep on it. Shit, there he is. Let's go."

They walk towards the doorway of the office and are greeted by a less-than-impressed Phillip Tatton. He shakes his head and lights a cigarette as they approach. "Hope you're here to tell me Michael Tanner's banged-up for good."

"We wanted to ask you some questions about this place, nothing that will take too long. We know you're a busy man, Mr Tatton," says Clarke, sickeningly appeasing. "Any recent contracts in the city in the last, say, two months?"

"We only do the city, so yeah. What's this got to do with Michael Tanner?"

"We found one of your industrial bolts lodged in the tyre of a vehicle that's of interest to us. Any idea how it got there?" asks Jo. She notices his eyes narrow, and his lips start to curl. He is either getting angry or confused. His eyes dart between Jo and Clarke, overcompensating that there is nothing to hide.

"We get around. Contracts all over the city and, yes, including the last two months. Do I need a lawyer?"

"No, there's no need for that, Mr Tatton. If you can just tell us where the contracts are, and we will be on our way. Leave you to get on with your business," says Clarke.

Jo is surprised at how quickly the information is turned over, but she doesn't trust it. Surely, he has all angles covered and will back up false information if questions were ever raised or the wrong people come knocking. So far, Edge Lane Enterprises is looking legit.

"Thanks for your cooperation. We'll be in touch," says Clarke, patting him on the shoulder and leading Jo back to the car. "There we go, all makes sense, told you it would be a dead end."

"He's got contracts in most places. This doesn't help us narrow anything down. It can't be a coincidence, surely. The main suspect, Tanner. His taxi. A bolt from Tatton's company, the father of Tanner's ex. Something isn't adding up," says Jo, finishing the remains of her doughnut.

"Maybe it does add up. Here, look at this." Clarke shows Jo his book of dates and notes about what goes on at Chaloner Motors. "When Michael Tanner's car was in the lockup, Tatton used it for two or three jobs. Not him directly, but you know what I mean."

"So you think the bolt could have come from one of those jobs, rather than from one of our crime scenes? Makes sense." Jo can't believe she is agreeing with him. "What else do you think about the cases? You're so set on Michael Tanner. You must have a theory."

"Look, we've got a man with a restraining order, a history of mental health problems, and his semen was found at one of our crime scenes. He ran from you and Gillespie when you found him, and one of his receipts has been found in the bedroom of Faye Williams, who was also killed in cold blood. What part of thinking it's Michael Tanner is ludicrous?" asks Clarke.

Jo finds herself agreeing with him again. She needs another doughnut.

39

'Cable Cars' is the type of taxi rank that makes you wait outside in the rain for your car to be ready. It doesn't offer luxurious seating areas or shelter from the elements, and it is not a place any woman would want to find herself waiting alone for a ride home, late at night. The walls of the operator's office are decorated with nude pictures and calendars, and the toilet is indicative of this being an all-male establishment. Mould adorns the taps and sink plug, and a bottle of hand soap looks old and untouched. The floor is wet, and the toilet seat is missing.

"Help you?" asks Graham, leaning against the door frame, smoking.

"Hello to you too," replies Gillespie. "I've spoken to your boss. Interesting chat."

"Yeah? Good for you."

"You didn't mention that you have been in trouble for bringing a car back in a real state."

Graham shrugs his shoulders. "Ages ago. I cleaned it up and forgot about it. What's the boss man been saying about me then? He's never here and wouldn't have a bloody clue what I do for this place." He looks like he hasn't seen a shower in a few days, or a razor. His clothes are too big, hiding his bulky frame. He spits when he talks and scratches his genitals far too often for Gillespie's liking.

"I need to see every pickup and drop-off from your taxi, the same way we did for Michael Tanner's."

Graham walks to the operator's room and starts bringing up the schedules from the last three months. He curses while he does it, but it doesn't take him long to print it off. He hands it to Gillespie and continues to express his frustration and every other word is a profanity.

Before Gillespie can respond, they are interrupted by a knock at the door. Graham shouts, in a less than professional manner, "What do you want? Money?"

Gillespie looks towards the door and is surprised to see Emily Spencer standing there, who looks just as surprised to see him.

"Gina said don't be late tonight. She's cooking your favourite tea," Emily says, leaving as quickly as she can. Graham doesn't acknowledge what she has said.

"Daughter?" asks Gillespie.

"Fuck no. Sister-in-law. Pain in the arse too. Always a drama of some sort. Anything else I can do for you or is that it?"

Gillespie pieces together the information circling his brain. Could this be the person Sophie Sheridan spoke about? Why else would Emily be here? These days, there are too many coincidences for anything to be random.

Later, he walks across town and buzzes to be let into the building where Sophie works. He knocks on the big blue door, worried that he will be interrupting another vital moment in someone's therapy. Luckily for him, she is available and busy moving furniture. He helps her move the desk and the couch, and then helps her move it back when she changes her mind. A woman's prerogative.

"Graham Pierce? Yes, I know that name. Can I ask why you want to know?"

"He might be a person of interest. Tell me if I'm wrong but is he the same Graham you mentioned when we spoke about Emily?"

"We didn't '*speak about Emily*', Detective Gillespie," says Sophie. "But yes, that's him. He's her brother-in-law."

"The one who makes your skin crawl?"

Sophie thinks about the things she has heard from Emily. Creepy and sleazy, yes. Nothing actionable. "Why is he of interest?" she asks.

"Just looking into him and a few other people about the murders in Liverpool. He doesn't exactly give me 'stand-up guy' vibes. I was there earlier when Emily popped in."

"Really? That does surprise me. Although I'm glad to hear she's out and about again after her setback the other day. For what it's worth, I don't think your assessment of him is inaccurate, but I've never met him. I'd like to keep it that way too."

"Is there anything I should know?" asks Gillespie. He knows that, like Sophie, he can't say too much about his case, but anything is valuable at this point.

"Nothing concrete. From what Emily says, she can't wait to get out of that house. He comes home late, if at all. He drinks, smokes, invades her personal space, that sort of thing. Once, she told me that her sister, his wife, found photographs of women on his phone, which he'd taken in the park or on the street. These women didn't know they were being photographed. When you can't walk around somewhere like Chavasse Park on a sunny day, without some pervert photographing you, where can you go?"

Gillespie makes his excuses and leaves, afraid he is about to take the blame for a world of misogyny. He sits on a bench facing Liverpool Cathedral, which towers over him. It would be the perfect place for a Batman signal to be positioned. His phone pings with a WhatsApp message. It's Jo, updating him on the dead end at Edge Lane Enterprises, and calling Clarke every name under the sun.

He warms his hands up and replies, *'That sucks. C is a dick, but harmless. Anyway, I have something to cheer you up. We have another suspect to look at."*

40

"Jesus Christ, I've just told you. I don't know where they came from," says Graham.

After he came home late last night, Gina went through his pockets and found a pair of knickers. Scrunched up, with a 'Supergirl' logo on the front.

"They haven't bloody well just appeared, have they?" shouts Gina, grasping the knickers in her fist. "You better start talking now, or you can pack your bags." She stands, waiting for an explanation that will set her mind and nervous system at peace.

"It was probably one of the lads having a laugh, or maybe I found them in the back of a taxi. You don't trust me at all, do you? I don't appreciate my partner treating me this way," he says, remaining calm and composed, like a veteran gaslighter.

"Are you not even bothered that I'm upset? Don't you care about what goes through my mind when you don't come home, or when I find girl's knickers in your pocket?"

"Of course I do, and I'm sorry that you've got yourself so upset over nothing." He sits in his armchair and taps on his knee. "If you calm down and think about things logically, rather than overreacting, you can come and sit here, and I'll tell you about my day. You can tell me a bit about your day too." He taps his knee again, and Gina sits down.

"I'm sorry. I think I'm hormonal or something," she says, unknowingly pathologizing herself.

"You know me, I never hold a grudge. I forgive you."

As they kiss on the armchair, the front doorbell rings.

Graham sits and thinks about the knickers and photographs. He smiles and starts to feel aroused but is disturbed by Gina walking back into the room, accompanied by a familiar face.

"Hello again," says Gillespie. "Mind coming with me for a chat down at the station?"

"I'm not going anywhere with you. This is bloody harassment. First, you come to my work and now my home. Gina, why would you let this filth into our home?" He spits out his words in anger.

"It won't take long, Mr Pierce. A couple of questions to help with our inquiries and I'm sure you'll be home in no time." Gillespie hands Graham his coat and nods to a uniformed officer to accompany him to the car waiting outside.

Gillespie asks Gina about her relationship with Graham. Have there been any problems? Has she noticed any unusual behaviour lately?

She doesn't mention the photographs on the phone. Nor does she mention the nights he goes missing. She keeps the knickers in her pocket, out of sight.

Before Gillespie reaches the car, a phone call from Jo sets off his 'Yellow Submarine' ringtone. It irritates him but he hasn't got around to changing it.

"Dental impressions from Michael Tanner are due back today," says Jo. "Clarke kept him here overnight. Reckons he missed a check-in at the front desk so at least he'll be around when we get the results through." Jo takes large mouthfuls of a steak sandwich, before asking, "How are things on your end?"

"Super. I'm on my way back in with Graham Pierce. Do me a favour and do a background check. I'll be there in ten."

Jo puts her phone down and wipes her greasy hands on her trousers. A tiny piece of steak has lodged itself between her teeth and she fiddles with it, whilst running a background check on Pierce.

He was arrested for driving under the influence of alcohol ten years ago. *'Excellent safe recruitment by 'Cable Cars' I see,'* she thinks. A caution about noise in the last year. A neighbour reported yelling and screaming coming from his house. Police cautioned him and Gina but were satisfied it was only a domestic argument. Apart from that, Pierce is clean.

Although aren't all successful criminals clean?

41

"For the purpose of the tape, Dr Jolene Linnet has entered the room," says Gillespie, not missing the opportunity to use her full name. No doubt she will bring it up later. He looks at the background check and drops his shoulders in disappointment.

"Can you tell us again about your relationship with Michael Tanner?" he asks.

Graham Pierce sits across the table with his arms folded, protected by his lawyer who, somehow, arrived at the station before he did. Gina must have rung for help the moment Gillespie left the house.

"No comment," says Graham, with an obnoxious smirk on his face.

"Did you spend much time with Michael Tanner outside of work?"

"No comment."

"What's your relationship like with Emily Spencer?" Graham and Jo are both confused by the question.

"No comment."

"Did Michael Tanner ever share intimate stories or fantasies with you?"

"No comment."

"Do you have fantasies?" asks Jo, leaning across the table. The *'no comment'* response was delayed this time.

"Do you fantasise about women when they're in your taxi? Do you think about what you could do to them? Or what you *would* do to them?" Jo speaks softly as if she is intrigued and aroused by the suggestion. It appears to work. Graham smiles and unfolds his arms. "I'm only human. What about you?" he asks Jo, looking her up and down.

"I asked first," she says, smiling. "You're a big strong guy. I bet you could dominate anyone in a struggle."

The micro-expressions are written all over Graham's face. His lips curl and his eyebrow raises. This body language is almost invisible to the naked eye, unless you have a baseline for normal behaviour, and know what to look for. Graham's lips pout partially and Jo knows he is reliving something. A thought. A photograph. Or maybe a kill. She lets the silence continue to build up tension and anticipation.

"Or maybe I'm wrong," says Jo, retreating.

"You're not wrong," Graham says, taking no notice of the lawyer advising him to be quiet. "I could do all those things to you and more."

"I don't believe you." Jo knows the only way to get information from a man like Pierce is to wind him up one way or another. "I think you're just the same as all the other guys I know. Full of words but no action."

"You don't know what I'm capable of, but I'm happy to show you," he says, grinning like a predator about to snack on its prey. Again, Jo remains silent, luring him into her dance. Gillespie watches and listens, uncomfortable but enthralled. "I could do anything I want to you. You wouldn't be able to stop me. You wouldn't want to stop me."

"And if I resist?" asks Jo, leaning into the conversation.

"That just makes it better for both of us," he replies. He starts to say something else when there is a knock on the door.

'For fuck's sake,' thinks Jo. The tension in the room is broken when Officer Summers pops his head around the door. "Sorry to disturb you, but there's an urgent call for you both," he says, sheepishly.

"I think my client could do with a break now anyway. We need to discuss a few things in private and I'll also need any evidence you have that suggests my client must remain here," says the lawyer, but Gillespie and Jo are already heading out of the door.

"That was impressive," says Gillespie. "I nearly confessed my own fantasies in there."

"I almost had him. Another five minutes and he would've cracked like an egg," replies Jo, snatching the phone from Mark and putting it on loudspeaker.

"Jo? It's Tara." Jo immediately turns off the loudspeaker, indicating to Gillespie to get them some coffee, but he stays and strains to hear the conversation.

He can only make out bits of information, but he hears enough to understand that the dental impressions from Michael Tanner are not a match for the bite marks on Anne-Marie Swift's body or those found on Faye Williams. He opens his phone and signals to Jo that he will call Clarke and have Michael Tanner released.

"You still there, Jo?" asks Tara.

"Yeah, sorry. It's disappointing news but we do have another possible suspect. How come you rang the office?"

"I tried calling you, but your phone was ringing out. I was worried about you." A silence hangs between them.

"It's on silent in my bag, sorry. Thanks for the thought though. Anyway, best get back to it. See you soon."

As Jo puts the phone down, she spots a bag of crisps on the desk and helps herself. Michael Tanner is an odd one but, without the bite mark evidence, there is nothing to indicate he is the killer. There is still the semen in the alleyway, but that's been explained satisfactorily. The receipt in Faye Williams' bedroom could have come from anyone in the shop. Michael Tanner isn't their prime suspect anymore, but Jo considers the possibility that he may be involved, just not working alone.

She gets up to find Gillespie, but almost runs into him in the doorway.

"Gillespie, I want to run something by you. What if Michael Tanner is involved, but he's not the killer? Think about it. Graham Pierce, or someone else, could be the sadist and murderer, but Tanner could have helped arrange it all or watched the girls and reported back. I'm not sure yet, but it's something to think about. There are numerous pairings in criminal history where one is the alpha male, and the other is the quiet submissive partner."

"Can you class someone as submissive if they're dead?" asks Gillespie.

Jo looks at him, confused and caught off-guard.

"Michael Tanner was found dead in his cell an hour ago."

42

Jo and Gillespie march to Clarke's office for answers but find him giving the long-awaited statement to the press. He tells the audience that he is doing 'everything that he can', and that the primary suspect in the murders was detained last night and killed himself, in fear of being punished by the full force of the law.

Clarke is well-presented and his uniform is adorned with medals, for the sake of the media. His chin dimple and piercing blue eyes make him a favourite with photographers who know how many likes they will get on social media posts. He waves goodbye to the reporters as if he is a political hero, addressing his followers. As he leaves, a reporter asks a question about his plans for becoming the commissioner in Merseyside. Jo and Gillespie are surprised to hear him confirm that the plans for his promotion are underway.

"What the hell happened to Michael Tanner?" asks Jo.

"You heard me out there. Killed himself. Guilt and fear will do that to a criminal," replies Clarke.

"Why would he kill himself? He was only in holding because he missed his check-in," says Jo. "What aren't you telling us?" She grabs Clarke by the arm and isn't deterred when he glares at her. "What is it?"

"Look, I locked him up to teach him a lesson. Gave him a talking-to, showed him some crime scene pictures and gave him a glimpse into his future. Prison. Revenge. That sort of thing," answers Clarke. "I wanted a confession and I guess it looks like I got one."

"Suicide isn't a confession to anything. Who ruled it suicide anyway?" Jo is following Clarke and struggling to keep up, as he heads for the staircase. The crisps from earlier start to repeat on her. "Unless you've just presumed suicide which, as you know, isn't procedure."

"Procedure? You're the ones that built the case against Tanner," retorts Clarke, spitting as he speaks. Gillespie checks his own breath to make sure the smell isn't coming from him. "It doesn't get much clearer than this. He slit his wrists with a sharp piece of plastic. Must have smuggled it in or found it somewhere. The place is a bloody mess. No pun intended."

"CCTV catch it all?" asks Gillespie.

"There was a fault. CCTV has been out for two days. Anything else, Mr and Mrs Marple?"

"Tanner didn't kill any of our victims. We got the dental impression comparisons through, just before your press conference," Jo says, as she stands in front of Clarke, who looks confused. "The dental impression from Tanner wasn't a match for any of the bite marks on our victims."

Clarke is startled and doesn't say anything. He looks at Jo and Gillespie, trying to piece it all together. "Why would he kill himself then?" he asks. "If he was innocent, why would he do that?"

"I'm not saying he was innocent. Maybe he didn't act alone, I don't know. We'll never know now. So, congratulations on your fear tactics. Very impressive," says Jo, clapping her hands. She knows she is antagonising him but, at this moment in time, she doesn't care. Bob Clarke has just driven a potentially innocent man to suicide.

She is the first to leave, shaking her head as she walks away. Gillespie takes a cigarette and places it behind his ear. It's an old school-detective thing.

"What was that about?" asks Gillespie. "You're never making commissioner, and you know that. There's no way your role in Phillip Tatton's operations will go overlooked. No way in hell."

"What role?" asks Clarke.

Gillespie looks at him, confused.

"Where's your proof that I've got any such role, in any such operation?" asks Clarke, moving closer towards him. "CCTV? Gone. Tatton? Not going to talk to you. My logbook? Destroyed. So, what role?"

Gillespie stares at him in disbelief. Clarke has made all the evidence, and traces between him and Tatton, disappear. No one else knows about what he and Jo found. They didn't tell anyone and didn't file any reports. How could they have been so careless?

Clarke waits for an answer and, when he realises that he has the upper hand, he smiles and pats Gillespie on the shoulder before sprinting up the stairs.

Gillespie sits down, thinking about the chain of events that has led him to this point. He feels like he hasn't slept properly in weeks.

He smells like he hasn't showered in days. The excessive use of Lynx body spray can't hide the blood and sweat that got him to this point in the case. With Michael Tanner now dead, Gillespie realises that he might be able to get some direct answers now from the dentists he has already spoken to. They can't release patient information before, but they can if a patient is dead.

He works his way through the local dental surgeries that have already turned him away. '*Has Michael Tanner ever been a patient in your practice? Do you have any records about a Michael Tanner? Has anyone called Michael Tanner made an appointment in the last twelve months?*' A string of negative responses is broken when a dental receptionist confirms that they have a Michael Tanner on their records and that he matches the description given by Gillespie.

'*Holy shit,*' thinks Gillespie, as he runs down the stairs in pursuit of Jo. He runs over to where she is standing, drinking coffee and fiddling with her phone. He doesn't know where to start, so it all comes out at once. Clarke's return to his plans to become a commissioner, and the name of the dentist where Michael Tanner was treated.

"Jesus Christ." Jo sits and takes it all in. She is furious with Clarke, but more so with herself for not thinking ahead and having it all backed up. "That's great news about the dentist. Not sure what good it will do, now he's dead, but it's still worth speaking to them."

"That's what I thought. I'll head there now."

"Wait, you're not going to like this. Graham Pierce has been released," says Jo. "I'm sorry. I know you wanted to nail something on him."

"How's he been released already?" Gillespie thinks about Emily Spencer and Sophie Sheridan, and how he could have helped them.

"His wife has given him an alibi for the night Faye Williams was murdered, and the night we found Gemma Woodcock. Reckons they were home together all night," says Jo. "Lawyer got him out of here as fast as possible. If you want to bring him back in, we need something else on him. Shit day, right?"

"Total shit. I need to stop off at home first, grab a wash, and then I'll pay a visit to the dentist."

"Good, you are rather ripe," replies Jo, distracted by her phone.

"Anything interesting?" he asks, nodding towards her phone.

"Oh no, nothing. Just sending a message to Tara. She had no idea about Michael Tanner."

"Do you normally put kisses on your messages to the medical examiner?" asks Gillespie, sneaking a peek at her phone and laughing. She pushes him away and puts her phone back in her pocket. "Go to the dentist, Dickhead. You could do with a Silkwood shower at home too," she laughs, her face feeling flushed with embarrassment. Either that, or the fact that the reply from Tara also has a kiss at the end of it.

43

Gillespie walks over to 'Dental Pride', the surgery that confirmed they have Michael Tanner on their records as a patient. He rings Sophie Sheridan and shares as much as he can about Graham Pierce, asking her to contact him if anything new causes her concern. She thanks him for looking into it and reassures him that if she hears anything from Emily about Graham that she will follow the proper channels, but will let him know as a courtesy.

As he crosses the road towards 'Dental Pride', he spots Bob Clarke walking into the surgery. He watches through the window and sees Clarke speak to the receptionist and then take a seat.

"What are you doing here?" asks Gillespie, walking into the surgery.

"I could ask you the same," replies Clarke.

"I'm here to get information about Michael Tanner. I'll ask you again, what are you doing here?"

"Same as you, of course. Linnet told me where you were heading, and I thought I'd join you," says Clarke, indicating that he should approach the receptionist.

A short stocky woman sits in a swivel chair behind the reception desk. Her long nails tap the keyboard and Gillespie notices that her mobile phone is open on WhatsApp, with memes coming through thick and fast.

"If you want to take a seat, I'll have those records for you shortly," she says.

"I don't want the records, at this stage. I just want to know a few things. Can I ask a couple of questions?"

The receptionist nods and folds her arms.

"Has Michael Tanner been diagnosed with any dental condition in the last twelve months?

Tap, tap, tap on the keyboard. "No," she answers.

"Has he been given any medication prescribed by the dentist?"

Tap, tap, tap. "Mouthwash for dry mouth, tooth mousse for sensitivity, and antibiotics for an infected socket after a tooth extraction."

"Great, thanks. What about things like gum disease?" asks Gillespie, still not finding what he wanted.

Tap, tap, tap, and a loud huff. "Nope. As I said, you can have all these records if you wait a while."

"No, that's fine. Thank you, you've been very helpful," says Gillespie, deflated. He sits down in the reception area and Clarke sits across from him.

"Why don't you get back to the station, or wherever it is you and Linnet are off to next? You could both do with a break," says Clarke. "With Tanner dead and that new suspect of yours having an alibi, there isn't much more we can do."

Gillespie holds his tongue, knowing that the frustration of the last few weeks of death is bubbling inside of him. He shakes his head and gets up to leave when the receptionist slams a file on the counter. “Seeing as though you’re still here, and you did ask for them, here are the files.”

He takes the files and leaves the surgery. He doesn’t realise that he has dropped one of the records from the file. Clarke picks it up and turns to the receptionist who is holding out her hand, waiting for him to return it.

“That’s OK, I’ll give it to him back at the station,” says Clarke, folding it up and putting it in his pocket and showing the receptionist his police badge to remind her of his status.

The receptionist glares at the badge and looks him up and down. “Sir, I know you are just doing your job, but I’m afraid I can’t let you leave here with that record.”

“That man is one of my detectives and he has the rest of the files, so why can’t I leave here with this one?”

“Because your detective isn’t a patient at this surgery, Mr Clarke, and you are. If you return to the waiting area, the dentist will see you next.”

44

Gillespie sits in a café on Mount Pleasant Street and flicks through Michael Tanner's dental report. Nothing from the last twelve months bears any significance to the cases. Tanner had teeth extracted but had no false teeth. Previous X-rays show cracks in the molars, supposedly caused by teeth grinding. Gillespie makes a conscious effort to relax his jaw.

He continues turning pages, looking at appointments in December, July and April, then moves back to the end of the twelve-month period. He doesn't notice that he has gone too far back and, by the time he realises, he is looking at dental notes from two years ago. Gillespie almost chokes on his digestive biscuit as he spots a handwritten note from the dentist. '*Patient is advised to use any of the products below, as often as possible, to improve oral hygiene and reduce risks of halitosis.*'

Some of the products are familiar. Sonic dental scaler, Corsodyl mouthwash and plaque removal tools. Some of the products, however, are not so familiar. Gillespie searches a few of them on his phone and looks at the ingredients. It is jargon to him, but one ingredient stands out. Xylitol.

Michael Tanner had a history of dental issues, and it seems likely that he was using a few products with the same ingredient found at some of the crime scenes. He scoops up the papers and shoves them back into the file, in no particular order. It might give the receptionist something to make a meme about. He sends a message and asks Jo to meet him at the medical examiner's lab in ten minutes.

Jo's phone is on silent, but she is already at the lab, talking to Tara. Jenna has finished early for the day and has been given the rest of the evening off. Without giving Tara time to change her mind, she grabs her bag and leaves the building.

"Now we're alone, let's talk," says Tara, making coffee for them both. "Sugar?"

"Just one, please," replies Jo. She can't have four like she normally does. That won't look good in front of a medical examiner.

"I still haven't been asked to review Michael Tanner's death," says Tara, as she stirs the coffee and opens a packet of biscuits. Ginger Nuts. Boring, but good for digestion. As she turns around, she sees that Jo has her head in her hands, crying. Her heart breaks a little.

She puts the coffee cups down and walks over to Jo, putting her arm around her. She doesn't hurry her or tell her to stop crying. She doesn't ask her to share what is wrong or give affirmations about how everything will be OK. She just holds her.

"Sorry. I don't know where that came from," says Jo, wiping her eyes and reaching for a biscuit. "It's all a bit much sometimes, you know."

Tara nods and hands her a tissue. She stays close to her, with a friendly hand on her shoulder.

"They were just kids. Anne-Marie, Faye, Gemma, and God knows who else. Their whole lives were ahead of them and now they're just cold bodies in a morgue, and I don't know what else to do."

"You've done amazing on this case. It's not over, but those families know that you and Gillespie are doing everything you can." Tara wipes a tear from Jo's eye. "You're not responsible for Michael Tanner's death either. You followed the evidence, and it all led you back to him."

Jo sniffs. "I don't blame myself for his death. I blame Clarke. He's the one who should be feeling like shit." She drinks her coffee and wipes the snot that has started to form, with her sleeve. "Great look this is, isn't it?" she laughs.

"I've seen worse," replies Tara, pointing her head in the direction of the post-mortem table.

They both laugh and, for a second, Jo feels relaxed. Safe. The tension in her body falls and Tara allows her to let go.

"Thank you. I can't even remember why I'm here. I just walked and walked, and this is where I ended up," Jo says.

Tara wipes the remaining tears from her eyes, and brushes fallen strands of hair behind her ear. "For what it's worth, I'm glad you did," Tara says.

The brief silence is comfortable but broken by banging on the door. Tara walks over to let Gillespie in, and Jo puts her hair back to how it was. She likes it messy.

"This is the worst lock-in, ever," jokes Gillespie. He senses tension in the air when neither of them laugh. "I've got news, I think. I wanted to run it by you both." He recounts his trip to the dentist and what he has read in Michael Tanner's dental records. Tara reads through the list of recommended treatments and tools, while Jo continues to drink her coffee.

"This could make sense," says Tara. "Many of these recommended products contain lots of chemicals that we found in the substance at the crime scenes, notably the Xylitol. Why is it handwritten though?"

"I rang the receptionist and asked that question. She wasn't very helpful and won't win any 'employee of the year' awards, but she said that they usually stamp everyone's records with that. They had run out of ink for a few days though, hence it was written," he replies, as he takes a Ginger Nut.

"That adds to the evidence against Michael Tanner but, realistically, it could still be anyone. Why are you pursuing this when you already know the dental impressions aren't a match?" asks Tara. Taking another biscuit, Gillespie shrugs his shoulders.

"You want extra reassurance that it wasn't Michael, don't you?"

Gillespie nods and sits next to Jo. They both look deflated. Beaten. Everything has been leading up to charging Michael Tanner with the murders. The receipt. The semen. The alleyway. The restraining order. The whole case is collapsing and neither of them knows what to do for the best.

"Look, you can only go on what you see. The first rule of being a medical examiner. Sure, there is a lot of evidence that makes Michael look like your killer, but biology doesn't lie. He didn't bite those girls. He didn't have allergies and didn't leave the lambskin traces, and he didn't have gum disease which was found on Amy

Tatton's garden door. I'll take the biological evidence over a receipt and restraining order any day." Tara pauses to let her words sink in.

"What was Clarke doing at the surgery?" Jo finally asks.

"I asked him the same thing. He knew where I was going and thought he'd lend a hand. Covering his arse more like," replies Gillespie. "If he makes commissioner after being in bed with Phillip Tatton, and now this stunt with Tanner, I'm handing in my badge and gun."

"You don't carry a gun," says Tara.

"I'm 'handing in my badge' doesn't quite have the same ring to it. It sounds like I am giving my ASDA lanyard back to the store supervisor. Everything's much cooler on law and order, don't you think?" he jokes, then pauses before aiming a comment at Jo. "I didn't think you would give Clarke the time of day after what's happened."

"I'm not. After his little show with the media, and on the stairs, I'm staying as far away from him as I can. Bob Clarke and my temper are not a good match on any day, let alone today."

"Why did you tell him where I was then? That was your perfect opportunity to send him on a wild goose chase and get rid of him for the day." Gillespie searches the cupboards looking for more exciting biscuits. "You can always go and buy some biscuits, Harry," says Tara.

"She told you my name? I can't believe you told Tara my name," he says. "Well, if we are on a first-name basis now, Tara, then I politely request that you get some 'Classic' bars or 'Penguins' next time you do a shop run."

"I didn't," says Jo.

"It's fine. I forgive you for telling her my name. We're old friends now, right Tara?" says Gillespie, smiling and throwing his arm around Tara.

"No, Gillespie," says Jo, standing up. "I didn't tell Clarke where you were."

45

There is an extra chill in the medical examiner's lab, and they all feel it. Jo is consumed by anger and disgust towards Clarke for his role in Michael Tanner's death, but she still wishes Gillespie had come to the lab later than he did. Tara remains logical about everything, offering alternative reasons as to why Clarke may have known where Gillespie was going.

"Perhaps he heard you on the phone. Who knows? It's not like him being there has done any harm," she says, attempting to diffuse the tension. "I bet he knows where you both are right now. Isn't it his job to know?"

Gillespie is angrily biting Ginger Nut biscuits and Jo shrugs her shoulders.

"I guess," says Jo. "Anyway, where do we go from here?"

Tara clears the table and places flipchart paper and a pen in front of them.

"Group work?" asks Gillespie, sarcastically. "How come, when I need to find something, it takes me hours, yet you magically produce flipchart paper of all things?"

"Regroup. Go back to the drawing board and everything you know so far. There must be things that need looking at again or new ways to get information."

Tara sits with her pen, ready to make sense of everything about to be discussed. She writes down the victims' names and key medical evidence, then colour-coordinates everything that overlaps. Next, she writes down the current profile of the offender. Male, 20 to 45 years old.

"What else?" she asks.

Jo provides an overview of the current profile, aware that it is falling apart. The killer is a marauder and lives locally. He has enough physical strength to dominate a woman and not be injured in a defensive struggle. He uses the gym, or has a job where being fit and physical is beneficial. The forensic awareness at the scenes suggests he's an organised killer, rather than a disorganised one. He's choosing his victims. He's choosing the disposal sites for the bodies. He knows what the teams will be looking for, hence leaves no incriminating evidence.

"Anything else?" asks Tara, in awe of the way Jo's mind works.

"He's angry. He has slit throats and killed Faye Williams' dog when he didn't have to. He enjoys it. Killing is cathartic for him. He's not remorseful. He pulled Anne-Marie's body across the ground like it was luggage. He's angry. At a specific woman maybe? Financial stress? An inner conflict or rage is driving the behaviour."

"He's a psycho. Add that with the red pen," adds Gillespie.

"A psychopath would have zero remorse about anything or anyone and is purely driven by self-gratification. The nature of the killings appears chaotic, but the lack of evidence, including DNA, shows that it is not. If he is a psychopath who has started killing, I'd expect to see more bodies. This man can control it. He probably has a job or reputation that requires control," says Jo.

Tara adds some of the lab findings alongside what Jo has said. The lambskin fibres, bite marks, Xylitol and other shreds of evidence.

"What about victimology?" asks Jo. "We should add that."

Tara discusses the patterns she has identified across the victims, but it's not much. Female, student age, living in Liverpool's inner-city centre or studying there. All of the voyeur victims had long-term medical issues. Anne-Marie Swift was asthmatic. Faye Williams was diabetic. Gemma Woodcock experienced migraines, and most were on some type of medication. None of them matched physically.

Gillespie adds that all the victims had family who would miss them. They all had social media accounts but kept them private. Nothing suspicious or useful was found on any of the accounts. Photographs from Anne-Marie's birthday night out had not helped. The mobile phones that belonged to the victims showed nothing out of the ordinary. No recurring names that couldn't be accounted for, and no nuisance messages. Friends and family all showed genuine remorse and couldn't think of anyone who would want to harm their loved ones. No secret boyfriends or girlfriends. No jealous exes or bitter feuds. One thing the girls had in common was that they were popular.

"What about suspects?" asks Tara, keeping them on task.

"Michael Tanner was the prime suspect. He could be placed at the scene of Gemma Woodcock's murder, and there were links to Faye Williams and Amy Tatton," says Gillespie. "Graham Pierce has links to Michael Tanner and 'Cable Cars', and he's an unsavoury character. I'd have put money on it that he was involved, but he has an alibi."

"Bearing in mind the up-to-date profile and the evidence, would you still regard Michael and Graham as suspects?" asks Tara, playing devil's advocate.

"They both live in the city centre. I wouldn't say either of them are fit, or in their prime, but they could both stand up for themselves or appear threatening," replies Gillespie.

"Graham Pierce more so. Tanner was up to his neck in antisocial behaviours, but I don't see how he would have the forensic awareness that we've witnessed. On the other hand, Pierce is a manipulator," adds Jo. "At one point, I thought maybe they were working together. Pierce as the dominator and Tanner as the submissive, but the profile indicates that this isn't a duo. Plus, Tanner didn't have any allergies."

They pause and look at the frustrating jigsaw of information. Tara adds her own conclusions. "We know the bite marks aren't Tanner's. Can we get a dental impression from Graham Pierce, along with an allergy test?"

"Doubt it. He has an alibi for two of the nights when a body was found. His lawyer got him out of that station as quickly as you could cook a Pop-Tart," answers Jo, suddenly feeling hungry.

"I'll give Clarke a ring, see if he can pull some strings and get him back in," says Gillespie, begrudgingly leaving the room to make the call.

Jo and Tara sit and look at the flipchart paper. Several murders, and numerous voyeur cases. "In your professional opinion, what would have caused the switch from voyeur to murder?" asks Tara, as she moves closer to Jo.

"A trigger of some sort. A bereavement perhaps, or a breakup? Anything that causes the offender to become that bit more unstable, or to lose the control they've been trying to exert. Gillespie has always said it seems strange to have escalated so quickly, but I've seen it before. Not often, but it happens."

Tara nods and thinks about the things that she has seen throughout her career. Some things stay with you for life. "Between my career and yours, I bet we have seen it all. Sometimes the bodies come in and they look so peaceful, regardless of how they died. Other times, they look like practice."

"What do you mean by 'practice?" asks Jo.

"Like it's the first time someone has caused harm to another person. One time, I examined a body that had been repeatedly stabbed in the stomach, but the cause of death was choking on a rat. The killer, who was a woman by the way, thought that if she stabbed her boyfriend in the stomach and left a hole, he'd bleed out. What she didn't realise was that she had stabbed her boyfriend so deeply that it ruptured his spleen and caused massive internal bleeding. He bled from the mouth and that's where some nearby rats went to. Long story short, one got stuck. My point is that people get better with practice."

"Anne-Marie Swift; was she practice?" asks Jo.

"Her throat was slit. The wound wasn't particularly smooth or jagged. Based on what I saw, I would say it was inconclusive. Based on my instincts, no. It didn't feel like a practice or someone's first time." Tara stood to clear the cups and plates. "What's that look on your face?"

"It's just my face; I always look like this. What are you trying to say?"

"Nothing. I like your face," she says, smiling. Jo smiles back as Gillespie returns. Before he can speak, Jo stands up, grabs her bag and asks him, "Were there any hits with the search from previous crimes where lambskin was found?"

"No, but I've asked them to widen the parameters."

"What if the killer didn't escalate from voyeur to murder? What if he was already a killer? That would explain the forensic awareness and the organisation. Get your officer to look at murders and accidental deaths in Liverpool over the last ten years. Look at the people that were interviewed too. I bet you Pierce's name pops up." She swings her bag over her shoulder. "What is it?" she asks.

"It's Graham Pierce. Seems like his wife doesn't remember being with him on the nights in question, after all," replies Gillespie.

"I knew it. Told you, didn't I, Tara?" Jo is startled to see that Tara is already watching her.

"That's not all," says Gillespie. "She now remembers finding a pair of knickers in his pocket."

46

Emily Spencer arrives for her admission interview for an art course. She is wearing the smartest outfit she could put together from her disorganised wardrobe. A black and white striped shirt with a blazer over it, and a pair of straight-cut trousers she has borrowed from Gina. She hopes that the interview panel will consider her bottle-green leather boots as quirky and becoming, as an artist would wear.

She waits for her name to be called. She has the last interview of the day and isn't sure whether that is good or not. Will it make her more memorable or will she be rushed through because they have seen enough?

"Miss Spencer, you can come through now," says a woman with a clipboard.

Emily stands and swallows her nerves. She could vomit right now but that wouldn't be the best first impression. She picks up her portfolio of drawings, smiles as though a coat hanger is wedged between the corners of her mouth, and walks into the room. Informal pleasantries are made, and Emily is introduced to the three people on the interview panel.

"Tell us about yourself," says interviewer number one.

She takes a few deep breaths, like Sophie has advised her to, and resists the urge to tell them anything too truthful. "I'm Emily and I have a passion for art." The interviewers smile and wait for more. "I've been practising art ever since I can remember."

The tension increases and the silence feels never-ending. Should she add more? What else do they possibly want to know at this stage? Surely, they don't want her life story. They glance at each other and Emily notices a 'look' between them. As interviewer number two draws a breath to ask the next question, Emily hears herself speak.

"I don't like much in my life. It's not been great so far. I've experienced enough trauma to last a lifetime, but art has always been a friend. Something to turn to when there is no one else. Something to share my anger and heartache with. I don't draw because I'm good or because it's fun. I draw because, well, what else can I do with all my thoughts and feelings?"

The interviewers nod and make notes. They look at each other and give approval for the next question to be posed. They become more answerable. *What style of art will you pursue in your course? What are your preferred mediums? What are your goals after college?*

They ask Emily to leave her portfolio with them and collect it the following day, after they have determined her current working level. Emily wonders if they ask everyone to do this, or if they are just tired and want to get home.

As she leaves the building, sweat drips down her back and her shirt clings to her. She exhales and, as the nerves and tension leave her body, she is surprised by how dark it is. *'No wonder they wanted to get home,'* she thinks to herself. *Did they think I was unprepared? Did I present myself as committed? Did I come across as troubled?*

She is startled when her phone vibrates and she answers without checking who it is.

"Emily? Hi there. It's Julie Richards from the college. It was lovely to meet you earlier."

"You too," says Emily, confused why she is ringing.

"We looked at your work after you left. It's good, with lots of potential. We were very impressed with your interview. You clearly have great resilience and a desire to make something of your life, despite your troubles."

Emily is waiting for the 'but'.

"We'd like to offer you a place on the course, and we are very excited to have you join us." Emily wonders if she heard that correctly. "So, I'm starting the course in a few weeks?" she asks.

"That's correct. We'll send some admission paperwork and introductory materials in the post and see you at registration. You can collect your portfolio then, or come back for it tomorrow, whatever is best for you."

Emily offers her thanks and, even as she puts her phone away, she can't quite believe that she did it. In the same month that Marcus Gaines almost jeopardised her recovery and relationship with Sophie, she got herself into art school. She decides to wait until she gets home to tell Gina, in case Graham answers the phone.

The last train to Liverpool Central Station pulls up with a screech. The station is almost empty but that doesn't stop the clammy heat from making her uncomfortable. It always smells like damp laundry that has been left wet for days in the dryer. As she leaves the station and walks to the top of Bold Street, she sticks out her thumb to hail a black cab. Several drive past, already occupied. She rings 'Cable Cars' but the line is engaged.

She sits on the steps outside the bombed-out church, thinking about how long it would take to walk home. When 'Cable Cars' is still engaged fifteen minutes later, the decision is made for her. She walks and turns onto Brownlow Hill. The absence of traffic and beeping horns is not surprising at this hour. Rush hour though, is a different story.

She puts her earphones in and walks at a faster pace. At the bottom of Brownlow Hill, she walks past an abandoned car park and thinks about crossing it as a shortcut. She looks to see if anyone is around but, since she is alone, she decides to stick to the side streets for safety.

As she is about to cross the road, out of habit she turns to check for traffic and notices someone in the distance, walking towards her. She crosses and looks at her watch. Twenty minutes from home. Her feet are hurting in the boots. She wants to sit down but the bench is occupied by a man wearing his hood up. Instantly, she thinks the worse. *Will he grab me? Will he steal my bag and run off? Will he say something obscene?*

As she hurries past, wishing there was another route she could take, she hears the man's keys jangle as he stands up. He tries to speak to her, muttering something under his breath. Scared and focusing on what is behind her, Emily walks straight into someone else.

"Oh, I'm sorry. I wasn't looking where I was going," she says.

"It's OK," he says. "I saw that fella trying to talk to you and thought you could do with a hand."

The hooded man walks off in the opposite direction, still muttering to himself. He has a blanket and a carrier bag of belongings. Emily feels guilty that her first thought was for her own safety, rather than the dire circumstances of a homeless man. Still, the anticipation of danger dissipates.

"Thanks, I freaked out there for a moment," she says, looking at her saviour and straightening herself up.

He has a kind face and, under the flicker of a streetlight, she sees him more clearly. He introduces himself as Tom, and she is taken aback by the dimple in his chin, slightly crooked teeth, and the most unique pair of eyes she has ever seen.

47

"You dropped this," says Tom.

She turns to see that she has dropped her hand sanitiser. A new black cherry scent. "Thanks, it must have fallen out when we bumped into each other."

"No problem, Emily," he says.

She walks further down the street, regretting her decision to walk rather than wait for a taxi. She replays the chance encounter in her mind, embarrassed that she seemed so relieved to have retrieved her bottle of hand sanitiser.

Tom with the nice eyes. Tom with a nice face. Tom with the comforting Liverpool accent. Tom the friendly guy. Did she tell him her name?

She turns to look behind her. He is still there, walking. Of course he is, he was on his way somewhere before they clashed. He seems to be walking in her direction now, despite going the other way earlier.

She crosses the road. He doesn't.

She starts to calm down, but Tom has almost caught up with her. She takes her phone out and calls Gina. Talking on a phone is a good deterrent when you feel on edge or want to look busy. Her call drops out, so she rings again. No answer. Gina is either at work or asleep.

"Hello again," says Tom.

She jumps and clings to her phone as she pretends to look confident and calm.

"One second, Mum." Emily holds the phone to her shoulder. "I'm on the phone," she continues, excusing herself from the encounter with a white lie.

"Sorry, didn't mean to interrupt," he says, as he holds his hands up and walks past. As he is about to cross the road, her phone rings and her lie is exposed. He walks back to her. "Bad signal or a really good one?" he laughs.

She laughs and tries to enter the security PIN on her phone. Her hands are shaking. She is cold and nervous, and the phone isn't recognising her PIN or fingerprint.

"Where are you heading?" Tom asks. "I can walk with you if you want. I don't live too far from you."

With sudden realisation, she knows that she didn't tell him her name or where she lives. Adrenaline floods her body and her muscles become tense. Her insides feel like they are spinning but he looks calm. He looks like he is waiting for an answer to his suggestion. He looks friendly, but her body doesn't lie. It has been in danger before, and it recognises it now.

Without hesitating, she kicks Tom in the shin hard enough for him to double over in pain. She runs down the street, too out of breath to shout for help. She doesn't want to slow down to ring anyone, as her body is on autopilot and she can do nothing but run. The last time she ran like this was from Marcus Gaines. She had threatened to expose him, and he had battered her until her lips were so swollen that she couldn't talk.

Out of breath, she hides underneath a parked car. It's a tight squeeze and the ground is wet, but she can't run any further. There are no houses to knock at, just closed businesses. She holds her breath as much as she can, but her lungs feel like they are in spasm.

She can see his feet walking towards her, with a slight limp caused by her kick. She is glad she caused him pain. He moves closer to the car but walks past it. This old Ford Focus has given her the shelter she needs. She rests her head on the ground and allows herself the time and opportunity to regain her breath and composure. When she can't hear any footsteps, she slides herself out from underneath the car, grazing her chin on the ground.

She has almost pulled her bag free from the car when she feels a jolt to her neck.

Tom has grabbed her by the neck and now throws her to the ground. She tries to scramble but she loses her balance and falls on her back. She kicks and tries to move away as he comes closer. The nettles and weeds sting her hands and a sharp shard of glass pierces her finger. She stalls and Tom grabs her by the waist. He is strong; much stronger than he looks.

She kicks and screams, but his grip is too tight. She tries to claw at his face, but she can't reach him. She wants to scratch those eyes right out of his head with her bare hands. He drags her off the pavement and into the garden of a derelict house. It has tall overgrown bushes and there is an old wooden shed in the corner.

He throws Emily into the shed and the door swings shut behind them. She knows this fear all too well. She is trapped.

She grabs a rusty shovel and jabs at him. If she can push him into the shed door, it will break and she can run. Run like before. She jabs and he swerves, like a practised routine. The wood splinters in her hands and she drops the shovel. As she bends to reach it again, Tom kicks her in the face with the same force and finesse as if he were taking a goal kick.

Blood spills on the ground and Emily holds her face in her hands, screaming and crying. The blow to her head leaves her disorientated. Every sound is muffled, but she can hear shouting. Tom is shouting. She can't make out what he is saying. She can't hear him telling her how much of a bitch she is and how she will be thankful when he has finished.

She feels the tugs at her trousers. Gina's trousers. The button and zip are being ripped open. He is on top of her.

She still can't hear what he is saying. Everything sounds like she is underwater, but she can smell him. His breath is warm on her face and neck, and smells like a week's worth of morning breath. She feels helpless. She wills herself to be conscious enough to fight back. The flashbacks of Marcus Gaines are all that she can see. His smiling face when they met, and his puppy-dog eyes, asking her to let him record her. It is Tom's breath on her neck, but it feels like Marcus's. It is Tom's hands on her legs, but they feel like Graham's. Fucking Graham.

While Tom's hands claw at her, Emily's fingers claw at the dirty wooden shed floor. More splinters stick under her nails, piercing her like little swords. She tries to grasp anything within reach but only finds dirt. She takes a handful and smears it over Tom's face. He inhales it and starts to splutter, losing his grip on her. She manages to wriggle free and takes another handful of the dirt, which has spilled from an old bag of garden soil. She charges at Tom and forces more into his mouth and eyes. As he falls back, she runs.

Out of the shed, out of the garden, and down the street to the only place her body wants to go.

48

"She rang me last night and said she was here. I came as fast as I could," says Sophie.

"You did the right thing calling me," replies Gillespie.

Emily had run to Sophie's office. The safest place she knows. It was locked but, the moment Sophie put the phone down, she raced over to Huskisson Street and held Emily as she wept.

Now, Sophie struggles to hold back her tears. "I don't know what's happened yet, I rang you straightaway. She was shaking and crying. Terrorised. I'll never forgive myself if her brother-in-law…"

"Let's speak to her together. She might feel more comfortable if you're there," says Gillespie, with his hand on Sophie's shoulder. "Do you need a minute?" Sophie shakes her head and wipes her eyes. She takes a deep breath and puts her professional face on.

"Emily, you remember Detective Gillespie?"

Emily nods as she recoils. Sophie sits next to her so that Gillespie doesn't. She doesn't know what has happened yet but she knows that, whatever it was, it will have triggered Emily's previous trauma. PTSD doesn't vanish, even with all the work Emily has put into managing it.

"He's going to ask you some questions about what's happened. Is that OK with you? He's a friend." Sophie doesn't break her attention from Emily. She can see that her clothes are torn, and her fingernails are filthy. Flashes of what might have happened flicker through her mind. The worst cases.

"Hi Emily, I'm Detective Gillespie. You can call me Harry, if you'd rather. As Sophie says, I'm here to help. When you're ready, could you tell me what happened?"

Emily continues to sit and shake, with her arms tucked into her body as tightly as possible, as if she is hiding something shameful. Gillespie sees the ripped clothes and looks for other visual clues. Soiled hands and nails. Cut on her chin. Black eye and bruised cheek. Bloodied nose. Someone has done a number on this girl, or tried to.

"Can you tell me how you hurt your face?"

Emily doesn't answer but she winces, as if remembering that her face is injured. She reaches up to her nose and flinches.

"I kicked him," she says. "I kicked him in the shin, but he found me. I hid from him. Under the car. I thought he was gone. I thought he was nice. He gave me my hand gel back."

Gillespie looks at Sophie, both understanding the fragmented nature of the shock.

"Who was he?" asks Gillespie.

"He knew my name. I don't remember telling him. He knew it though. Tom."

"He said his name was Tom?" asks Sophie, thinking back to their sessions for any mention of a Tom.

"He dragged me to a garden. In a shed. I was just walking home," says Emily, as if watching it play out before her eyes. "I couldn't hear anything. After he kicked me. But I could feel him."

Sophie's heart is breaking. Emily has worked so hard and overcome so much already. To see her injured, and God knows what else, is soul-destroying.

Gillespie and Sophie listen as Emily recounts the night. The gel. The car. The shed. The soil. She gives clear details, from previous experience Gillespie assumes. She tells them where it happened, when it happened, and what happened. All that is missing is the 'who'. They have a name, Tom, but that is likely to be false.

"Emily, would you come to the hospital with me? Sophie can come too. We need to get you looked at. Get your injuries treated." He pauses. "And we'll need to collect any forensic evidence. Fluids, fibres; anything that can help us catch who did this to you."

"And a rape kit," says Emily. "You need to check for semen, right? What will happen after that? This time, I mean." Her matter-of-fact comments catch Gillespie off-guard.

"After that, we'll go to the station and a dedicated officer will be assigned to you. They'll be your single point of contact and will make sure you get all the help and support you need while the case is investigated."

Emily nods slowly, but the tears fall fast. Sophie moves closer and takes Emily in her arms. '*If I can't show a patient some love and sympathy after this, when can I?*' she thinks.

"I'll make a few calls," says Gillespie, leaving the room. He calls the station and arranges for a dedicated officer to meet them at the station and to contact Gina. He rings for an ambulance to take

Emily to the hospital. He would rather take her to the hospital himself, but the CPS will want the usual protocol to be followed so that the case is airtight if it goes to court. Finally, he rings Jo. "What's up?" she asks, as she has just woken up.

"We might have something. I've just interviewed a girl who was attacked tonight. I'm not sure, but it could be our guy."

"What's the connection?" asks Jo, stumbling out of bed to throw clothes on.

"I don't know how reliable this is, but she said she heard him say something about 'the other girls'."

"Anything else?" Jo isn't convinced of the connection just yet.

"She remembers his breath being disgusting, and he kept trying to bite her."

The line goes quiet. Sexual assault victims often recall smells and tastes over facial descriptions, but it is pertinent to this investigation, and the biting is a clear connection. "I'll meet you at the hospital," says Jo. "I can be there in twenty."

"OK. I'll go in the ambulance and ask Sophie to follow in her car. One more thing. She's Graham Pierce's sister-in-law."

49

Jo arrives at the hospital, aware that her shirt is creased and her socks are odd. Victims take priority over ironing and anyone who doesn't agree should take a running jump as far as she is concerned. She is escorted to where Emily is being treated and meets Gillespie and Sophie outside the room.

She has heard about Sophie from Gillespie but makes a mental note to tell him how modest he has been about her beauty.

"They're almost done with the examination," says Gillespie.

Jo notices that his arm is around Sophie and looks away. Whatever is going on between them will need to stop. She is part of an investigation now which makes her off-limits.

"What are the chances of Graham Pierce, one of our suspects, having a sister-in-law who gets attacked?" asks Gillespie.

"Could be a coincidence. Or maybe one of his friends or associates liked what he saw in Emily," replies Jo. "Did she recognise this 'Tom'?"

"No. If it's the same man then that rules out Graham Pierce. I showed her a few pictures before the examination, with her permission. She didn't even recognise Michael Tanner."

Jo looks in through the window, but it is covered with privacy glass. No one can see in, and no one can see out. Hospitals are part of the job. They go with the territory, but that doesn't stop them from reminding her about Susie. Jo visited more than her fair share of hospitals when looking for her sister and identifying bodies that turned out not to be hers. You never get the smell of hospitals out of your pores. If it isn't for the fact that she has checked that Eddie Doran is still in prison, he would be on her suspect list.

"What about Marcus Gaines?" asks Sophie. "He wanted to meet Emily as part of his rehabilitation. She said no, understandably. Maybe this is revenge for rejecting him."

"I already sent someone to the prison to speak to Gaines," says Gillespie, moving to the end of the corridor to make a call.

"He likes you, you know," says Jo, looking at Gillespie but with her attention on Sophie.

"We're just friends. Not even that really."

"Keep it that way. He's a good guy. You'd be risking his career now if anything happened."

"I can assure you that nothing will happen. In case you haven't noticed, we're standing outside a hospital room where my patient is being treated and examined after a serious assault. I'd appreciate it if you kept the big sister routine for someone else."

Jo nods and smiles as she opens Gillespie's notes. She instantly likes Sophie.

"She reported a wedding ring," Jo says out loud, directing her remark to Gillespie.

"She wasn't sure if it was a wedding ring or not, but it was silver with a sword on it," says Gillespie, walking towards them and waving his phone. "Gaines had nothing to say. We can show Emily some pictures of his known associates and see if she recognises anyone. Everything OK here?" he asks, as a nurse comes out of the examination room. She indicates that Sophie can sit with Emily and tells them that Gina is on her way to the hospital. Jo and Gillespie follow her to the small family room.

"She's doing OK. She's a brave kid," says the nurse. "She's got a bite mark on her thigh but it's very faint. Signs of rape are present, as expected. She's bruised in her genital area and thighs, and there are injuries to her face. The lab will send test results as quickly as they can, but we might not get them back until late tomorrow."

"That's fine. We know someone who can make sure they are given priority," says Jo, thinking of Tara. "Any seminal fluid?"

"Not quite," replies the nurse. "I did find something but, for obvious reasons, I can't give it to you without sending it to the lab. Maybe *your person* can get that back fast for you too." Jo spots the inflexion and tone in the nurse's words. There is a thin line between sarcasm and spite.

"I found a condom," continues the nurse. "Likely it came off in the struggle. She probably didn't even know it was still inside her."

50

"Nothing under the fingernails," says Tara. "Just soil and chips of wood."

Jo and Gillespie rang her while they were still at the hospital, and she has put a rush on the results. She doesn't like to use her rank for priority testing but if this is the killer they are looking for, then he has just made a mistake and time is precious.

"The bite mark is too faint to get a proper comparison to the others, but my best guess is it's the same. You can see even fainter indentation where the false or eroded teeth are," Tara reports. "The condom is confirmed as lambskin." She is sickened, yet pleased, at the confirmation but Jo gives her a 'well done' look anyway.

"What else does it tell us?" asks Gillespie.

"Examination inside the condom didn't find any semen. Emily got away before that could happen, but some fluid was tested and gave us some genetic information. Nothing that's a match for

Michael Tanner, Graham Pierce, or any of the other people you asked me to look at."

"Well, Tanner's dead and Pierce was neither identified by Emily as her attacker, nor on the streets last night. He was in the station after his wife admitted she gave him a false alibi. Seems like Mr Pierce has a thing for watching women work out in the park. His phone is full of pictures that were taken covertly. None of our victims," says Gillespie. "He claims the knickers were found in the back of a 'Cable Cars' taxi and he pocketed them 'for a laugh'."

Jo excuses herself from the medical lab and goes outside. She sits on a bench a few metres down the road and lights a cigarette. She hopes Tara doesn't come out and see her smoking. Graham Pierce hasn't been ruled out, but she isn't hopeful that his dental impression will be of any use. That means their suspect list has shrunk to zero.

What new information has Emily Spencer's attack brought to the case? It occurred within the 'Circle of Danger', so no surprise there. The offender hasn't changed geographically. Emily is a fit and healthy young girl who has been resourceful and strong enough to fight off her attacker, but he still managed to cause serious injury and force her to the shed.

The ring is interesting, but why? A silver ring is as common as anything. It has a symbol of a sword on it. What does that mean? Probably nothing. These days you can get anything on a ring. Jo noticed Tara wearing a 'love is love' ring when they first met, and she used to own one with a picture of a cherub on it.

This 'Tom' was charming at first, disarming even, so the social skills and professional status are still accurate in Jo's profile. He appears to target young women who work or study in Liverpool. No clear connection has been established between the victims of the voyeurism or the killings. There must be something to link these girls. It's not physical. They all looked different. It isn't age. There isn't a 'type' of victim that the killer seems to favour. Is it someone they all knew? If so, how did they know him?

Jo walks back into the medical lab, keeping her distance from Tara until the three pieces of chewing gum she scoffed before entering have their desired effect. She sits and catches up with what Tara and Gillespie are talking about.

"It's not rare but it is uncommon to find many people with heterochromia in a small geographical area. It's a condition where someone has different coloured eyes. It can be a genetic trait or the result of trauma, among many other things, and is caused by different levels of melanin in each eye. Normally our irises have similar levels of melanin, which gives the distinct appearance of our eyes being the same colour, even if they differ slightly. In someone with complete heterochromia, the levels are so different that the eyes can be completely different colours, as is the case of Emily's attacker. One of his eyes is blue, with very little melanin, and the other is green, with average levels."

"Does that help us?" asks Jo.

"It's certainly a characteristic that could narrow down your suspect list, but that would require you to have a list to begin with," replies Tara. "I didn't mean that to sound as harsh as it did."

"It's fine. You're only saying what Clarke and the rest of his boys' club are thinking," says Gillespie.

"This might help though," says Tara, printing off a list of addresses. "My team managed to identify the specific make of the condoms and here's a list of the pharmacies that stock them. Thought it would help."

Gillespie takes the list and smiles. "Only two places?" he asks.

Tara smiles and replies, "And one of them has been shut for refurbishments for the last six months, meaning anyone who needs them has to pick their scripts up here." She pulls up the address of the pharmacy using Google Maps. Gillespie and Jo recognise it instantly.

Chaloner Street.

The same street where Clarke and Phillip Tatton were caught on camera.

51

He looks at himself in the mirror.

His eyes are still bloodshot from the shit she threw at him. He uses eye drops to swill his eyes clean, but each movement feels like small shards of glass scraping along the surface of his eyeballs. He will have to wear his glasses tomorrow but that will reveal too much, and it isn't his time yet. The scrappy bitch saw his eyes and had nearly blinded him. He hadn't expected the fight. She always looked so introverted. So unaware of the world around her.

He looks at his teeth. A few are crooked. A few are rotten. The medication helps but it will be a while before anything tastes right again. He picks at the plaque on one of his teeth and it doesn't move. In anger, he forces dental floss between them. A stinging sensation shoots through his gum, which starts to bleed. The pain hurts but feels good. A relief. A burst in the bubble of fury. Blood drips into the sink, drop by drop. He clenches his teeth together and stares at his lips as blood seeps through.

He is angry with himself. He followed his plan, like before. There is no room for ad hoc changes or improvisation. If someone wants to get away with a crime, they have to be three steps ahead at all times. Know the target. Know the location. Know the ending.

The ending should have been exhilarating. A relief. It should have been him walking out of there alone, not him writhing in pain.

The birthday girl had screamed like an infant. She got into the car willingly. She was on the streets alone, with no friends. She had assumed that the smiling clean-cut man was a safe bet. How wrong she was.

The one with the dog. The dog had been expected, as she walked him every night. It had to die, as being mauled by a dog was not part of the plan. A dog is a man's best friend until there is something to compete with it. Then it is just a disposable obstruction.

He has learned from the others. Walking too close makes people uncomfortable. Personal space is a British delicacy and standing too close is a major red flag, no matter who you are. But walking too far behind increases the risk of losing your target in the side streets, hidden down other side streets.

The knife isn't necessary, but it is efficient. The slow death from bleeding out is like watching a coin roll round and round the charity boxes placed in supermarkets. It goes on for a while but, then suddenly, the coin is gone. Their eyes accept fate, and the look of terror turns to defeat. Their last breaths slow down, muscles relax their grip and they circle the drain, like the coin, before it drops.

When it's over, you want to put another coin in.

52

The pharmacy on Chaloner Street doesn't open for another half hour. The car park where CCTV revealed Clarke's relationship with Phillip Tatton is metres away. Clarke has managed to distance himself from Tatton and destroy any evidence that implicates him in any wrongdoing. His plan for promotion to commissioner is back on track and, within a month, he will be the figurehead of Merseyside Police.

The commissioner. Responsible for the totality of the police; the voice of the people, and the one with the power to hire and fire the chief constable. It makes Gillespie sick to his stomach that corruption from the top can, potentially, spill down and flow into the city.

Jo knows that it already does. The politics and power at the top of any institution are always corrupt. The people at the top usually have several sociopathic markers. Charm and affability, but with a lack of remorse and empathy. The characteristics of most leaders.

Whether it is law and order, or education, the people who call the shots make sure they aren't the shooters. They want to win the war without taking part in the battle. Prepared to sacrifice every lamb required. The bad apples that can spoil the barrel.

Dickheads, according to Jo.

"How does Clarke have one of the best crime-closing stats, when the average crime rate for the city is on the up? That's like saying a college has a 100% pass rate on a course but failing to say that 60% of the cohort dropped out halfway through," she says.

"His stats are mostly based on thefts and burglaries. The averages for the city are skewed by influxes of knife crime and drink-driving but a closed case is a win, whatever the crime," Gillespie says, shrugging his shoulders.

"He hasn't always been in Liverpool though. That stint of his in Glasgow must have put his stats behind, surely. If I was going to take a sabbatical, I'd go to Vegas," says Jo. "And I'd time it so that Adele or Cher was the resident show."

Gillespie shrugs his shoulders again. "Clarke was deployed there for a year to help put a new training regime in place for a new academy in Glasgow. He came back early. Only stayed for seven months. Seems he left under a dark cloud that no one wants to talk about."

"A dark cloud around Bob Clarke? Never," Jo laughs. "I'd like to put a dark cloud around his …"

She is interrupted by a tall woman who is unlocking the door to the pharmacy. She is looking at Jo and Gillespie out of the corner of her eye, trying to hurry through the door. As Jo starts to approach her, the woman waves her away and says, "The methadone clinic isn't open until tomorrow."

Gillespie laughs and steps forward, showing the woman his badge. Jo tries to flatten the creases in her shirt and tidy her hair. She isn't offended by the woman. At least she has assumed that Jo is a *recovering* addict.

Inside the pharmacy, the woman turns on the lights and brings the room to life. She opens the blinds and the early warning signs of a hot day seep through the slats. Leaflets about self-help and alternative services adorn the walls. The irony is not lost on Jo. The GP surgeries advise you that help can be accessed online, and online services refer you to pharmacies, who give you advice on self-help. The worst game of treasure hunt.

"Do you stock lambskin condoms?" asks Gillespie. He quickly remembers the importance of context and adds, "It's for a case we are working on. Our evidence says this is the only pharmacy that stocks them in the city centre."

The woman does not break from her routine. She flicks several buttons on computers that look unintentionally retro. Heater fans work excessively as the hard drives desperately try to boot up the system. Finally, she sits and swaps her Converse trainers for salmon-coloured heels.

"I'll have to check the inventory to see if we have any in stock right now but, yes, we do normally dispense them. You can only get them on prescription though."

"Can you give us a list of who is prescribed them?" asks Jo. "It would really help with …"

"Absolutely not." The woman cuts Jo off before she can finish her subtle pleasantries. "That would be career suicide. If you want to access that type of information then … well, I don't know. But it certainly isn't in my job description to give out that type of data."

Jo looks around the pharmacy and pretends to read a self-help leaflet on 'How to manage pain'. She watches as Gillespie offers flattery and old-school gentlemanly respect, but the woman still refuses to help.

"Can I show you some names and pictures, and then maybe you could just nod or shake your head if they are in your system? That wouldn't be against the rules, just a slight bend. For little old me?" asks Gillespie. "It will save my partner here coming back later." He gives a nod in Jo's direction and the woman scrunches up her face. She has taken an instant dislike to Jo, and the feeling is mutual. Frustrated, she shrugs her shoulders and starts tapping at the computer.

"Go on then, but quickly. Janet has called in sick today so I'm doing the work of two people on a one-person wage," she says, in a flippant and bitter tone.

No results for Michael Tanner. Nothing in the last year for Graham Pierce. A nod for Phillip Tatton, but she refuses to divulge anything about him. She clearly knows a thing or two about his reputation.

"Why are you so interested in lambskin condoms?" she asks, as she realises that she could be playing a role in an important investigation. '*She looks the type to read 'Agatha Christie' on holiday,'* thinks Jo.

The woman continues with her questioning. "Are they central to your case? I don't suppose many people use them. We stock them but only because we were asked to. If we didn't have patients who want them, we wouldn't have any at all. You'd have to wait a week before we can order some, and that would put an end to any impromptu or romantic plans. Imagine that." She sips her coffee and her imagination is fast at work.

Jo and Gillespie know to not interrupt and let someone keep talking, as they might volunteer useful information without realising it.

"The man who gets lambskin condoms from us only comes about once a month, so we only order a couple of boxes to keep in the shop. On the other hand, he needs Fexofenadine too, a medicated antihistamine. Now, that is a common prescription." The woman continues to ramble. Gillespie and Jo let her.

"My sister always says I might meet Mr Right at work. I don't see how. That would mean he is our 25-year-old pharmacist assistant, Juan, or one of the customers, which would be messy. Mind you, there's always Mr Tatton, who looks dapper in a suit, or Mr Swift, who looks like he needs a good meal. His daughter died not that long ago."

There it is. The piece of information that suddenly makes this visit to the pharmacy worth it.

53

"Is Mr Swift the father of Anne-Marie?" asks Jo.

"Yes. Terrible business that," says the woman in the pharmacy, whose name tag says 'Barbara'. "Poor kid. She comes in here, or used to, every month for her inhalers and spacer. I threatened to leave this job when I saw all this on the news. Young Anne-Marie and then Faye Williams. Two of the loveliest girls you could meet. Makes a difference when you deal with polite people, but why should I put my life at risk? I should be paid danger money for working here after all this carry-on."

"What about Gemma Woodcock? Was she a nice person too?" asks Gillespie. Jo has learned to observe rather than rub the woman up the wrong way.

"Didn't know her so much. She used to come in for migraine medication. I only know that off the top of my head because I checked when I saw her on the news. Didn't come in often but, the last time she did, she looked like she'd been dragged through a bush. Young people and their partying. I wouldn't trade places with them for all the tea in China."

Gillespie makes quick notes whilst she talks. Faye Williams, Anne-Marie Swift and Gemma Woodcock had all used this pharmacy, at some point. The only pharmacy that stocks lambskin condoms. '*Does Emily Spencer also frequent this pharmacy?'* he wonders and makes a note to check this later. Nothing about Emily, or her attack, has been released to the press yet.

Jo is also putting the pieces together. The one thread that the girls have in common so far, apart from their untimely deaths, is this cramped and stuffy pharmacy. She makes a mental note to run a background check on Barbara and her colleagues. Better to be safe than sorry. The likelihood is that whoever is targeting these women is meeting them here. That means customers, staff, and residents are people of interest.

Gillespie writes down the names of all the people who work in the pharmacy, including those who have left within the last twelve months. Barbara is only too happy to disclose information about her colleagues. Gillespie understands why she will never find Mr Right at work, or anywhere else for that matter.

Jo and Gillespie sit outside the pharmacy. They exchange the pungent smell of tablets and Barbara, for the exhaust fumes. Chaloner Street is as busy as ever. Lorries drive by on their way to deliver fresh produce to supermarkets. Buses glide past, delivering herds of workers and students across the city.

"Shall we knock on Mr Tatton's door and ask him outright which condoms he uses? It's worth a shot," jokes Gillespie.

"He matches the profile but so does Graham Pierce. Phillip Tatton has access, as we are literally steps away from where he keeps and borrows cars. He has the money, the physique and the means to get around the city, whenever and however he likes. He could easily have seen all the victims around this pharmacy," says Jo. "And he's angry. Like, seriously angry. The authority and power he has in the city must have him wound up as tight as a cat's arse. Maybe he attacks women for release, or maybe it makes him feel more dominant. Maybe he can't get it up and violence is his aphrodisiac."

"What about Amy Tatton? I can't see him watching and perving over his own daughter. He's a piece of work, but there's nothing to suggest incestuous urges." Gillespie lights up a cigarette and offers Jo one. She accepts and is suddenly aware of how hungry she is.

"Maybe Pierce or Tanner watched Amy Tatton," replies Jo. "Pierce could have been working with Tatton and stepped out of line. Went off plan. It's not like he's a straight arrow."

"Pierce was in the station when Emily was attacked, and Tatton doesn't have this hetero thing," says Gillespie, looking back through his notes. "Heterochromia. The eye thing."

"Could be wearing contact lenses. Have you ever seen him wear glasses?"

"No, but then again, I never really looked. Too busy making sure he doesn't break my kneecaps."

He flicks his ash behind him and checks his messages. Sophie has replied and confirmed that Emily gets her antidepressants from Chaloner Street Pharmacy, which means it is the first overlapping factor between all the girls.

"What does that do for your profile?" asks Gillespie.

"It gives us our common denominator across the girls. Apart from being similar in age and from Liverpool, there's nothing else so far that ties them together. Someone knows them or has observed them here. If our killer follows his prey like a twisted predator, then he could have followed any of them. We need to see the CCTV. See when they've been in and who was around." Jo stubs her cigarette out onto the floor.

"Where are you going?" asks Gillespie.

"To see what Tara makes of this new link. See if there's anything we're missing about the ailments the girls have."

"Yeah, right. Give her a kiss from me, won't you?" laughs Gillespie.

Jo gives him the middle finger as she puts her sunglasses on and walks down the street.

54

Emily is sitting on her bed, surrounded by her art. She is trying to complete one of the introductory assignments for her course. The university has said that they understand her circumstances and are happy for her to start in the second semester, but she is determined to get on with her life. She doesn't want to let what just happened define her, the way Marcus Gaines had.

She grips the pencil so tightly that her fingers turn white. She tries to conjure up pleasant images to draw; a honeybee sitting on a sunflower or a cat cleaning its paws. However, all that comes to mind is the shed. The shovel. His face. His blue and green eyes.

She throws her art onto the floor and screams with frustration. Gina opens the door, startled, and without saying anything, sits next to her and holds her hand. There are no words that can bring comfort. Gina knows, from previous experience, that all Emily needs is to know that she is there, ready to cuddle her when she wants, and ready to hold her when she cries.

Graham has gone.

Gina threw most of his clothes and belongings out of the front door, into the street, exactly twenty minutes after she changed her statement to the police. She has lied about being his alibi. She has lied for love, but the knickers and photographs on his phone are not love. Love isn't following other women and taking pictures of them without their permission. Love isn't finding used knickers in your taxi and keeping them in your pocket, for God knows what.

As far as she is concerned, Graham should be locked up or sent to wherever perverts are sent. Chemical castration is too good for him. When Gina first met him, he was seeing someone else. He chased Gina and asked her out until she said yes. She should have known then that his persistence and aggression are a huge red flag.

She has put up with a lot from him. His nights out and his sleazy friends. One time, he didn't come home after a night out and, when he did finally knock on the door, he was so drunk he had soiled himself. Another time, he came home battered and bruised after a night at the casino. He had racked up so much debt that the security team had beaten his face until he agreed to pay them back another way. It was then that Gina found out he was delivering errands for Phillip Tatton. One week, it could be drugs in the boot of his taxi. Another week, it could be following someone home and reporting back. The debt must have been insurmountable because he had continued these errands and was in too deep to get out.

He could have anything and anyone he wanted, as long as he continued to run the errands.

55

"OK, thanks for getting back to me so quickly." Jo puts the phone down and waits for Tara to come back with their coffees.

When she left Gillespie, she messaged a friend from her training days. Lea joined the Investigative Psychology course at the same time as Jo, but had relocated to Glasgow halfway through the year when she met her current boyfriend through an online dating app. There is something ironic about a trainee criminal profiler finding love through the internet.

Tara moves her seat closer to Jo, so the sun isn't shining so brightly in her eyes. She laughs to herself when Jo adds two more sugars to her caramel macchiato, but doesn't comment. Tara has learned that Jo needs her sustenance, and she can see why. Spending your days trying to think like a killer, or get inside the mind of a twisted offender, can drive anyone to live for moments of literal sweetness.

"My mate said Bob Clarke's a well-known name where she works. Something of a legend," says Jo.

"What is your fascination with your boss? I don't know why you have it in for him. You must be exhausted with work, let alone with this vendetta against him."

"Vendetta? Do you want to see Bob Clarke as the next commissioner? I sure as shit don't. He might have gotten rid of the evidence but, I'm telling you, he's as corrupt as Phillip Tatton. The two might look like they're on different sides of the law, but they are definitely lying in the same bed," says Jo, slurping her coffee, even though it's far too hot. "Are you telling me you think I should let him crack on?"

"I wouldn't tell you what to do at all, but I think Bob Clarke himself isn't the issue. The problem lies with the corruption of anyone with power. Do you think I don't come across it myself? Even in my position, as medical examiner for the city, my professionalism is tested every day by the pen-pushers and the politicians. Do your job the best you can and go home, that's what I think," says Tara, wiping up the excess sugar that Jo has spilled.

Jo nods to pacify her and continues with the story. Clarke moved to Glasgow on a secondment and, according to Lea, he came home early because he botched up a case. A woman was found dead, hanging from the ceiling. He arrived at the scene first and cut her down. His fingerprints and footprints were everywhere. Forensics couldn't establish whether it was suicide or foul play."

"That's a schoolboy error. Why would he do that? He knows that would stuff up the crime scene analysis," replies Tara, slightly more interested in him now.

"Aha, this is where it gets interesting. The victim was his then-girlfriend. His wife had stayed in Liverpool while he went to

Glasgow. She was recovering from a stroke but had insisted that he go. Guess he found something in Scotland that he liked, and not just the shortbread."

"So he found her, cut her down in a panic or in desperation to save her. Understandable. Not the affair, of course. If I'd met someone I really liked, or loved, and found them hanging from the ceiling, my first instinct would be to cut them down and try to resuscitate them, despite my job," says Tara.

"I guess. But still, he had an affair and then fucked up the case. Bob Clarke was not looking like the face of the new training program at the academy anymore. He came back, picked up where he left off with his wife, and that was that."

"How is he still expecting to make commissioner?" asks Tara. "Surely that mistake will be on his record for the rest of his career. It would be a political nightmare if it got out that a high-ranking officer disturbed the scene where his mistress was found."

"We come back full circle to the corruption at the top. Seems like Clarke has made friends with the right people. Gillespie has worked with Clarke for most of his career and I don't think even he knows about this. If it wasn't for Lea, I wouldn't either." Jo finishes her coffee and wipes her mouth with her sleeve.

Tara watches Jo eating her muffin. Crumbs fall onto the table and she wipes them onto the floor. Jo couldn't be any more different, but that is a good thing, as Tara spends all day working with the dead, in a clinical and methodical way. There is something refreshing and attractive about the way Jo doesn't give a fuck about anything.

"Do you want to get a drink with me later?" asks Tara, smiling.

"Can't, sorry. I'm heading over to Phillip Tatton's office." Jo wipes her mouth with a napkin.

"After that, then?"

"After that, I'm going back to the station. I need to put a new report and profile summary together," Jo replies, oblivious to Tara's invitation and intentions. "Come with me if you want. I plan on giving Phillip Tatton some latex gloves to hold for me and see if he starts anaphalactising."

"Do you mean *anaphylaxis,* the life-threatening allergic reaction? You can't be serious."

"Sure I am. He won't let us test him and we can't get answers from the pharmacy about his prescriptions. I figure if I ask him to hold onto the gloves while I fix my shoe, or something else a damsel in distress would do, I'll know if he has a latex allergy."

Jo stands up to leave, brushing excess sugar and muffin crumbs from her trousers. She takes her hair out of her bobble and ties it back up again. Tightly.

"You coming?" she asks.

"I think I better had. You might need medical assistance but, for the record, I completely disagree with this plan."

"I know you do. It's noted and officially on record that this is not your plan."

Jo is about to open the door for Tara when she stops. "Got any latex gloves?" she asks.

56

Gillespie is sitting in the CCTV review room, watching many hours of footage from the pharmacy on Chaloner Street. He rolls a coin between his fingers and chews the edge of his polystyrene coffee cup. Trailing through the footage will take days, especially since Barbara can't offer specifics about when the girls were in the pharmacy. He plays the tapes at five times the normal speed and is amazed at how empty a pharmacy can be at times. So far, he has watched Barbara restocking shelves, drinking coffee, and pulling her knickers out of her arse.

"There you are," says Clarke. "Coffee?"

Gillespie nods, but only because coffee is the one thing that will get him through this CCTV trawl. He has three other people watching different files to lighten the load but the monotony of the task is making coffee look like the nectar of the gods right now.

"Here, shove up a bit," says Clarke, handing him a coffee and pulling up a chair beside him. "Anything of interest come up yet?"

Clarke sips his coffee and puts his glasses, pen and pad on the desk in front of him. The coffee is hot, and the steam makes him look blurry-eyed.

"Nothing yet. Just Barbara diligently working. I never realised how boring it must be to work at a pharmacy. It seems like nothing more than a pickup point for bags of medication."

"Keep at it. I need to wrap this case up like it's a Christmas present. You and Linnet need to find some way to tidy this up and get Graham Pierce's name all over it," says Clarke.

"The same way you wanted Michael Tanner's name all over it?" asks Gillespie. "That didn't work out too well for you, did it? Or for him." Clarke gives him 'the look'. The one that a superior gives when you are skating too close to the ice.

"Dreadful business. Suicide. Must have had something to hide. That's my opinion," says Clarke.

They keep their eyes on the CCTV footage from the pharmacy.

"Michael Tanner didn't kill anyone. You put him in a cell to scare him. Phillip Tatton paid you to arrange an accident." Gillespie looks at Clarke. "That's my opinion."

"Luckily, your opinions don't mean jack shit." Clarke picks up his belongings and walks to the door. "Let me know when you have something, and it better be quick."

Gillespie opens a window to air the room. Coffee, testosterone and bullshit do not make for comfortable TV viewing. He presses 'Play' on the next file where Barbara takes a stock delivery and sticks two fingers up at Janet.

In the next frame, a young girl comes to the counter. Emily Spencer. Her face is blurred but Gillespie would recognise her anywhere. When you watch someone cry and tell you about being raped, their face is etched in your memory forever.

He writes down a description of everyone in the frame. Barbara is serving at the till. An elderly lady is buying some vapour rub. A tall man, wearing a red baseball hat, who appears to be too engrossed with stock on the shelves to show his face to the CCTV camera. Gillespie sends a message to the other officers who are drowning in footage and instructs them to meet in the break room as soon as possible.

As he walks out of the stuffy room, the bright lights and coffee aroma hit him like a truck. Officers are entering the break room, looking as worn-out and square-eyed as him.

"We'll go around the room one by one. Tell me if you have seen any of the victims and, if so, who was in the pharmacy at the time or anything suspicious that you might have observed. Summers, you go first," says Gillespie.

One by one, the officers report very little. Lots of foot traffic in the pharmacy but nothing untoward or worth getting excited about. As Gillespie begins to think that this is a fruitless exercise, more positive reports are given.

One officer spotted Faye Williams in the pharmacy on three occasions. During one of these, there was a tall man in the queue behind her, wearing a red hat.

Another officer had watched footage of Anne-Marie Swift collecting her prescriptions with her dad and, then again, when she returned her empty inhalers. During her return trip, a man in a red hat also collected a prescription.

It turns out that Mark Summers saw Gemma Woodcock on tape but he doesn't recall a man in a red hat. He admits to being distracted by his phone at various intervals. When Gillespie asks him to bring up the file in front of the other officers, there is no man with a red hat in the recording.

However, Gillespie spots a man of a similar height, wearing the same coloured trousers as in the other recordings. He may not have made the connection, had it not been for the light reflecting off his large silver ring.

57

"A man in a red hat wearing a silver ring? I'll look like a clown if I give that description to the media," barks Clarke. "Give me one of the recordings and I'll see if we can release an image. See if anyone recognises him."

Gillespie hands Clarke a memory card containing the recordings of interest. He has made backup copies, in case it is lost and a folder on Dropbox in case natural disasters strike all the cards simultaneously. It's always better to be prepared.

"Barbara, the woman who works at the pharmacy, says she recognises the image but can't give us any personal information about who he is, his address or his medications," Gillespie says, as he dials Jo's number.

"Leave this with me," says Clarke. "I'll see what I can do straightaway and what favours I can call in to get the information we need from this Barbara. If a busybody pharmacy assistant is all that's standing between us and the killer, then it shouldn't be too hard to get her out of the way."

Jo has already filled Gillespie in on Clarke and his rookie mistakes in Glasgow. It's tough to lose someone you love, even if you have been having an affair and your sick wife is waiting for you to come home. Gillespie shrugs off the moment of sympathy for Bob Clarke. It seems like lying has always been part of his DNA. That's probably what makes him a good political player and keeps him a step ahead of everyone else. If he can get past iron-clad Barbara, then maybe he will make it to be a commissioner after all.

Gillespie looks through the photographs on his phone. Old family pictures when they were happy, with the whole world in front of them. Before his wife got mixed up with the wrong people, doing the wrong things. It is a slippery slope. It starts with sampling a free product on a night out, usually some cut-to-death lines of cocaine. Then you owe someone a favour, so you sell a few grams to your friends. After that, you're in it up to your neck. Possession and distribution charges don't go away because you feel like you can't say 'no' to someone. Especially if that person then blackmails you to take bigger risks.

Gillespie found out too late to intervene. His wife was already selling drugs outside the school gates. He should have known. It was his job as a detective to know. It was his job as a husband to know.

When the police came knocking and accused his wife of assaulting another woman, in a moment of panic, he stepped in and provided a false alibi. The investigation leader who took his statement convinced him to retract it and then proceeded to destroy any evidence that the alibi existed. It was the investigation leader who made it clear that Gillespie's children would be worse off with both parents in prison.

Gillespie doesn't think Clarke will make a good commissioner, but he did make a good investigation leader.

58

If it ever comes to it, he knows that Emily Spencer can identify him. She is a loose end that needs to be tied up.

He knows the pharmacy is compromised, as the police will have worked out the connection. The epicentre of the investigation. The place where he first laid eyes on the girls.

Anne-Marie Swift was vocal about her birthday night out. It wasn't hard to follow her home and learn her routine.

Faye Williams was a regular at the pharmacy, as she picked up her insulin and dropped off her sharps boxes. Finding out where she lived took less than an hour. A stroll through the city in a swarm of people rushing to-and-from work. Liverpool rush-hour was the camouflage he needed to follow her.

Gemma Woodcock was a chance encounter. She came for migraine medication but only when she had a flare-up. Had he not needed condoms for his time with Anne-Marie and Faye, he may not have come across Gemma. He was immediately enthralled by her. She looked like a party girl, wearing last night's makeup and hair. She had been too hungover to realise that he was only a few steps behind her the whole way home. She had been too self-absorbed to recognise him from the pharmacy when he greeted her at the coffee shop where she worked a few hours a week.

Although it was a serendipitous meeting, she became more useful than first anticipated. It was easy establishing a connection between her and Michael Tanner. Michael was obsessed with Amy Tatton and he spent a lot of time in that alleyway.

Poor Amy. Lovely girl. Any boy would be lucky to have her.

He had watched Michael pleasure himself enough times to know that, every Friday night, he went to the alley and watched Amy stumble home from nights out, with his hands down his pants. He knew Michael's DNA would be all over the alley. All over the ground and the wall where he wiped his hands. All he had to do, to put the police on to Michael Tanner, was leave a body next to the DNA. Gemma Woodcock to be precise.

Isn't it funny how fate brings people together in the most fortuitous way?

59

Jo and Gillespie sit in the canteen at headquarters. Even when empty, the smell of grease from a deep-fat fryer lingers in the air.

"Any joy with Tatton and the gloves?" asks Gillespie.

"Nope. Told me to go fuck myself when I asked him to hold onto them."

"Probably a good job. It wouldn't have been admissible evidence if he had died from an allergic reaction on the spot."

"That's what Tara said. She reckons anything about the allergy is going to have to come from a blood test done in the proper settings by a professional, or else it won't hold up at all."

"What else do you two talk about when you're together?"

"This and that. Work most of the time. Why are you so curious? Jealous?"

"Just wondering when you'll ask her out," says Gillespie, with full confidence that this should be her next move.

"I'm not asking anyone out. Besides, why would Tara want to go out with someone like me? I'm always working. Always eating. Always look like I've just got out of bed, and I've been married to a man. That's hardly going to rack up the winks on any dating advert, is it?"

She shakes her head and opens a tube of Pringles. "I think she might have asked me out earlier. I'm not sure. I just pretended I didn't hear her. Rather than turn up for a date that turns out to be an informal autopsy report. Pringle?"

Gillespie reaches for a crisp but her hand is already back in the box, so he politely declines.

"This pharmacy's a real breakthrough for us. Clarke's doing his best to find a way around Barbara and the other staff who have embargoed the customer records," he says, ignoring the huff from Jo. "Can that really be it? The only connection to the girls and the offender is where they get their prescriptions?"

"It doesn't matter how big or insignificant it turns out to be, the overlap between the victims is what it is. That's all you can work with," says Jo, clapping her hands to lose the crumbs. "Links to universities and being students is all very well but, in Liverpool, you can throw a stone and hit a student, so it doesn't mean much."

She hasn't pursued the student link because of the location of the crimes. The city centre is full of various universities and other educational establishments. Even those who want to study outside Liverpool have numerous options on their doorstep. You can stand outside St Johns Shopping Centre and choose twenty people at random, and most would be female students. The maths alone made Jo quickly determine that this wasn't the victims' connection.

"What's your professional verdict on the man wearing the red cap and the ring?" asks Gillespie.

"The ring and the symbol bother me," replies Jo. "I've read that something similar used to be given to people who have helped the community in some way. Paramedics, armed forces, police; that type of thing."

"It's not going to help us narrow anything down unless we see him wearing it," says Gillespie.

"What's more telling is that the man in the red hat doesn't look like someone you would cross the road to avoid," continues Jo. "Today, women are more scared than ever to go out after dark or be alone walking through the streets. Fear drives the decisions that women make when they are making plans. How will they get to their destination? How will they get home? Who will know that they have arrived safely? What's the backup plan in case they find themselves stuck somewhere? Who can they ring if they want to be on the phone walking through a dimly lit area? Even getting a taxi from A to B needs serious thought to weigh up the risks. Women and girls don't just talk to anyone. They don't just accept lifts from anyone. Sadly, safety is the first thing that influences our decisions. Despite this, the killer managed to follow these victims and learn their routine. He was able to be in front of them and in control before they realised what was happening. The way an expert burglar might be in your bedroom, with his hand over your mouth, before you even open your eyes."

"Maybe they recognised him from the pharmacy, or they didn't see him as a threat."

"Whoever it is, he doesn't look like a threat. He appears normal. He appears to be safe, at first glance anyway. Who makes us feel safe?"

As Gillespie starts to answer, he realises she is asking a rhetorical question.

"People whose job it is to make us feel safe. Police, doctors, firemen; they are all safe people. As well as taxi drivers whose identification clearly matches their face, and who have pictures of families pinned up in their car."

Gillespie knows Jo well enough to let her carry on talking when she is in profiler mode. Her mind is actively looking at all the jigsaw pieces and trying to decide which are relevant to this particular puzzle. He takes a handful of Pringles whilst she is too busy to eat.

"We've determined that he found his victims at the pharmacy. We know the locations don't have much in common, except that they were somewhat secluded within the 'Circle of Danger'. The bodies have all been found outside, presumed to have died where we found them. Even the voyeurism took place outside. Consistently. Do you know why they stick to being outside for their crimes?" asks Jo.

Gillespie shakes his head.

"Safety. Too much risk indoors. Too much effort to get inside someone's house. Too much skill is required. Offenders who commit their crimes outside tend to be more impulsive and less experienced. It's easier to escape outside if something goes wrong, like when Emily Spencer fought back and ran for her life."

Gillespie furiously writes notes, trying to keep up with Jo and her jigsaw-solving.

"Committing your crimes outside *and* in the dark, well that's just another sign of inexperience," she continues. "Easy to escape and less risk of being seen and identified. Less chance of someone missing you. The wife or girlfriend thinks you're out with the lads or at work but, instead, you're hunting your next kill. The kids are in bed, you've done your bit, said 'goodnight' and read them a story, then it's out to rape someone."

Memories of reading bedtime stories to her children, when they were little, bring Jo out of her hyper-focused state. Flashbacks come rushing back of saying 'goodnight', for what would be the last time, to her sister, Susie.

"To put all that in a nutshell," says Gillespie, flicking through his summary of notes. "The man in the red hat is likely to look approachable and have a job or hobby that makes him seem safe to women. He might have a family or girlfriend at home, so he only commits his crimes at night. He isn't experienced enough to commit his crimes indoors, and always needs an escape plan in case something goes wrong?"

Jo realises something that hasn't occurred to her before now. The darkness, and the preference for a secluded area, isn't about the body not being found. It's about confidence. The killer is worried about his plan not working out as intended. He has a backup plan because he knows there is always a chance that things can go wrong.

Because in the past, that's exactly what has happened. Someone else had gotten away.

60

"I'm coming," shouts Janice Gregson, as she runs to open her front door.

She greets the man in front of her, waiting for him to introduce himself. Over his shoulder, she sees her neighbour carrying groceries in from the car. The sun is shining hotter than usual for May, so it is a good day to get washing on the line.

"Sorry to disturb you, won't keep you long. I'm here as part of your neighbourhood watch scheme. I don't want to alarm you but there have been reports of young lads attempting to break into gardens. Mind if I check your gate? They've been gluing coins to the door as a sign to others that it's a safe house to break into."

Janice looks for an ID picture on the lanyard but it is back to front and her house phone is ringing. She looks back and forth, and signals for him to come in with a hand gesture. She runs for the phone and hears the front door shut as he enters and wipes his feet.

"Shit. Missed it. Why don't people ring for longer? I'm not the bloody 'Flash'." Janice sits for a second to catch her breath, annoyed that the phone had redirected the caller to her answer phone before she could press the green 'accept call' button.

He stands in the hallway, waiting to be invited into the living room.

"Look, my garden gate's bust and has been for years. If someone wanted to break into my house, then they would have done it already. Not that I've got much worth taking. All my money goes on cigarettes, washing powder and medication," says Janice, folding her laundry. "I didn't even think I was still on the neighbourhood watch. Is that still a thing?"

"Oh, yes. It's a vital part of the community and a great way to help keep each other safe. Have you been paying your monthly sub?" he asks.

"Nope. I used to give this lady a quid whenever she knocked. I don't know what for or where it went. In fact, I haven't seen her around for a while. Maybe she saved all the money and took herself off to Barbados. Good on ya, girl, if you did."

As she opens the front door and signals, as politely as she can, for him to leave, the timer on the oven starts beeping in the kitchen.

"For fuck's sake," she curses, while running into the kitchen and slamming the hallway door behind her. She leads a chaotic life. She has two small children and raises them alone after her husband left her for another woman. '*Bitch,*' she thinks.

The children are out for the day with a friend, leaving Janice to do her chores and then enjoy a quiet afternoon, binge-eating and watching back-to-back episodes of 'Killing Eve'.

She turns the oven off and walks back into the living room. She sits down and pours herself a glass of white Zinfandel from a half-empty bottle and looks at her phone. She has hours yet before the kids will be back in Liverpool, so she decides to head upstairs for a quick shower and change of pyjamas. Fresh pyjamas make every TV binge better.

The hot water is running, spurting from the shower head like a tropical rainstorm. Steam gathers in the bathroom. She lets the water run down her body and Avon shower gel glides over her skin. The heat relaxes her muscles and eases the tension from her hectic morning. She closes her eyes and relishes the peace and sensation of water falling around her.

The bathroom door creaks.

She opens her eyes, with her senses alert and tuned into the room. She stands still, summoning up the courage to move. She puts her fingers around the edge of the shower curtain, with water still trickling down her face. One. Two. Three. She takes a deep breath and pulls the shower curtain back with a scream.

Nothing.

The room is as it should be. Towel ready and door ajar, so she can hear the music from downstairs.

She puts her head back under the shower, satisfied that she is alone. She laughs as she thinks of the horror movies she has seen. This would be the ideal moment for someone to hide behind the shower curtain and clamp their hands over her face when she steps out of the shower. Or the classic movie scare where the showerer sees a silhouette on the other side of the curtain. Those scenes are overused but deeply terrifying every time. Much scarier than the 'Psycho' shower scene. At least the victim was stabbed to death immediately. She didn't have those ten seconds of realisation that there was an intruder there, about to do unspeakable things.

She laughs as she turns the water off and dares herself to peek behind the shower curtain. She throws the wet towel into the laundry bin and brushes her hair. Fresh pyjamas at this stage would only end up wet on her back.

Her body cools down as she sits on the edge of the bed. Her skin is red from the influx of antihistamines. She focuses on the breeze coming in through the window, the cool air hitting her skin, and the scent of Patchouli lingering on her clean body.

She lets her eyes feel heavy and is peaceful as she enjoys the quietness. Complete silence runs through the house.

Silence?

'Why has the music stopped?' she wonders. She listens for the faint melody of 'Fleetwood Mac' from the music channel she left on the TV, but she can't hear anything. She takes the towel out of the laundry basket and creeps onto the landing at the top of the stairs and stands, listening.

Nothing.

Edging her way downstairs, she gently wraps the damp towel around herself and pushes the door of the living room. The TV has been switched to mute.

She glances into the kitchen. The oven is off. The apple pie she was cooking is now on the chopping board next to the sink. The bottle of white Zinfandel is in the recycling box. She feels the hairs on her body stand to attention, and her skin begins to tingle as it senses danger.

She is not alone.

She feels the tension run through her veins and her muscles lock with fear. She spins around and reaches for the front door. Who gives a fuck if she is only wearing a towel?

The door is locked. She fumbles around for her keys, trying to keep her breathing quiet even though her heart wants to burst out of her chest with terror. She hears a creak upstairs. She stops still, like she has looked directly into the eyes of Medusa. Slowly, she lifts her head to look up the beige carpeted stairs.

She sees the edge of two black shoes. Her eyes fill with tears and she keeps very still. With her hands behind her back, she fumbles for her keys. She wants to scream but her body has decided against it.

The black shoes move down a step. Then another.

The crash of her keys on the ground awakens her body. She snaps out of freeze and into flight. She bangs on the door, screaming and desperately trying to capture the attention of anyone walking by. Perhaps the lady who collected the pounds and went to Barbados.

As she bangs on the door and screams for help, she feels a gloved hand force itself over her mouth. Her towel drops to the floor as she tries to rip the fingers from her face. She bites down hard to get loose, but the grip only gets tighter. She is dragged back upstairs, her feet and legs kicking in the air. '*What about the apple pie? What about the kids coming home?*'

Her cries are muffled. She cannot wrestle the hand away from her mouth or the arm that clings around her waist. Her feet find the floor and she uses the momentum to push herself backwards, putting all her weight on her attacker. He loosens his grip, and she steals the moment to run back towards the stairs. He grabs her hair and pulls her back so hard that she slams into the wall, her head first. She loses her balance and drops to the floor, dazed.

She feels another blow to the back of her head, causing her to almost black-out. She can still feel her body being tugged and jolted. She cannot see or hear anything but knows that he has dragged her to a bedroom. Kieran's bedroom. She recognises the glimpses of football wallpaper and trophies on the shelf. Kieran is only five years old, but he is already a confident goalkeeper.

As her senses start to coordinate, she feels a burning sensation on her wrists and tightness on her ankles. She is immobilised. Her hands are tied behind the back of the chair. The chair where Kieran plays with his 'Lego'. The chair that three-year-old Gracie bumped her head on last week.

"Please, what do you want?" cries Janice.

He stops what he is doing and turns to face her. She sees no remorse or hesitation in his eyes. His multicoloured eyes. She must have concussion, as his eyes seem to change colour depending on which one she is looking at.

He does not respond. He moves closer to her and places his cracked lips next to her neck. The smell of his breath makes her stomach turn. She is terrified for her life, but her tears are of regret.

She had let him into her house. He had looked so normal and smart. His name sounded familiar. A name you hear around Liverpool and associate with authority.

He stands up, gazing down at her, focused on her chest. She realises she is naked. Helpless, naked prey.

He takes the knife out of his bag and moves towards her, blade first. He pauses for a second, indecisive about what to do next. She lets the tears roll down her face. She is exhausted. Injured and exhausted. Yet the terror is only just starting.

He moves towards her and starts to undress. She closes her eyes and prays that her children don't come home early, and that her children are not the ones to find her. She knows what's about to happen and there's nothing she can do.

All she can think about is that the apple pie will go to waste.

61

"How is she?" asks Gillespie.

Since Emily's attack, he and Sophie meet for coffee once a week. Only a brief coffee, but it is beneficial to both. Gillespie can check on Sophie and Emily, and Sophie can get informal updates on the case. If they enjoy each other's company too, then that is a bonus.

"She's managing. Which is not the same as doing fine or recovering. How does anyone recover from being raped and almost murdered, let alone when it has happened before?"

Gillespie is familiar with rhetorical questions.

"When I first met Emily, she used to come to the sessions and try her hardest not to say a word. Her sister had arranged it and she wasn't a willing client. But she came back, week after week. She wanted to be there. She wanted my help but she didn't want to talk."

"So what did you do? How did you get her talking?"

Sophie waited for Emily to feel ready and ensured that the office was a safe space, if nothing else. Sometimes she sat drawing whilst Sophie did her admin, and sometimes they chatted about everything but Marcus Gaines. After two weeks, Emily was sharing her art and her ambitions about art school.

"One day she started telling me about how she had met Marcus Gaines. The rest is …"

"History," says Gillespie, butting in.

"Confidential, is what I was going to say," replies Sophie. "My heart has been broken for that girl more than it has for any man."

"She's lucky to have you," says Gillespie, brushing his hair back out of his eyes. "I guess not everyone has someone to talk to."

"There should be more done to promote the help that is available. Everyone is so focused on reporting rape that they overlook the worry that victims have about not being believed, or feeling ashamed or judged. That's why there are support services now, to listen and help rebuild your life and confidence, without the pressure to report the attack."

"It should be reported though. How else can we nail the bastards? If my daughter was raped then I'd want the police to do all they can."

"If your daughter was raped, wouldn't you want her to know she can tell you without being pressured into doing something she doesn't want to?"

Gillespie thinks about the question. He knows if anyone hurt his kids, he would be prepared to serve a life sentence for doing whatever was needed. But if they couldn't speak to him, then they would suffer in silence. Somehow, that is even worse.

"Do we have any of these services in Liverpool? They must be hard to fund if they are private."

"There are a few across the city centre. Don't go knocking on doors and asking questions. It's a safe space for a reason," replies Sophie, standing and putting on her coat. "People who use these services have been through enough. They don't need to be reminded about what happened. Spare a thought for the people who see the news and what has happened to these girls. Then spare another thought for the people who have experienced it themselves."

Sophie smiles and leaves money on the table towards the bill. Gillespie watches her as she gracefully disappears out of the door and into the hustle of the city centre. Inside it is cool and spacious. Outside it is humid and the dense population makes walking through town feel like an involuntary game of 'Tag'.

He thinks about their conversation. He has never thought about it this way before. Why would he? He is a detective and it is his job to catch the bad guys. He contemplates finding out where the city-centre services are located and poke around for some names.

For all he knows, the man they are looking for may have other victims. He commits crimes outside, in the cover of darkness. He worries about making mistakes, because he may have made some in the past.

Nothing in the system matches the parameters of the recent cases. Bite marks. Lambskin. Throats slit with a knife. Rape. Murder. Anger. Organised crime scenes.

Then again, crimes escalate and criminals evolve with practice. A mistake is a steep learning curve. A mistake that goes unreported is lucky.

62

An urgent meeting has been called at headquarters, and Jo just makes it in time. She is followed by Clarke who enters the room and takes a seat, facing the rest of the officers. The meeting is about possible leaks from inside the station. Local reporters have been asking questions about the significance of the silver ring and the 'Dental Pride' surgery.

"I'm not saying anyone here is the leak. Not an intentional leak anyway. Be vigilant. Assume you can be overheard when you discuss the case outside of the station. Hell, assume you can be overheard in the car park," says Commissioner Grant. "These reporters are bloodthirsty. They all want to be the one to report it first. They don't give a shit about how their reports affect our case."

Everyone in the room is dismissed but Clarke asks Jo and Gillespie to stay behind.

"Detective Gillespie, good to see you," says Clarke, more polite and professional than usual whilst in earshot of the commissioner.

"As you know, I've been keeping a close eye on this investigation. How about we run through the latest profile and evidence?" He glances back at the commissioner to make sure he is listening, but he isn't.

"Did you get laid last night?" asks Jo.

"Excuse me?" replies Clarke.

"Nothing. How did you get here so fast? I barely made it from a few streets away, but you got here from New Brighton."

"Keep up, Linnet. I've been staying close to HQ a few nights a week for the last year. When I say I am all in for my career, I mean it. Do you think murderers and robbing bastards stop while I switch trains at Hamilton Square or look for change for the tunnel? Now tell me, what have you got? It better be good."

Gillespie gives him an update and, in return, asks how 'Operation Barbara' is going at the pharmacy. Clarke has given the media a still image of the man in the pharmacy footage but has not revealed its location.

"Seems that Barbara is on an extended holiday. Gone away for a few months on a sabbatical. Maybe your ugly mug was the nail in the coffin, so to speak. Have to wait until she's back to speak to her. Meanwhile, I've got someone trying to get us access to the pharmacy records. It will take a while though. Red tape." Clarke looks over at Jo, who is texting on her phone. "Keep a tight leash on that one, Gillespie. Don't be led astray."

"Yes, sir. Although I wouldn't let her hear you say that."

Clarke mumbles something offensive about Jo and picks up his glasses and bag. He makes a quick exit when he sees Commissioner Grant leave the room.

"Well?" says Jo.

"What?" replies Gillespie. "I didn't say it, it was him."

"What was?"

"Nothing. Was that Tara on the phone?" asks Gillespie, trying to divert her attention.

"No. I sent my daughters a message last night. It's got blue ticks but I've had no replies. I guess I'm still on the periphery. At this rate, I'll have to join TikTok to keep up with their lives."

"Are you not on TikTok?" he asks. "I thought viral dance routines and accident-prone cats would be your kind of thing." She hits him on the arm. Hard.

His phone rings. Jo wonders what it will take to get her daughters to message her everyday again. She's not asking for the world. Hello, or a goodnight message is all she wants. Which is a good job, because she has blown their worlds apart.

"Let's go downstairs. We've got a walk-in," Gillespie says. "He reckons he killed Faye Williams and the others."

They enter the interview room where Tom Underwood is sitting. He is looking around the room for CCTV cameras. "Am I being recorded?" he asks. "If I am, does that mean I need a lawyer?"

"You can have a lawyer if you want one." Gillespie purposefully leaves this open and vague. "My colleague tells me you have something to tell us. In your own time, Mr Underwood."

"That girl. I did it. It was me. I killed her. I killed her dog," says Tom.

Jo and Gillespie nod and let the silence fill the room. If he wants to talk, let him.

"I followed her from her street. I watched her walk her dog. Then I did it. It was me."

"What did you do?" asks Gillespie.

"I killed her. I fucked her and then I killed her," laughs Tom.

Gillespie feels sick to his stomach. "Did you kill the dog before you fucked her? Or after you killed her?" Gillespie asks the ambiguous question, unconvinced that Tom Underwood has ever met Faye Williams.

"Before. Had to get it out of the way. The damn thing could have attacked me."

"Do you recognise any of these photographs?" Jo puts pictures of three girls in front of him. "Yeah, I do. All of them. I recognise them all. That's who I did. That's who I killed." He looks directly at Jo. "What happens now? Are you going to take me to jail? If you don't, I'll do it again."

"You're free to leave, Mr Underwood," says Gillespie.

63

Jo and Gillespie leave the room and make way for uniformed officers to escort Tom Underwood out of the building.

"How did you know?" asks Clarke, who was watching from the observation room. "You better be right about this, Linnet, or else you won't work long enough to pick up another payslip."

"The pictures I showed him were fake. I had Gillespie include three photographs of stock pictures of girls in the file before we entered the room. I had a feeling this wasn't our guy."

"I'll ask you again then, shall I? How did you know? Or are you not answering any of my questions today?"

"The profile doesn't suggest that our killer has had enough. He hasn't finished. Plus, there's no way our guy would walk in and submit to a defeat. He isn't the submissive type. He's arrogant and egomaniacal. The only way he's going to stop is if we make him."

Clarke looks at Gillespie and shakes his head. This is his default response when he has nothing to add or when he has been proved wrong.

Jo continues, "I'm more confident in the profile than ever. Tom Underwood has a criminal record. Petty theft, drunk and disorderly, but nothing violent or risky. Plus, he works as a till operator in a supermarket and is single."

Clarke goes to say something, but Gillespie stops him. He knows it is always best to let Jo think out loud.

"Tom Underwood is the opposite of our guy. Where Tom is in a monotonous job and has no restrictions on his time, our guy is in a position of trust and thrives on risk. He kills at night because it's safer for him. He's less likely to be spotted. But he also has to wait until night-time because of family or career responsibilities that limit his availability."

"Put it in a report and email it to me. We need everyone to be up to speed. It's no good having a working profile that only you two know about," snaps Clarke, leaving the room. He opens the door so quickly that it almost knocks the receptionist over.

"Someone here to see you, Detective. Asked for you specifically."

Gillespie and Jo follow the receptionist into the comfort room. It goes unnoticed by Gillespie, but Jo recognises it as the room where dedicated officers support rape victims.

"Hi, my name is Detective Gillespie and this is Jo Linnet, my partner."

Jo notices that the woman sitting across from her is frightened. Her hands are clasped together tightly like she is holding onto something. A secret, or a pain. Her legs are firmly shut together. Closed body language like this is either a sign of defensiveness because there is something to hide, or nerves because they are about to reveal something.

"Can we help you in any way?" asks Jo.

"I hope so. I'd like to report a rape."

"Are you comfortable talking to us both or would you prefer to just talk to me?" asks Jo.

"No, it's fine. It was a long time ago. I doubt there's even any point in me being here."

"You've done well to come and speak to us, Miss …" Gillespie pauses for the woman to provide her name. It is more friendly than asking a victim to identify themself before going through the events that brought them to the station.

"My name is Janice Gregson."

64

Janice Gregson arrives at the station, intent on telling her story to the police. She doesn't know if it will help, but it may be relevant to what is happening to the young girls in Liverpool.

"I saw on the news that the person you're looking for wears a big silver ring. That got me thinking about what happened to me. He wore a ring. A silver one, with a symbol on it. I don't recall what it was. It's funny the things you focus on when you think you're about to die," she says.

Janice tells Jo and Gillespie the details of her ordeal. The way his hand clamped over her mouth when he dragged her upstairs. The way she was battered and thrown against the wall. The way he tied her up and raped her.

She leaves nothing to the imagination. She has replayed it a million times over in her head.

"Do you mind if I ask you some other questions, Janice? They might seem a bit odd, but it would be helpful to our investigation," says Jo.

"I don't mind. You can't ask me anything that I haven't already thought about."

"What did he say to you? Was there anything specific about his voice or what he said?"

"When he was lying on top of me, he kept telling me to move up and down, and that I wasn't doing anything for him. I think he meant sexually." Janice takes a sip of water. "When he couldn't get inside of me, he kept saying, 'Help me put it in'."

"What did you say to him?" asks Jo.

"I couldn't say anything. For the most part, he forced my hand inside my mouth so I couldn't scream. I gagged and vomited all over my hand, which he found disgusting."

"Apologies if this next question seems insensitive but did he threaten you verbally?"

"He didn't threaten me verbally, no. But he was demanding. Asking me to put it in. Telling me to move. It was like I was an object significant only for his sexual needs." Janice stares into the distance as if reliving it again. "Sometimes I wish he had killed me."

"Why do you think he didn't kill you?" asks Gillespie.

"I think he intended to. He had brought a large knife with him, in a bag. After he was finished with me, he tied me up again. Before he could do anything else, the doorbell rang. It was my neighbour. She had taken a parcel for me the day before and was dropping it off. Can you believe that? Saved by a stroke of luck. If I hadn't ordered a new hose pipe or taken an extra shift the previous day, I wouldn't be sitting here now. The bell rang. He panicked, then waited until it stopped before he left via the back door."

"You mentioned his different coloured eyes," says Gillespie.

"Yes, at the time I thought I was severely concussed and seeing things. He had one blue eye and one green. I thought that was just something in the movies."

"And the silver ring?"

"I saw it on the news. I've been following the cases. Those poor girls and their families. My kids are still too young to know what happened, but they know that someone hurt Mummy." Janice looks to Jo for reassurance. A maternal drive that seeks out other women. "I saw the ring and I thought it might be the same man who attacked me. He wore a silver ring. I only noticed it because it hurt like hell when he slapped me. It was like being struck with a rock. Solid."

She pauses, deep in thought, before asking, "Is it my fault that those girls were killed?"

"It's not your fault. It's not anyone's fault except the person who attacked you and killed those girls. You've been extremely helpful, Janice, and incredibly brave in talking to us and answering our questions. Is there someone we can call for you?" asks Jo.

"Not really. I didn't tell anyone who knows me. I spoke to someone in one of those places that help but don't pressurise you to report it. They saved my life. I just hope this can help someone else."

Gillespie opens the door and signals for Officer Summers to stop what he is doing and escort Janice home.

"We will get an officer to drive you home. If there is anything else you would like to tell us, or if there is any support we can provide, please do not hesitate to get in touch." says Jo, giving Janice her direct contact number.

Officer Summers approaches Gillespie, but he turns and makes a quick exit when he sees Janice Gregson.

65

Mark Summers sits in the office chair adjacent to Gillespie. Jo stands against the window, contemplating how quickly the smoke alarm will go off if she has a quick pull on a cigarette.

"Officer Summers, thanks for coming in. Miss Gregson was helping us with a few things. She has been very helpful today," says Gillespie. "Unlike you. What happened earlier?"

"Toilet dash. Sorry, I must have eaten something dodgy last night."

"Nice ring," says Jo, watching as Mark wipes his sweaty hands on his trousers. She doesn't buy into the toilet story but then again, she is suspicious of everyone. "Bet that makes a right knuckle-duster." The silver ring is chunky and has a faint engraving of a sword.

"Thanks, it was my dad's. He was a fireman, but he died a few years ago. He was given this ring when he saved five children from a fire in a hospital ward. They were post-op and couldn't walk. He put them all on a bed, drips and everything, and wheeled them out."

"Do you always wear that ring?" asks Jo.

"Just sometimes. It was the anniversary of his death a few weeks ago, so I dug it out and have been wearing it as a sign of respect. The guy was my hero," says Mark, smiling. "Look, I know it must have looked unprofessional when I dashed to the toilet, but I didn't want to get caught short. Not in front of your victim."

"You got any allergies?" asks Jo, as she sits next to him. "Sometimes when I wear jewellery, my fingers turn green. When I wear the good stuff, the real stuff, I break out in eczema."

Mark shakes his head.

"How did you know that Janice is a victim?" she asks.

"I presumed. You were in the comfort room."

Mark isn't giving much away and, without being under caution, Jo and Gillespie cannot ask much else, so they let him return to work.

"What do you think?" asks Gillespie.

"Fits the profile in some ways. Professional, approachable, athletic build, and somewhat charming. Has the ring. It's all a bit too easy. A possible connection to an early victim. He was there when we found Gemma Woodcock, but no surprises there. If he's guilty of that, then we're all suspects."

Gillespie shrugs. "I'm going to dig. See if Officer Summers has any connection to Phillip Tatton. Maybe it's a pair of offenders after all. Profiles have been known to be wrong." He clenches his teeth as soon as the words leave his mouth.

"My profile isn't wrong. You can't just change a profile to suit the suspects. We're definitely looking for a single offender. I've spent what feels like a lifetime going over the voyeur reports and the kills. The consistency between the voyeur cases, plus the consistency across the murders, all point to one offender. If there were two or more people, there would be things that don't fit. The rapes are vaginal, each time. The bite marks are on the thigh. Even Janice Gregson had a bite scar to show us."

Gillespie nods.

"Go back to the voyeur cases if you're not convinced. Look at what the victims have said. 'I saw a figure of a man' and 'I saw a figure peering through the window'. It's always a man or a figure. Singular."

"And all the voyeur cases were at night too," adds Gillespie. "The victims, including Amy Tatton, had returned home at night, and realised they were being watched."

"It answers your question though, about how someone can escalate from voyeurism to murder," says Jo. "He made a mistake with Janice Gregson. The neighbour disturbed him, he panicked and he ran. He was so close to the kill. That's why he commits crimes outdoors now. He can't risk being disturbed or caught again."

"He didn't escalate from voyeurism to murder," says Gillespie. "He turned to voyeurism following his near-miss with Janice Gregson."

"Exactly." Jo stands and puts on her coat. "He didn't evolve at all. He switched lanes."

Gillespie stands to follow her.

"And then switched back, with a vengeance."

66

Following the possible connection between Janice Gregson and Mark Summers, Gillespie has requested that all his male police colleagues, within the age parameters of Jo's profile, volunteer their blood. They can't waste any more time on false leads. The budget bulldogs will not be happy when they hear about this.

Tara is at the old HQ running the blood tests. These are voluntary but failing to volunteer would raise a red flag.

Gillespie has his blood taken, as does Clarke. They both watch closely as Mark Summers has his blood taken. He isn't happy about it but makes a big show about having nothing to hide, and asks, "What happens now?"

"The blood will be sent off for testing. In a few days we'll have the results and hopefully be able to rule you all out," replies Tara.

"I didn't think any blood was found at the scenes," he states.

"We can do all sorts with blood tests, Officer Summers. With this blood, we can run DNA checks, allergy tests, and much more.

Thank you for volunteering today." Tara kills him with kindness, as he walks off, deep in thought.

"I take it not everyone knows we got DNA from the condom inside Emily Spencer," Tara says to Gillespie. She has used her connections to get the results back quickly from the condom and evidence collected from Emily, as well as in the shed where she was raped. The DNA isn't proving useful yet. There are no matches to any offenders already in the system. The blood tests at HQ will probably be rolled out across the city. It will cost a small fortune but, with a predator on the loose and Merseyside Police under the microscope, it will be money well-spent.

"How soon can we get Summers' blood results back?" asks Gillespie.

"The whole batch will be sent off in the next hour, so a day or two most likely. The labs will have to pull an all-nighter or else the blood will coagulate and be useless. I can put Officer Summers at the top of the list."

"Can you put Clarke at the top of the list as well, please?" asks Jo. "I want to know if he's allergic to anything that I can get my hands on."

"Sure. But that's not me aiding and abetting," laughs Tara. "Seeing as it's you, I'll get onto it straight away." She smiles at Jo and holds eye contact until Gillespie interrupts them, by saying, "It makes me sick to think my DNA will now be on record."

"Scared some kids you don't know about might come looking for Papa?" jokes Jo. "Look at this, the geographical profile still fits." She opens a map of the city, marked with the reported voyeur cases and murders, to which she has added the markings where Janice Gregson and Emily Spencer were attacked and raped. Even with these new cases, the 'Circle of Danger' is still intact.

Liverpool's inner city isn't that big, compared to the likes of London or Manchester.

Once you run out of places to leave a body, the challenge is to find somewhere else for the next time. You only have to look at Jeffrey Dahmer and Dennis Nilsen to see that repeatedly killing people in the same location increases the risk of being caught. Each crime adds a geographical risk. A dot on a map. A higher police presence in an area. Citizens are more alert about their safety. The optimum way to reduce the risk of being caught is to find, if possible, a new location each time.

"Did you see the way Summers got out of here like a whippet? He's hiding something."

"Give it up, Gillespie. He was sweating like a pig in your office earlier. He'd need control and nerves of steel to be the killer. He's not the guy, I'm telling you," says Jo. "We're looking for someone organised, who remains calm in stressful situations and isn't overpowered by adrenaline. Remember Peter Sutcliffe? He abducted his victims and hid bodies left right and centre. He got away with it for so long because he was as calm and organised in his crimes as he was in day-to-day life."

Jo thinks about the bite marks. '*Why would someone, so organised and in control, bite their victims? Up until now, the bite marks are part of a ritual. Are they an impulsive action, or do they provide more than that? Maybe the biting is merely a way to mark the victims. Some offenders want to leave their mark like the numbers they put on victims in German concentration camps.*'

She remembers learning about a case where a man broke into houses at random and looked for females who were sleeping alone. He drew a cross on their cheeks using a kid's paintbrush which had been dipped in acid. The women had no idea until they woke up and looked in the mirror. He had left his mark before leaving.

'Do these bite marks demonstrate the same purpose?' she wonders.

67

"Where are you?" asks Tara.

"Don't judge, but I'm following Clarke. I'm sitting in my car, drinking coffee and eating a protein bar, watching him put petrol into his car," replies Jo.

"Seriously? Who eats protein bars anymore?"

Jo recognises and appreciates the lack of judgement about following Clarke.

"I'm starving. Did you need me for something? Only I think Clarke is about to … oh, he's gone. I'd make a terrible private investigator."

Tara has the results back regarding Summers and Clarke. Both are positive for allergies. More specific tests are needed to determine what they are allergic to. There is some bad news. The remainder of the blood coagulated while the other tests were being done and there was just enough to test Clarke against the DNA found in the condom.

"He's not a match. I'll arrange for another sample to be taken from Summers," says Tara.

Jo throws her head back in frustration.

"You still there, Jo?" asks Tara. "I know it's not what you wanted to hear, but it's good news."

"I know. I just hoped something would come back on Clarke. I'm not dropping it. That business in Glasgow, and then with Phillip Tatton. I don't know what he's up to, but he's sure as shit up to something. If I'm wrong, I'll give up chocolate for a month. No, for a week."

"There's one other thing. I didn't ask for this to be done with all the samples, but I know how important these two people are to you and Gillespie. I tested the blood for any signs of infection or bacteria."

"Checking for STDs?"

"Not quite, although that would have come up. I was thinking more along the lines of dental or gum disease. Xylitol is still an unknown substance and, paired with the vague results you got back from Amy Tatton's garden door, I thought it was still worth checking out."

"And?" Jo asks as she licks her fingers clean.

"Officer Summers and Bob Clarke both tested positive for gum disease."

68

He sits on the grass in Chavasse Park, which is only a short walk from the office. The sun is intense but he is under no illusion. It will probably rain by lunchtime and be muggy for the rest of the day. Such is global warming.

Children run around him playing with a frisbee. Teenagers sit with earphones in, and tapping on their mobile phones. These days it is sociable to just be out and about; you don't have to actually engage with each other.

A woman is looking at him over the top of her magazine and smiling. He smiles back and she blushes. If he waits, she will come to him. She has long brunette hair and is wearing denim shorts. Quick to pull off. Easy to rip open.

She sits beside him. "Are you working or just here for pleasure?" she asks.

"Just resting. You?"

"Same."

She brushes bits of grass off her shoes. As she bends down, he can see down her vest top. She is wearing a pink bra. She wants him to see it. It's not the same when they want it.

"I must say, you look very smart in your uniform," she comments.

"Thanks, perk of the job."

"Will you tell me off if I drop litter on the ground?"

"Of course. I'm an officer of the law. I can't let things go unpunished."

"My name's Claire," she says, holding out her hand.

"Nice to meet you, Claire." He reciprocates the gesture. "My name is Mark. You can call me Officer Summers."

69

Gillespie has arrived outside one of the casinos run by Phillip Tatton. Jo was unsuccessful in her attempt to trick him into holding the latex gloves, but Gillespie is following his gut feeling. Tatton is up to his neck in something that is connected to the murders.

Before he is out of the car, a heavy-set man in a suit approaches, doing his best to look like the Terminator, with sunglasses hiding most of his bloated face. Without exchanging pleasantries, Gillespie understands he should follow.

They walk through the casino. Men sit around the poker tables and look like they have been there all week. The room is dimly lit, and cigar smoke circles under the lampshade. No clocks, so people don't know how long they have been there. Bottomless drinks as long as you are betting. Even Gillespie recognises positive reinforcement in action.

The Terminator leads him into an office at the back of the casino, where Phillip Tatton is waiting. "Detective Gillespie. I assume you're not here to part with your wages," he says.

"No, but I could be of use in a different way, if you're interested."

Tatton extends his arm, inviting him to sit.

"Bob Clarke," says Gillespie. "Chatty bugger when he gets going, isn't he?" Tatton doesn't flinch or offer any indication of interest. Gillespie knows he needs to step the pitch up.

"He's told me everything. You, Michael Tanner and the cars at Chaloner Street. I bet you didn't think he would be silly enough to keep it all written down."

Tatton glances at the Terminator, who has taken a gun from the inside of his jacket. Gillespie spots a silver ring. Tatton shakes his head, warning the Terminator to slow down.

"Whatever that whiny, ambitious prick has said, it has nothing to do with me," replies Tatton.

Gillespie senses the imminent danger and retreats. "Yes. Maybe I got it wrong. Clarke's a pain in my arse. I just thought you might be able to help me … find some relief."

"I'm not in the business of relieving people, Detective."

"Of course not. Never mind. I'll see myself out."

He stands up to leave and glances at the casino security cameras. There are at least fifteen cameras, yet four of them are picking up a feed from the same table. Where the high rollers play. Men and women with money to burn and time to kill. People who are aroused by the thrill of the gamble.

The CCTV will pick up any cheating, card counting, and any big wins. That's when Tatton and his terminators go onto the casino floor, watch the winning players, and ensure they don't leave the casino. The house always wins.

Gillespie takes his time putting his coat on, while scanning the cameras for familiar faces. He glances back to the high rollers' table and sees a man and woman join the game. The man has his back to the camera but is smartly dressed. The woman looks a little underdressed, and knocks back a whisky as soon as it has been placed in front of her. She waves to the waitress and orders another, keeping one hand on the gentleman's shoulder. *'A display of affection, or a signal to others that they are together?'* wonders Gillespie.

The man orders a drink and exchanges a large wad of fifty-pound notes for poker chips. *'Another display for the attention of their competitors.'* The waitress must have said something as she walks away, because the man turns to answer her. That's when Gillespie sees him.

Mark Summers says, 'Yes.' He does want ice.

Gillespie tries to hide the recognition as he heads towards the door. The Terminator steps aside and allows him to reach for the handle.

The last thing he remembers is a blow to the back of his head and blacking out as Phillip Tatton towers over him.

70

Gillespie's head drops. Blood runs from the nape of his neck, round to his chin. Droplets fall to the floor like a slow-leaking tap. He tries to move his hands, but they are tied together. The heavy-duty rope burns his skin as he tries to wriggle a wrist free.

"Good afternoon, Detective. Thought you might be staying for the night," says Phillip Tatton, flanked by the Terminator and Mark Summers.

"What have you done?" slurs Gillespie, as he spits blood to the floor. "Where am I?"

Summers drags him off the floor and onto a chair in the middle of the room. A lightbulb hangs overhead. The heat from it becomes unbearable as the Terminator lowers it gradually.

"High wattage. Been on all day. No protective sealant on the glass. One touch and you'll be marked for life," says Tatton, pointing at the lightbulb. "Jimmy here tends to drop things. Short attention span. Ain't that right, Jimmy?"

The Terminator grunts.

"Summers," says Gillespie, "I knew you were guilty. Where's the girl?" He strains his neck as he tries to find relief from the intense heat.

"She's where I want her to be, for now," laughs Summers.

"You're a piece of shit," says Gillespie, before Summers punches him in the stomach repeatedly.

"There's more where that came from," says Summers, wiping the sweat from his forehead. "You're pathetic. You walk around with your floppy hair, stinking of ale, followed by that slag, Linnet. Day after day. Running around, trying to put all the pieces together. You don't have a fucking clue who you're messing with."

He picks up a plank of wood and strikes Gillespie in the face. A rusty nail tears his skin. It feels like his face has been slashed with a Stanley knife. The man who painted acid on his victim's cheeks comes to mind.

"Summers, stand down," commands Phillip Tatton. "Detective Harry Gillespie, what am I going to do with you? You had to come here and take advantage of my hospitality. You and your bitch partner have been sniffing around me for too long, like dogs on heat. She's got a real hard-on for me, Jolene Linnet."

Gillespie makes a mental note to tell Jo about that last bit, if he ever sees her again. She will laugh her head off.

"And you," says Tatton, slapping Summers, "I told you to be more careful. Stay away from my businesses, I said. What did you do? You got some heat on you and came straight to the casino. Dipshit."

"I didn't know he'd be here. Maybe it's you that's got us into this ..." Before Summers can finish his sentence, the Terminator grabs him by the scruff of the neck.

"Do you want a seat next to the detective?" asks Tatton, remaining calm. "I didn't think so. Shut the fuck up and let the grownups talk. Capiche?"

The Terminator throws Summers to the side of the room, while Tatton crouches beside Gillespie. "He hasn't always been this useless. His dad and I served together. Two tours in Afghan. He's the reason I opened the casinos, you know. He bet me I couldn't do it. The irony."

Tatton laughs. "He asked me to keep Mark busy. Bung him some money here and there for running errands. I paid for his education you know. Financed him while he did his police training."

"He's a bent piece of shit," spits Gillespie.

"Can you really be a bent copper if you go into the force with ill intentions? The plan was he'd be my inside man. Literally. Give me the heads up on any drug raids in the pipeline, so we could get there first. A 'rob from the rich, sell to the smackheads' type of thing."

"Yeah, you're a real Robin Hood alright," says Gillespie. His wrists are blistering due to the friction of the rope. Sweat runs from his pores with the heat of the lamp bulb that continues to be lowered.

"He got a taste for other things then. Girls. It's always the bloody girls. Am I right?" asks Tatton.

The Terminator nods, although Gillespie is not sure the man even speaks English.

"In the end, the only thing I needed was for Mark to keep an eye on our friend, Clarke. Make sure he kept our Chaloner Street agreement to himself. I had Clarke down as a squealer but, to be fair, he lasted longer than I thought. If Clarke becomes

Commissioner, then who knows, soft shite here could rise through the ranks to become Chief Constable, with a nudge here and there."

"What about Amy?" asks Gillespie. He knows it is a risk bringing Tatton's daughter into the conversation, but he has to know the truth. "Did you count on Summers taking a fancy to her?"

Tatton nods towards the Terminator, who lowers the lamp bulb again.

"That wasn't me. You know it wasn't me, Uncle Phil," says Mark.

"Shut the fuck up, you useless prick," shouts Tatton. "We all know it was that scumbag, Michael Tanner. I don't care if he was a firework short of a display or not. He violated my daughter. Left her terrified in her own home."

"You've got no proof," says Gillespie. "Neither do we. Not now he's dead."

"I know boys like Michael Tanner. Can't keep it in their pants. Do you think I didn't see him in the alleyway? I chased him off more times than I care to remember. That's why Mark helped me out. Slipped Mr Tanner something he could cut himself with. Had a little word with him. Told him he could go on his own terms or be raped in prison every night by his cellmate. Next thing. he winds up dead; looks like a suicide and my Amy can sleep at night again."

Phillip Tatton orders Summers to finish Gillespie off.

"What about the other girls? Don't you care that you're complicit in the rape and murder of the others?" shouts Gillespie. The Terminator forces his hands down on each side of the chair. He can't move. He is cuffed to the chair.

Tatton has gone. Summers walks over, with free reign to finish the job however he wants. He takes a knife out of his pocket. A long blade glistens against the silver ring that Daddy Summers gave him.

"Shall I tell you what I'm going to do to the girl from the casino?" he asks. When Gillespie doesn't answer, Summers slips the tip of his knife under his fingernail and flicks it off. Gillespie almost passes out with the pain. He thinks about Jo and her Pringles.

"I'm going to take her somewhere nice. Would she like that, do you think?"

He flicks another nail off. The exposed nerves on Gillespie's fingers feel like they are sizzling with the pain. Red-raw, the nerves pulsate. He thinks about his kids and promises to be a better dad.

"First, I'll be nice. Then I'll be flirty. I'll take off her pink bra, no sweat."

Another flick. Another nail. "Stop, please. Don't hurt her," whimpers Gillespie. "Take me instead. Just let her go."

"I don't think you're following me. I can hardly do to you what I'm going to do to her. You could always watch, I suppose."

The Terminator shakes his head and says, "Get on with it."

He can speak English after all.

71

Jo sits in Tara's car. They have been working late, going over the medical records and the profile in the lab.

"I'm telling you now, the killer is organised. His record-keeping would put your spreadsheets to shame," says Jo.

"I think that might be the hundredth time you've stated that he's an organised offender. Why don't you get a good night's sleep and we can regroup, with Gillespie, in the morning."

"It's more than being an organised criminal. He's an organised person. I bet he keeps a diary. Not a fluffy 'I heart Gillian Anderson' type of diary." Jo looks at Tara to see if she has picked up on the Freudian slip. She hasn't. "He'll keep a diary or records of the girls. That's what following them is about. Learning their routine. Rating them out of ten for obscene things. It's what happened with Jack the Ripper, you know?"

"That's right, and James Maybrick," says Tara. "He was from Liverpool too. Kept a diary about the people he killed, but he commuted in and out of London. That's not the same as whoever killed our girls."

"I know it's not the same. I'm just saying that I wouldn't be surprised if he kept records. That's how he would have known about the timings."

"You've lost me," says Tara, taking off her seatbelt to face Jo.

"His notes will have included how long he would have to commit his crimes. He'd have enough information to know whether he has to be quick, or whether he has time to play with. He'll know he can stay longer in the areas where houses are more secluded. It's a classic horror movie nod."

Tara looks at Jo, shrugging her shoulders. "I'm more of a sci-fi buff myself."

"Remember Drew Barrymore in 'Scream'? Nice big house, miles from anywhere. Remember Neve Campbell? Huge house, out of the way of everyone. In fact, by 'Scream 3' she was isolated, and yep, he still got to her. Our guy legged it from Amy Tatton's but spent considerable time in Janice Gregson's. He picked Anne-Marie up in the taxi and didn't kill her until much later. He took his time. Because he knew he could. Premeditated, organised, and learning from each one."

Jo pauses to drink her can of Pepsi Max. Tara nods and smiles.

"I bet you think I'm annoying, don't you? I do tend to hyperfocus and ignore people when I'm thinking," says Jo, sheepishly. "Sorry about that."

"Actually, I think you're pretty incredible."

Jo was planning to finish the rest of her McDonald's fries but it doesn't seem like an appropriate time. "Thanks."

"The way your brain works is fascinating. I wish I knew half the stuff you do, so I could figure you out more," says Tara. "Do you want the rest of my fries?"

"I thought you'd never ask," says Jo, smiling. "I have to go soon."

"Do you want me to …"

"You're pretty amazing too, you know," says Jo, interrupting her. "I mean, all the time you spend with dead bodies and you're still more sociable and pleasant than me."

They sit laughing, and Jo realises it is the first time she has really laughed in years.

"Will you go straight to bed when you get home?" asks Tara. "I might watch Buffy. My favourite episode, 'Doppelganger' is what I watch after a tough day."

"Season three, episode sixteen. It's a classic."

Tara smiles. Impressed.

"Do you think Willow already knew back then?" asks Jo.

"One hundred per cent. When you know, you know. You know?" replies Tara.

They laugh again, and Jo finishes her McDonald's meal. "I better go. I might drive by HQ on my way home though, to see if Clarke is still about. I know what you're going to say, but I can't shake it. Call me biased, but I can't stand the guy."

"Please don't. I'd hate to be at home all cosy, thinking about you driving around. Not knowing whether you're safe or not." Tara puts her hand on Jo's leg. "Gillespie would say the same too."

"Doubt it. He's ghosted me tonight. Probably crashed out in the corner of The Red Arms."

"Either way, please just go home. For me?" asks Tara.

"Well, when you look at me like that, how can I resist?" Jo smiles and gets out of Tara's car. A sleek black Audi R8. She heads for her car. The opposite of Tara's.

She waves to Tara and pulls out. Instead of turning left for home, she decides to turn right and go the scenic way, past HQ. She will go straight home, but it won't do any harm to do a drive-by.

Tara quickly puts her car into gear and takes the same right turn. If Jo is going to do something stupid, then she is going to stop her.

72

"You'll have every cop in Liverpool looking for you. My partner knows where I am," says Gillespie, fighting the urge to vomit due to the pain. Bile bubbles at the back of his throat. Bile and blood.

"I doubt that very much. You've been here for hours and not heard a dickie bird from her," replies Summers, scrolling through Gillespie's phone. "Your daughter? Nice. Just my type," he says, holding up a photograph.

"Don't you fucking dare," shouts Gillespie. "I'll fucking kill you."

"She's a bit young, but I can take one for the team."

"You're sick. I hope someone shoots your fucking dick off."

"A bit over the top don't you think? I'm not the only man who likes it rough sometimes."

"Rough? You mutilated those girls. You raped them and killed them. You're such a sicko that you even let someone rape Janice

Gregson and let them get away with it." Gillespie turns to vomit, but he swallows the bile. *'It's like drinking battery acid,'* he presumes.

"What the fuck are you on about?"

"You know what you did, you fucking dog."

Summers sits on a chair in the corner. Gillespie lifts his head to see what is taking him so long. Phillip Tatton will expect him to be dead and buried by now.

"I had nothing to do with that. She was a friend of a friend. It was none of my business what happened to her. Anyway, Phillip said to keep out of it."

"Maybe you can't trust Uncle Phillip after all then."

"He would never. He can't even get it up for his wife."

The blood must have been dripping from Gillespie for longer than he realises. He is lightheaded, but the pieces of the puzzle are starting to arrange themselves.

Summers did not have a clue what Gillespie was talking about. He didn't rape those girls. He didn't bite them or kill them. And, if what he says is true, then Tatton can't have raped Janice Gregson or anyone else.

It is then that Gillespie realises what he has missed all along. Maybe it is his head injury or the adrenaline. He has missed that Summers is wearing glasses. Thin, hipster-style glasses. His eyes are both brown.

'Have I seen Summers wearing glasses at work? He didn't have glasses on when we spoke in the office, earlier this week. Or did he? Glasses are one of the things we are blind to.'

Gillespie tries to make sense of it. He knows he is missing something else.

Summers is wearing glasses now, which means he isn't wearing contact lenses. He may have been wearing glasses in the station, but Gillespie can't remember. If he wasn't, then he may have been wearing contact lenses, to make his eyes appear to be the same colour. This isn't making his mind any clearer.

Jo wears glasses when she reads small print, even though she pretends it's a lifestyle choice. Tara wears glasses some of the time. Clarke is never without his glasses. Was Phillip Tatton wearing glasses earlier? Gillespie can't recall. It's the 'Superman, Clarke Kent' thing.

The pieces start to fall into place.

Bob Clarke is never without his glasses. Gillespie has even tried them on when they were left on the desk. However, he has no memory of Clarke ever wearing the glasses. He carries them around every day but never wears them. He must wear contact lenses, which would hide his heterochromia.

Gillespie remembers the purple gloves in his coat pocket. Clarke had given them to him during the investigation of the shed where Emily Spencer was attacked. The forensics team only had extra-large gloves, so Clarke gave Gillespie a pair out of his own pocket.

It is all coming together.

Clarke had reason to be at every crime scene. He arrived at the shed before anyone else. The same way he had when he found his girlfriend hanging from her ceiling in Glasgow. Trampling through the crime scene probably wasn't a rookie mistake. A cover-up more like. Something to hide. No wonder he came running back to Liverpool early.

Jo is right. Gillespie has to get a message to her. She could be in danger.

But one thing still doesn't make sense. Bob Clarke's DNA is not a match for the fluids found in the lambskin condom.

73

As she drives past HQ, Jo sees Clarke standing outside, arguing with none other than Phillip Tatton.

Clarke is shouting and pointing towards the casino. Tatton stands calmly but, after a few minutes, he punches Clarke in the face and drives away. Clarke sits for a minute in his car, contemplating his next move.

Jo contemplates hers. This proves that her suspicions are accurate. He has been in bed with Tatton all along. No way is she going to let him become the next commissioner. The next one will have big shoes to fill when Commissioner Grant retires next month. Over her dead body will it be Bob Bloody Clarke.

Clarke starts his engine and drives towards The Strand, the main road that is home to many tourist attractions. The Royal Albert Dock sits in a haze of orange lights that bounce off the water. Restaurants and museums are illuminated at night-time, providing the perfect reference photographs for local artists.

The iconic Liver Building, a symbol of the city since 1911, stands over three hundred feet tall. Two Liver Birds made of copper sit atop each side of the building, the male looking over the city and the female keeping watch over the sea. Local legends suggest that the birds face opposite directions so that they do not see each other, mate, and then fly away. If this ever happens, the River Mersey will break its banks and Liverpool will fall.

Jo follows Clarke, glad that she is not on foot. He drives towards Brunswick Docks and pulls into the car park near the Delifonseca. Jo parks on the residential street, with Clarke still in sight. She recalls coming here with Susie to watch the ships dock, spend time in the soft play area, and taste the amazing range of cheeses at Delifonseca.

Clarke calls someone. His wife. He tells her that he will be home at the weekend and apologises for not being home more often. He apologises for not ringing her earlier. He seems to apologise a lot. For a moment, Jo sympathises with him. His wife is paralysed on the right side of her body after a serious stroke. The left side of her brain is damaged, causing Wernicke's Aphasia.

Jo shrugs the moment of sympathy off and gets out of her car.

Clarke is on foot now. *'Is he walking aimlessly, or does he have an intended destination?'* She follows him, making sure to stay far enough back to remain inconspicuous, but not far enough to lose him. She is too focused on him to realise that Tara isn't far behind her.

Tara has followed Jo. She is worried that she will get herself into some bother and now, here they are, walking the length of The Strand at night, in the freezing cold. She saw the argument between Clarke and Tatton but, as she doesn't have the facts, she refrains from jumping to conclusions about what the fight was about.

Although, she was secretly made-up for Jo when Tatton landed a punch on Clarke.

Tara thinks about shouting to Jo but decides that it will alert Clarke. She pauses to put her phone on silent, concerned that her alarm clock for Buffy will go off and draw attention.

Clarke walks past a long row of leafy conifers and makes a sudden right turn. The area is poorly lit and the turn catches Jo off-guard. She turns and her feet recognise a change in the ground. A steep ramp with a wobbly metal handrail supports her descent. In the dark, it feels like an extreme sport.

She wishes she had brought a torch, but she hadn't expected this to turn into an episode of 'Most Haunted'. Yvette Logan would have navigated this hill in the dark without a second thought.

As she approaches the bottom of the hill, she lets go of her grip and almost slips. Her shoes are covered in mud and sweat leaves her hair on the rough side of ready. Despite the darkness, she recognises the sound of River Mersey ahead. Lights from the Wirral look like fireflies in the sky. In the distance, a cruise ship is setting sail for someone's holiday of a lifetime.

Determined to catch up with Clarke, she takes a careful step forward and feels a sting in her neck. She turns to see him facing her with a syringe in his hand.

The last thing she sees before she passes out is Bob Bloody Clarke.

74

Clarke drags Jo's limp body out of sight. Unless someone is looking for her, they won't find her. At this time of night, no one will be exploring behind the huge slab of concrete waste that is tucked behind the overgrown conifers.

"You need to practise your stealth, Linnet. I clocked you back at the Deli."

Jo is coming in and out of consciousness. She can hear Clarke but can't fight him off. She is slurring her words, trying to ask questions.

"Relax, it's just a bit of Oramorph. Not intended for you, but at least it'll make you more compliant. Finally, Linnet, you might do as you're told." She tries to reach up and scratch his face. *'If I am going to die here, then I want his DNA on me. Tara will find it and use it to catch him.'*

He punches her so hard that she feels her jaw swing out of the socket and back again. The pain makes her want to scream and plead for her life, but she's not going to scream for Bob Clarke.

"Why can't you just leave me alone? It's ironic really that it comes down to me and you. Everything was going fine until you took a grudge against me. God knows why. All I've ever been to you is professional."

Jo musters up enough strength to laugh. Her face hurts but she forces the words out. "What's next, Clarke?" she asks. "You going to hang me like your ex-girlfriend?"

"How do you ...? It doesn't matter anymore," replies Clarke.

She feels him sit in front of her but still can't move her muscles to get up and run. Run or fight.

"You're right, that was my fault. We had fun and she fell in love with me. Soon after that, she wanted me to move in with her, leave my wife, and move jobs. Christ, I didn't even say 'I love you' back to her. She hounded me to leave my wife and, one day, I told her it was over and not to contact me again. The next thing I know, she calls me to say she's going to kill herself. I got there too late. Panicked. So yeah, it was my fault."

"Liar," slurs Jo.

"There's no point in lying now, Linnet. It's the end of the road for me. I either go on my terms, sit in a cell and rot, or let Phillip Tatton tear me apart. Literally." He stands over Jo. "Only now I don't have enough Oramorph to kill myself. Isn't that hilarious? You even managed to fuck my plans up for that."

"Why?" asks Jo. "Ring Gillespie. Get help."

"I don't think you'll be seeing him again. I thought his partner would have noticed he was missing by now." Clarke laughs, and then pauses to give her sedated mind time to catch up. "Such a shame too. I really liked that floppy-haired idiot. Saw his potential from day one."

Jo thinks back to the argument she witnessed between Clarke and Tatton. '*How could I have been so stupid? Gillespie wouldn't ghost me during an investigation like this. He is missing and I hadn't even clocked it. That would never have happened if it was the other way around. If I had needed help, Gillespie would be there, with or without backup.*'

"Besides," says Clarke, "there's no going back now. Sooner or later, you were bound to put it all together."

Jo looks at him, confused. The sedation is slowly wearing off.

"I'll spell it out for you, shall I?" He lists the familiar names. "Anne-Marie Swift, Faye Williams, Gemma Woodcock … you get the gist. I almost messed up with Amy, but I took some pleasure in seeing Tatton suffer. I wanted him to get worked up and have a heart attack but, in the end, his hatred of Michael Tanner became useful."

Jo feels lightheaded. Her instincts are right about Clarke, and her profile is right about the killer, but she hadn't connected the two.

"Your DNA is not a match," mumbles Jo.

"I don't what happened there. Fluke or fate, maybe? Or perhaps the lovely Tara Howden is flawed after all. Either way, here I am."

"Why?" asks Jo again.

"Because I could." This time, his voice is raised, and his tone is different. His words spit out like venom.

"Shall I do your job for you, Mrs Profiler? Let's see. A wife who can't walk or talk properly and relies on me for everything. I carry the weight of the force on my shoulders, have the best crime-solving rate in decades, but I've already been overlooked twice for the commissioner's role."

"Why the girls?"

"Why not? It was just a bit of fun at first. Following them home. Watching them. After a while, I wanted more. More risk. More power. I was in full control."

Jo tries to stand up. Her body feels like it is fighting gravity. She stumbles forward into Clarke, who grabs her and throws her down again. He takes the injection and stabs her thigh.

"Not so fast, Linnet. Seeing as though I can no longer throw myself off the docks wrapped in a blanket of Oramorph, I may as well go out with a bang. Literally."

"Bastard," says Jo, slumping over. If only Tara or Gillespie knew where she was. If only she can get herself together and reach for her phone. Or a rock, and smash Clarke's face in. Tears well up as she feels him tugging at her coat, starting to undress her. She decides that, given the choice, she would rather die and skip what came beforehand for the other girls.

"You're disgusting," she says. "Your wife is made-up that she doesn't have to sleep with you anymore. She doesn't have to 'help you put it in'." Jo dribbles while she talks. *'This sedative is a bitch,'* she thinks.

Clarke stops what he is doing and kicks her in the stomach. Repeatedly.

"I wouldn't fuck you if you paid me," he says, covering her with her coat.

"If I've got one more night, then I'm going to sort some unfinished business." He stands up, zips up his coat and looks around to check that they are still alone. "Emily Spencer is the only one left who can identify me. Without her, you're still the crazy lady who has a problem with men in positions of authority. When you wake up, Gillespie will be gone, Emily Spencer will be dead, and you'll never know what happens to me."

Jo hears every word but is unable to speak. As her eyes close involuntarily, she sees Clarke's shoes walking away from her, and the glint of his silver ring bouncing off the moonlight.

75

Tara is pacing up and down the main road, angry at herself for losing both Clarke and Jo. Calls to Gillespie are ringing out. A stupid driver had asked for directions. If she hadn't felt obliged to be polite to a stranger, then she would never have lost them.

As she rings Gillespie again, she sees Clarke on the other side of the road. Although there is no sign of Jo, she decides to continue the trail and get some answers of her own. She can ring Jo from the car. *'Where is Gillespie when you need him?'* she wonders.

Clarke gets back into his car at the Delifonseca. Tara does a quick three-point turn in her Audi R8 and stays close behind him. His driving is erratic. It would be a perfect resolution to the night if he gets pulled over for disorderly driving. Jo's phone is ringing out.

She follows Clarke all the way to Huskisson Street. He slows the car as he drives down a long row of houses and offices. Each one looks like something out of a history book. He pulls over across the road from a building with a blue door.

He waits and Tara watches. She rings Gillespie and Jo again. Neither of them answers. As she reaches into her glove box for her phone charger, she sees the blue door open.

Stepping out of the door is Emily Spencer. Tara recognises her from the crime photographs. She is followed by an older woman, who locks the door behind her. The woman appears to be saying a farewell to Emily. Neither is aware that Bob Clarke is out of his car.

76

Emily says her final goodbye to Sophie. In a few days, she is joining an art course in Manchester. She is relocating there with Gina for a fresh start.

Sophie has arranged for someone else to take over Emily's sessions, but insists that she sends her an original art piece one day. This is the part that Sophie dreads when she is too invested in her clients.

Emily walks away, waiting until her back is turned to let the first of many tears fall. She stares at the ground, willing her legs to walk faster so she isn't tempted to turn back.

Suddenly, a hand covers her mouth tightly and drags her into the road. She tries to scream but struggles to draw enough breath. Tara sees what is happening and jumps out of her car. "Get off her!" she shouts.

Sophie hears the shout and looks back to see what is going on. It takes no more than a second for her to recognise that Emily is in trouble. She runs down the street, watching as Emily is dragged further across the road. Tara is just behind Sophie.

"Let her go!" shouts Sophie. "Emily!" She runs at full speed into Clarke, knocking him and Emily over.

"Here, take this key. You know where I park, right? Go, don't look back. Just run," Sophie tells Emily, as Clarke stands up, grabs her hair, and stabs her in the side.

Emily is running down Huskisson Street, towards Liverpool Cathedral, where Sophie parks her car every day. It's a short walk, made shorter by a cut through derelict church grounds. Wanting to get to the car as soon as possible, she takes the shortcut. The nettles and weeds swipe at her ankles, leaving their sting. She trips over a broken headstone and cuts her shin. Limping, she makes her way past St James Gardens to Sophie's car at the back of the Cathedral.

She is unaware that Sophie has been stabbed and is lying in the middle of the road, desperate for help. Tara saw the blade enter Sophie's side and, within seconds, was putting pressure on the wound and watching Clarke chase after Emily.

"I'm fine. I can hold it. Please, you have to help Emily," pleads Sophie.

"I can't leave you. If you don't keep pressure on until help gets here …"

"I know the risks. The ambulance said five minutes, right? I'll be fine. Please, you have to help her. She needs you," says Sophie, pressing firmly on the hole in her side.

"OK. When the police get here, tell them I'm chasing Bob Clarke and that Jo Linnet's missing. And keep that pressure up," shouts Tara, as she runs towards the derelict church. Sophie lies on the road, alone. Her hand is covered in blood; sticky and warm.

It's late. The offices on Huskisson Street are closed. There's no reason for traffic to come through this way. Once a week, Emily has attended a twilight session with Sophie, so that she has a reason to be out of the house when Graham is at home.

Tonight was the last time Sophie and Emily would see each other for a while. It may be the last time Sophie sees anyone. She doesn't feel the pain, just her heartbeat slowing down. She manages to drag herself to the wall and rest against it. She feels faint. Like she could sleep.

She thinks about how she would give up her life so that Emily can have a fresh start. It becomes too hard to keep her eyes open. She rests them. Just for a moment.

77

Emily reaches the car and tries to open the door. She presses the central locking button so fast that the car opens and closes in quick succession. She tries again but to no avail.

She cries. Her hands are shaking and she drops the car key. She doesn't look back, terrified by what she might see. If she had, she would have seen a familiar face.

Tom picks up the key and throws it into the bushes.

"Tom … what do you want?" she shouts through her sobs.

"It's Bob, OK? Not that it matters now."

He throws her against the car bonnet. She spins around to protect herself, but she is too late. He slashes the blade at her neck, making a superficial cut, but the blood is enough to distract her.

"Oh, my God, stop. Please!"

Clarke punches her in the stomach. She doubles over and falls to the ground. From this angle, the largest cathedral in the UK looks like it extends far beyond the heavens.

"Now that the introductions are out of the way, could you do me a favour and stop talking? You're like an annoying fly in my ear, or rather, a whiney bitch." He kicks her face like a football. She lies flat out on the ground.

"When you ran away the first time, you caused me a lot of bother. Near enough blinded me with the shit you threw in my face. When I got back to the station, people are talking about heterochromia, the condom and the bloody lambskin. I knew the game would be up sooner or later. I just hoped it would be later."

Emily gets up and tries to stagger towards the main road, out of the cathedral grounds. She will not go through this again. She would rather be run over by a double-decker bus driving at full speed than let him touch her.

"There's nowhere for you to go. It's over," he says. "I wouldn't have chosen this place though. Even I have some lines that I won't cross but, of course, beggars can't be choosers." He looks up at the cathedral. "What have I got to lose anyway?"

He takes off his belt and wraps it around Emily's neck, pulling it until she gurgles and splutters. He tightens his grip as she tries to rip his fingers from his hand, but they are locked in place, hell-bent on finishing the job. She can feel his erection behind her.

The pressure builds in her head and her eyes feel like they will burst, like a balloon that is blown up too much. Her legs start to buckle, and Clarke throws her down.

Her face hits the ground, teeth first.

They scrape along the concrete as she tries to lift her head. She coughs, choking on the river of blood that runs from her nose, staining her lips. Her nails splinter as she crawls, burying them into the dirt. Her heartbeat resounds in her ears. Her face pounds like the skin of a drum being beaten until it rips.

She feels a blow to the back of her head. It strikes her like a bat to a baseball, a solid hit. The force spins her, leaving her blood-soaked face staring at the sky. Her breathing is shallow and her petite frame is limp. Her muscles give in to the numbness. She blinks, slower each time. Her eyes are heavy and her surroundings are out of focus.

Traffic and sirens are faint in the distance.

Unable to move, she closes her eyes and considers not opening them again. Tears roll down her cheeks. Her inner voice is screaming for help, willing someone, somewhere, to pick her up and carry her to safety.

She feels something move near her feet, followed by a pressure on her body. Fighting to open her eyes one last time, Emily Spencer finds herself face-to-face with evil. She locks eyes with Clarke, determined not to give him the satisfaction of being part of whatever sick fantasy he has in mind. He presses the knife to her face and moves the blade down her neck. Looking at her expectantly, he continues to move it down to her chest. Every flicker of fear and wince of terror reinforces his lust for control and power.

His smug superiority is interrupted by a sudden pain in his head. He falls to the side, shocked and confused. Blood trickles from his temple.

Tara knows she hasn't delivered a life-threatening blow with the thick branch, but she has bought them time. She pushes Clarke out of the way and pulls Emily up from the ground.

Emily is a dead weight. She has no coordination. She can hear Tara say, "Stay with me, Emily," but cannot reply. All she can do is hang on tight and hope that Clarke is dead.

"Come on, that's it. Keep moving, Emily. I've got you," says Tara, struggling to gather momentum. "The police are on the …"

Clarke kicks Tara in the back of her knee. Her legs buckle and she crashes into the iron gate ahead. She loses her grip on Emily, who falls to the ground.

Tara turns to see Clarke drawing back his knife. She resigns herself to an imminent death, knowing that his blood is on her hands, and Emily's hair is on her clothes. If he kills them both, there will be enough DNA evidence to charge him with their murders.

Tara closes her eyes and hears a voice she thought she would never hear again.

"Drop it, Clarke."

Over his shoulder, Tara sees Jo, who is pointing a gun at the back of his head.

78

"Let her go, Clarke," orders Jo, trying to stay focused on him rather than on an injured and terrified Tara. Her body aches like a bad hangover. She had come round from the Oramorph and had alerted the station.

Units raced to Emily Spencer's home address and Sophie Sheridan's office at Jo's command. She was picked up at Brunswick Docks, looking worse for wear but determined to make Clarke pay.

Now, with the Oramorph still tingling beneath her skin, she holds a gun. Her hands are sweaty and shaking. Her face feels twice its normal size. Her cheek isn't shattered but it hurts like hell.

"I knew I should have finished you off, Linnet," says Clarke, as he grabs hold of Tara and spins around to face Jo. "On the bright side, at least you get to see this."

He presses the knife blade against Tara's neck. A superficial cut but that could all change in a matter of seconds. Tara tries to keep calm. If she is going to die, then the last thing she wants is for Jo to live with guilt or regret.

"What do you want, Clarke?" asks Jo, biding time while the armed response unit sets up their perimeter. She hopes they will forgive her for borrowing a gun. "Do you want a legacy? Because you've got it. You're the Night Walker."

"Fuck off, Linnet. This isn't 'Game of Thrones'."

"OK then, let's start with 'why'? Why did you hurt the girls?" she asks, with her gun still pointing at him. She is likely to hit Tara if she takes a shot. *'Surely, she would forgive a temporary gunshot wound,'* she thinks.

"What do you want me to say, that I had mummy issues? Or that I snapped one day because of a trigger? I did it because I could."

"What about Janice Gregson?" Jo knows it is a risk mentioning Janice. Clarke has narcissistic traits. His ego is his baby. He is superior to everyone else, and the people in his life are only there as an instrument of progression. Jo uses this to her advantage. "You made a mistake with Janice Gregson. You thought you had hours. Your plan was spoiled. Interrupted. You should have thought ahead. You missed the detail."

"Fuck you, Linnet. I got inside the house. I took those risks. I charmed my way in. Everything was going the way it was meant to until some prick knocked on the door," he says, agitated. "She was for Tatton and Summers. I thought at least one of them would be implicated. Get them off my back."

"You didn't plan enough," says Jo, poking his ego. *'The more defensive he becomes, the more likely he is to hurt Tara but, to hurt her, he needs to move. If he moves, I will shoot.'*

"And Emily Spencer?" Jo looks to check that Emily is still unconscious and can't hear what she says next. "You fucked up there, didn't you? You managed to corner her in the shed, get a hard-on, overpower her and hurt her. All that planning and you go and leave the condom inside her. Come on, that's rape 101." She feels sick with her words but it's working. Clarke is focused on her instead of Tara.

"If you're so good, why didn't you figure it out? I'll tell you why. Because I'm better. I outsmarted you. I misled the profiler and the detective. I could have carried on, if it wasn't for her." He looks at Emily with disgust. "What are you going to do then? Shoot me? You'd take us both out. Not to mention the shit you'll be in for firing a weapon that's not yours."

Sophie was barely conscious when the armed response unit arrived at Huskisson Street. She told them where Emily was running to and, as soon as Jo heard Tara's name, she took the gun from the unit and ran.

"Phillip Tatton's at the station. He's telling anyone who'll listen about how you're his little bitch; his errand boy. Are you going to let him tell your story?" Jo plays on his ego and his need for control and power. She hopes that the same desires that drove him to prey on women will be his undoing.

"You're lying. He's gone. You'll never see him again. Once you kill a cop, you have to run, right?" asks Clarke, smiling. "And once you kill a detective, you have to disappear."

Jo tightens her grip on the gun, aware that he is trying to manipulate the situation. Even now, with a gun aimed at his head and a hostage in his arms, he thinks he can control the situation. Control the conversation. Turn things around so that she becomes the one who is tormented and distracted.

She thinks of Gillespie. His hair, his smile and his annoying jokes. She imagines him lying in a pool of his blood. Her hands get sweatier. She refocuses when Tara cries out. The knife is digging deeper into her skin and blood slithers down her neck.

"You'll be the last man standing, Linnet. My gift to you. You can live to tell everyone how you could have caught me. That you could have saved them all. You will see their faces and corpses every time you close your eyes. That's my legacy."

Clarke has his back to the gate of the cathedral. It is usually open for anyone to enter and find faith. Today, it is preventing evil from getting out.

Over his shoulder, Jo sees the armed response officers in position. She needs Clarke to move away from Tara, to give them a clear shot.

She continues, "Well, you've made your mind up, so get on with it. Finish her. Stick the knife deep though, you don't want to make a mistake like you did with Janice Gregson and Emily Spencer. And there's the time you almost got caught by Amy Tatton, not to mention the times you've had your backside smacked by Phillip Tatton. All in all, I don't actually think there's much to tell about you. I certainly won't be writing any books. Maybe a lecture on how not to commit a crime. Perhaps a journal about sexual dysfunction and lamb fetishes; that sort of thing."

Jo is pressing all of Clarke's buttons. She is no longer complying with his orders. He no longer has control of the situation. She lists all the mistakes he has made and highlights the things that will shame him and make him doubt his legacy. After all, a psychopath with narcissistic traits prefers to tell their own story, rather than have someone else do it injustice.

Clarke takes his arm off Tara but keeps hold of her hair so she can't run. He can't help but retaliate. "Does this look like sexual dysfunction to you?" asks Clarke, grabbing his erection and laughing. His urge to prove himself competent and in control provides the armed officers with the chance to take their shot. A bullet goes through his shoulder. He screams in pain and the knife drops to the floor. Tara grabs it.

Jo's only thought, as blood spurts across her shirt, is Tara. She grabs her and moves her to safety. They sit on the steps of Liverpool Cathedral, under the arches of sanctuary. Tara wants to check on Emily, but Jo stops her as the paramedics are already treating her. The best thing for Tara to do is let them work and get herself checked out.

Clarke is down. He is restrained on a gurney, with enough padding on his wound to ensure he lives to feel the full force of justice. He looks over at Jo, who sticks her middle finger up at him whilst she answers the phone.

"Tara, I'll meet you at the hospital. Make sure you get checked out before you leave here."

"Wait, where are you going? I'll come with you. I feel safer with you."

"They found Gillespie."

79

The Royal Liverpool University Hospital is filled with police officers from a range of ranks. Some sit in the family room and some sit in reception, but most are standing along the corridors, waiting for news. When one of them is down, they flock to show their support.

Jo and Tara sit next to Gillespie's bed. He was found unconscious, with multiple injuries and internal bleeding, in a room underneath one of Phillip Tatton's casinos. He would not have been found if it wasn't for Pink Bra raising the suspicion. She thought her potential boyfriend, Mark Summers, had been taken away forcefully by the Terminator. Worried for his safety, she rang the police, who eventually found Gillespie.

"I walked right past that casino when I was following Clarke. I was so focused on my grudge against him that I didn't even know when my partner was in trouble," says Jo.

"You couldn't have known, Jo. I walked past it too. There's no way we could have known what was happening to him," says Tara.

They sit in silence on either side of Gillespie's bed. His hair is matted with blood. The rest of him depicts a map of the torture that he experienced at the hands of Mark Summers and Phillip Tatton.

Summers has been arrested for the attack and Phillip Tatton is on the run, just like Clarke said. He has enough money to disappear for a lifetime, but he has ties to the city. Businesses, debts that need collecting, and his family. A man as cocksure as Tatton will come back. One day.

Jo wonders if Tatton and Clarke found each other through the police, or if they sought out like-minded people. Clarke is aroused by his authority and the fear he can cause. Although similar, Tatton shows remorse and is protective of his family.

Unlike Tatton, Clarke has demonstrated serious bias in his internal mental processes. His reality is that he is deserving of power and control. His needs and goals outweigh those of anyone else. He is the winner and the alpha. Somewhere along the way, he created a perception of the world where he is the only man that matters. In turn, this feeds his ego and desire for control. He crossed lines and laws and got away with it. The sexual arousal was probably unexpected.

He cast himself in the role of a champion but became the villain. Somewhere along the way, the thrill of taking risks and exerting control became a distorted search for intimacy. The women were objects; there to play a role for him. There to reinforce the created perception of himself.

"Would you have done it?" asks Tara. "Would you have shot him?"

Jo considers how close she came to pulling the trigger and shooting Clarke before he could kill Tara. Accepting that an injury to Tara was worth the risk. She would have lost everything if she had fired a weapon that wasn't hers, and she wasn't trained to use.

She didn't care. She would have shot him ten times if the armed response unit hadn't turned up. She would have done whatever it took to save Tara and take Clarke down.

"No," replies Jo. A white lie. "But I wouldn't have let anything happen to you."

"Not even when you told him to stab me?"

"Not even then."

They both smile and relax for the first time, in a long time, finding comfort in each other's company. Jo wonders if it is inappropriate to ask Tara to clarify if she did ask her out, back in the coffee shop. Instead, she continues to look and smile.

"Get your own room you two," says Gillespie, waking up. Even groggy, battered and bruised, he is in good spirits. Jo holds his hand and scorns him for going off on his own. Tough love.

Within minutes, she has recounted the events of Clarke's capture. The chase down Brunswick Docks, the bloody Oramorph and the cathedral. She leaves no details spared.

Gillespie tells his story. The casino, the CCTV, Mark Summers, the Terminator and the lightbulb.

"Is Sophie OK? What about Emily?" asks Gillespie.

Tara brings him up to speed. Emily has no internal bleeding but is being kept in for a few days for observations. Sophie was stabbed in the abdomen, but Clarke failed to puncture any vital organs. She is out of surgery and talking with Emily.

"She wants to see you," says Jo. "Sophie, that is. She's been worried about you."

Gillespie smiles.

"How about you, Jo, are you OK?" he asks.

Jo shrugs her shoulders. She's fine, apart from feeling like the blindest profiler the world has ever seen. It's not an exact science and is subjective, to a degree, but the profile was mostly accurate. What bothers her most is that she was just out-manoeuvred by Clarke.

"I'm OK. I have to give a full report soon. Questions are being asked about Clarke and how we didn't know it was him. I bet we are not the only ones to be fooled by the contact lenses. Plus, there are a few questions about me borrowing that gun. I thought sharing was caring?" laughs Jo, shaking off the seriousness of what lies ahead. "A profile needs a conviction in order to be validated. Until then, it's my subjective argument against their need for good public relations."

"I'm as much to blame as anyone," says Gillespie. "I should have listened to your suspicions. I was convinced it was Michael Tanner and, or Graham Pierce. Next thing I know, I'm gunning for Mark Summers and accusing him of the whole lot."

"He had us all fooled," agrees Tara. "I had Clarke's DNA sampled and tested again earlier. His DNA matched the condom."

80

Jo and Gillespie look at each other, puzzled.

"Firstly, you're meant to be resting. Secondly, what the hell?" says Jo. "Did you make a mistake?"

"Not quite. His DNA has been compared against what was found inside the condom multiple times now. At least forty per cent of the time, the DNA is a match," replies Tara.

"How does that happen?" asks Gillespie.

"Chimerism. A condition that occurs in animals and humans when the body contains the cells of two or more individuals. In other words, a person with chimerism can have two sets of DNA. It happens for multiple reasons; through blood transfusions, stem cells and bone marrow transplants. Some DNA from the donor is absorbed by the recipient. It's not likely nowadays, with the screening and quality control, but it's possible. Clarke has never had a transplant of any type though. My guess would be that he absorbed some of his mother's blood cells during gestation in the womb. I doubt he even knows he has it."

As Tara explains some of the characteristics of chimerism, the final parts of the profile fit into place. The heterochromia can be caused by the two sets of DNA, which would also explain the hit-and-miss DNA comparisons against the condom. Extreme allergies and immunosuppression conditions are common among people with chimerism, although the links may never be made. They may have no symptoms their whole life, and may only find out when they discover they have two blood types.

"So the dental issues, the Xylitol and the latex allergy are all part of this?" asks Gillespie, straining to sit up.

"The dental issues are just that. The allergy might be linked, but there are a lot of people with allergies who don't have chimerism," clarifies Tara.

"I still don't get it. I don't get why Clarke; a successful, albeit bent, copper would do these things."

Jo recounts the profile, more for her own reassurance than any other reason. "Clarke is a psychopath. He is driven by self-gratification, even at the expense of other people. His narcissistic traits and lack of empathy make him dangerous. With the added authority and power which his position in the police afforded him, he had the circumstance, personality and opportunity to become the person who has terrorised and killed across Liverpool City."

She continues, "Anne-Marie Swift likely got into the car that night because Bob Clarke looks normal. He is charming and appears safe. He had practice as he followed people, practised their routines, learned their movements and was always prepared. The crime scenes were organised, the choice of victim was organised, and his job provided the forensic awareness he needed to leave a crime scene free of evidence that could be traced back to him. He had access to Michael Tanner's taxi and the means to avoid anyone knowing he had used it. He made sure we made the link between Tanner and Gemma Woodcock too, despite the inconsistency with the bitemarks."

"I suspect that there are other attacks in Clarke's past that will never surface. Date rapes in college. Cruelty to animals, or others, for sheer pleasure. Something made him confident enough to enter Janice Gregson's through the front door and attack her in her own home. That was when he learned valuable lessons. Plan with more care. Eliminate the chance of disturbances. Be prepared for changes to the plan. Keep things outside for quick escapes, where required. Rape them quicker. Don't take too long to kill them next time."

"The move to voyeurism was practised. Dedication to perfecting the art of being invisible. Blending into the backdrop. Being in the same place, but undetectable, like the pharmacy. None of the girls had even looked at him. He saw something in them that made them appealing. Perhaps it was their lack of interest in him. How dare they not recognise him and his stature? Bob Clarke isn't someone you just ignore or fail to recognise," she concluded.

"That's it? His ego made him kill all those people?" asks Gillespie.

"Partly. He's a control and power killer. It's all about being in command. Being the most powerful one in the room. Showing others how dominant he is. He can take you and kill you, and still go to work the next day. He can rape you and dump you, without fear of being caught, because he is amazing at what he does. It's his ego, personality, attitude and opportunities. It's everything. The perfect storm."

"What about his wife? Has anyone told her?" asks Tara.

"Commissioner Grant personally visited her. He has known her for years and was shocked to see how ill she is. Clarke always said that his wife was recovering well, but the commissioner saw for himself that the stroke she suffered was devastating. She can't talk or walk. The assumption is that she has no idea what her husband has been up to. She was as fooled as everyone else."

"The BTK killer, Dennis Rader, was the opposite of what people imagine a serial killer to be like. Even the Yorkshire Ripper avoided suspicion in multiple police interviews before he was caught, by appearing normal. Clarke demonstrated these psychopathic traits until Emily Spencer escaped and was able to identify him. The monster was unmasked. The face of evil started to protrude from the cracks in the charade."

"They found more evidence in his rental apartment, which is almost in the centre of the 'Circle of Danger'. They found a red cap that matches the CCTV footage and detailed notes about the victims. Their routines, daily activities, and some grotesque ratings. Janice Gregson and Emily Spencer have already identified him. He's not going to see the outside of a cell anytime soon," concludes Jo.

She and Tara leave Gillespie to get some rest. He is lucky to have been found, but his injuries are serious. Rest is the best thing he can do for himself now.

"What's next?" asks Tara, stroking Jo's hair behind her ears.

"Now I have to go and give my report to the big bosses. I'll give them everything I know and explain the situation. They can't be too hard on me for trying to save a life, right?" asks Jo, putting her hair back to where it was.

For the first time since they met, Jo looks scared. A scapegoat will be needed before this mess gets to the media. Someone who missed the signs. Someone who should have known the person who matched the profile. Someone who was running around Liverpool with a gun and telling the serial killer to stab someone.

"I'll wait outside in the car for you. Whatever happens, tonight we'll sit on the couch, drinking wine together," Tara assures her. "And yes, there will be crisps."

Jo smiles and heads out of the hospital. She is ready to throw the bullshit back to whoever throws it at her first.

Acknowledgements

I could not have reached this point without the support and encouragement of an army of people.

Thank you to Michael Heppell and the team, who have taught me so much and given me the accountability I needed to get over the final line. Thank you to Christine Beech for brilliant editing and attention to detail, and to Matt Bird for his endless patience and wisdom!

Thank you to Paul and Richard for the endless nights talking about this book and beyond. I don't know how I got this far without giving you any spoilers!

Finally, thank you to Gemma and Brooke for your patience each time I locked myself away to write, and for sharing my excitement along the way.

About the Author

Laura Graves is a psychological crime and fiction author from Liverpool. She is a specialist in Psychology and Criminology. Her debut novel '**Hunted**' is the first in a new series and reflects her love of science, true crime, and psychological scares.

Printed in Great Britain
by Amazon

39343309R00199